WISDOM
BETRAYED

WISDOM BETRAYED

David, Bathsheba, and
The Man behind the Throne

A novel by

Don Clifford

Xulon Press Elite

Xulon Press Elite
2301 Lucien Way #415
Maitland, FL 32751
407.339.4217
www.xulonpress.com

Unless otherwise indicated, Scripture quotations taken from the New American Standard Bible (NASB). Copyright © 1960, 1962, 1963, 1968, 1971, 1972, 1973, 1975, 1977, 1995 by The Lockman Foundation. Used by permission. All rights reserved.

Paperback ISBN-13: 978-1-6628-2677-1
Ebook ISBN-13: 978-1-6628-2678-8

Dedicated to the memory of my long-suffering wife, Karen, whom I loved dearly and who faithfully endured so much pain in the loss of our three children.

Table of Contents

Introduction

I t is unusual for a work of fiction to begin with an introduction. However, this book is an unusual work of fiction because it is built so much upon biblical facts and characters. The story line is directly from the Old Testament book of Second Samuel. It is the familiar story of David and Bathsheba and the members of their respective families. But, the promise of this book is that there is much more to the story than is related in the brief biblical text.

There is actually a fascinating mystery hidden here in this book of the Bible. For some reason the author has omitted important details that might change how we interpret the story. The facts of the deeper story must be carefully ferreted out of the 2nd Samuel text. However, even with the discovery of the hidden texts, telling the entire story requires assumptions and speculations to fill in what is missing. Thus, the fiction. The resulting tale is quite possibly the most likely representation of the actual facts. So, what is fact and what is fiction? That's the question.

Why would important facts of a scriptural event be hidden from the casual reader? That's a good question. There may have been political or religious pressure on the author to keep certain facts untold. That's part of the mystery we may never know.

Of course, the Holy Spirit is the actual author of this entire episode and He might want His readers to enjoy a little mystery once in a while... Is that possible?

It is clear that the author of the biblical text has chosen to dangle several clues for the reader to find; clues needed to unravel the mystery. This introduction is here to point the readers to some of the clues, including some extrabiblical sources that can only be cited here. Where the clues can be found and how they can be fitted together to reveal the larger drama illustrates the need for this introduction.

Of course, the biblical story of David and Bathsheba is one of the most famous stories in all literature. The lurid tale of a hero of God falling into adultery and murder because of arrogance and lust is second in fame only to the story of Goliath in the life of David. The story is told very briefly in the second book of Samuel, chapters 11 and 12. On the surface, it is the story of a powerful and beloved king who happens to see a beautiful woman bathing in her back garden. He summons her to his chambers and takes her to his bed. She leaves, but she later reports to the king that she is expecting.

Not wanting to be identified as the father, the king summons the woman's husband home from the war and instructs him to go home and sleep with his wife. The soldier refuses to do so out of loyalty to his fellow warriors who are suffering in the field of battle. The king then sends him back to the front, bearing a letter to his commander, ordering him to put the man in the heat of battle where he will be killed. The commander obeys, the husband dies, and with feigned compassion, the king takes the wife into his harem.

The king is satisfied with his actions until a man of God brings him a message from the Lord God, condemning him for his evil actions and pronouncing dire consequences for him and his house. The king repents, but the child conceived in adultery dies. The king must live with the consequences of his sin. End of story.

Or, is it? While the biblical account is accurate, we are interested in what is going on that we are not told about. The first part of the mystery is solved by digging into some of the biblical material that most readers skip over; the listing of King David's Thirty Mighty Men in 2 Samuel 23. These men were closest to the king. Near the end of the list are the names of Bathsheba's father, Eliam, and Uriah, her husband. That's a surprise. With her husband and her father both being part of David's inner circle, it is clear that David had known Bathsheba before he summoned her while her husband was away. When David asked "Who was that woman?", he knew who she was.

We also learn from that same passage that Eliam's father was Ahithophel the Gilonite. That man was therefore Bathsheba's grandfather. That is an important fact because we read elsewhere (2 Samuel 15:12 and Chronicles 27:33) that Ahithophel is none other than David's personal counselor and advisor. The plot thickens. So, we learn that the great King David seduced (or assaulted) his personal advisor's granddaughter, who was also the wife and daughter of his personal bodyguards.

Knowing these facts, we can see immediately that there must have been a lot of emotional dynamics going on between Ahithophel, David, Bathsheba, Uriah and others. Without this information we wouldn't be able to understand why Ahithophel raged against David so vehemently in 2 Samuel 17. Ahithophel isn't mentioned in the brief biblical account of

David's sin, and not at all until years later when he shows up as an enemy of David, and as an ally of David's son Absalom, who leads a revolution against his father.

That is what this book is about: seeking to find and use scriptural clues to flesh out the brief biblical account. We use a fictional novel to allow us to freely investigate the back stories of the characters in this drama. That will help us to better understand the emotional dynamics between them. That understanding will hopefully illuminate spiritual and even practical lessons for our own lives.

Let's talk some more about Ahithophel since he is the title character of this book (The Man Behind theThrone). Most of what has been written in the literature about Ahithophel treats him as a dastardly character because of his apparent betrayal of David. However, very few writers have delved into the cause of his rebellion. In 1681, John Dryden published an epic poem entitled "Absalom and Achitophel"[1] (variant spelling). The famous poem is generally acknowledged as the finest political satire in the English language. However, the poem provides only a little insight into our character because Dryden simply uses Ahithophel in his satire to represent a scurrilous character in the political infighting of his time.

Rabbinic literature sees Ahithophel as a friendly adversary of David. David valued his wisdom and counsel, but the two men had a rocky alliance. Ahithophel is seen by the Rabbis as cursed because of his betrayal of David. In Jewish literature, the *Aggada*[2] says that Ahithophel's advice was on the same level as the Urim and Thummim in discerning God's will (note: the Urim and Thummin were small stones carried in the pocket of the priest's ephod, or tunic. They were used by the priests to inquire of the Lord). There is an intriguing passage in the

Aggada, where it is remarked that "Posterity has been favored with only a small part of Ahithophel's wisdom, and that little through two widely different sources; through Socrates, who was his disciple, and through a fortune-book written by him." We don't have the "fortune book," but we do know today that Socrates was familiar with Rabbinic teachings.[3]

Even though Ahithophel is not well known by most people, his influence was extraordinary. It has been said that this man was the most revered and respected advisor in the history of the kingdom. It has been written of Ahithophel by Whyte,[4] "David and Ahithophel were bosom friends from their boy-hood up. When David took the throne, Ahithophel was proud to lay all his magnificent gifts of sound advice and counsel at David's feet. David never made a law, nor gave a judgment, nor proclaimed a war, nor negotiated a truce, nor signed a peace, til Ahithophel had been heard and until his advice had been taken. It was, they say, as if a man had inquired of God."

Another Bible passage of interest is 2 Samuel 8:18, where we learn that David's sons are officials (chief ministers) in David's court. We see then that David must be well into middle age (50 to 60 years old) having served for many years as a ruling monarch. As members of David's court, his adult sons would be in close contact with Ahithophel. (We assume these sons are Amnon and Absalom, David's two oldest living sons. His second-born, Chiliab, must have died young or was handicapped in some way. He is never mentioned again in Scripture). Absalom's mother, Maacah (pronounced May ah' kuh) and his sister, Tamar, play important roles in the second part of this book.

Ahithophel's involvement with David's rebellious son, Absalom, is a mystery in the 2nd Samuel text. We are told simply that Absalom sent for Ahithophel, who was living at his family home in Giloh. We are not told why he was no longer in David's service at that time. Nor are we told why Absalom sent for him or why Ahithophel responded so promptly and vigorously to his summons.

Here is what Whyte[4] writes of Absalom's summons to Ahithophel: "Absalom had no head of his own, but he had what was better, for he had a head to know where greatness dwelt and he called for Ahithophel, whose head was like the oracle of God. A man whose heart rankled against David like hell itself. Ahithophel was worth 10,000 men to Absalom, and no one knew that better than David."

Other important clues about David's larger family are found in 2 Samuel 3:2–5, 5:13–16, and 1 Chronicles 3:1–9, and 14:3–7. In these passages, we learn of David's many wives and children (more than twenty) and allusions to his many concubines. If the reader is not familiar with these passages, they are recommended before reading this novel.

As Alexander MacLaren says in his book, *The Life of David*,[5] "A good man, and still more, a man of David's age at the date of his great crime, seldom falls so low unless there has been a previous decay of his religious life, hidden most likely from himself. And the source of that decay may probably be found in self-indulgence, fostered by ease, and by long years of command." Alexander Whyte put it this way, "David's power increased until the king of Israel denied himself nothing on which he had once set his heart."[4] Jonathan Kirsch writes in his introduction to *King David*[6] that "David illustrates the fundamental truth that the sacred and the profane may find full expression in a single human life."

One more explanatory note; the text of 2 Samuel 11–18 is a very short summary of events that omits many details. A careful reading of the passage reveals that the events reported are spread over eleven or twelve years. One purpose of this book is to present a possible scenario to explain this timeline of events.

One event seems to be inconsistent with several other passages. In chapter 12, verse 24, the text says that after their baby died, "David went in to Bathsheba and lay with her, and she gave birth to a son, and he named him Solomon." That statement is true. However, we know from the passages in chapter 5 and 1 Chronicles 3 and 14 that Solomon was the fourth son born to Bathsheba after the first baby died. Thus Solomon was the youngest of all David's several sons. The important historical fact the writer apparently wanted to document in the telling of this story was that King Solomon was also born of their union, which would surely mitigate the grief of their loss.

The fact that much detail is left out of this whole account is noted by Coffman's Commentary on 2 Samuel 15:7, which says, "It is evident that much more elaborate preparations had been made for this effort of Absalom to seize the throne than appears on the surface of this concise narrative." [7]

Many quotes from biblical passages are incorporated into this text. They are often paraphrased to fit into the flow of the story. The Bible used is the New American Standadrd Version (NASV). Much care was taken to avoid any conflict with the biblical text. A listing of the biblical texts incorporated into the story is included by chapter in the Appendix at the end of the book.

Since the book includes some lengthy passages from the Bible, the book is more semi-fiction than pure fiction. This book is not intended to be a scholarly commentary on the Scriptures, although it does seek to clarify and dramatize the brief textual story in keeping with current conservative interpretations. The intention is to "put some meat on the bones," simply filling in the open spaces in the scriptural account. Officially, it is Bible-based historical fiction, a novel written for the enjoyment of the interested reader.

Because of the popularity of this story, many readers will likely have existing concepts of the characters and events in their minds that differ from the author's in this book. That will probably be true of David himself. Most people are not aware of his behavior in his later years. Also, opinions of Bathsheba's role vary greatly. Was she an innocent victim, a willing participant, or even a seductress? David Wolpe says in his book *David: the Divided Heart,*[8.] "What we think about Bathsheba is more about who we are than it is about her." This subject is discussed more in the Author's Note at the end of the book, with the rationale of the author included. Happy reading.

PART I:

AHITHOPHEL'S REGRET

See to it that no one comes short of the grace of God; that no root of bitterness springing up causes trouble, and by it many be defiled. – Hebrews 12:15

Chapter 1:

The Patriarch

Adoting grandfather met with his small family to share their final meal together on a chilly spring evening before the impending departure. Lightly-woven window coverings had been pulled back to let in the fresh, cool air.

"Nonsense, Eliam! There is no reason for the king to remain in Jerusalem while sending the troops to Rabbah." The older man was adamant while washing his hands in a large basin of water drawn from the nearby town well.

"But Father, he has earned respite from the many battles he's already won," the middle-aged, muscular man said as he sat down at the wooden table where warm bread and a creamy yogurt sauce awaited the main dish.

A graceful, mature girl watched her father and grandfather debate whether King David should lead his troops or await messages in the palace. She turned to the servant who hovered nearby.

"Anna, the stew is ready. Please take it to the table now."

The servant girl bobbed acknowledgment of the request and went to the hearth where she scooped out the fragrant lamb stew into waiting bowls. Taking them to the table, she placed one in front of Eliam and the other before his father Ahithophel, who was now seated. After a quick smile and nod from the young woman who observed from the doorway, the girl scooped the first seasonal greens from a board where they had been laying to dry after earlier washing and placed them on a platter that she took to the table as well.

Just then, a bronzed man with a muscular form and impressive height entered the kitchen from the back entrance. No one paid attention to the battle scar on his neck any longer. It was part of his identity as a warrior—one of David's Thirty Mighty Men, just as his father-in-law Eliam was.

"Uri, come, sit down. We are about to pray the Lord's blessing."

The newcomer exchanged a smile with his young wife who was presiding over the meal and took a seat between the two men. The grandfather began to pray:

"Baruch atah Adonai Eloheinu melech ha olam..." *(Blessed are you, O Lord, our God, ruler of the universe).*

After Betta, short for Bathsheba, served a bowl of lamb stew to her husband, she stood contentedly watching the men consume the meal that she and Anna had cooked. There was plenty, and for a few moments, no one spoke as the men eagerly consumed the enjoyable meal. Betta and Anna finished eating alone, leaving the men to continue their conversation.

Finally, the young wife asked, "Father, why shouldn't the king lead his men into battle? He's not ill or beset by serious problems, is he?"

Ahithophel smacked the table with his hand. "There, even young Bathsheba can see it! Uri, you must have shared some military counsel with my granddaughter."

Uri grinned as he broke off a piece of bread to dip in the stew. "It's true, His Majesty's announcement surprised us all. But maybe something is happening behind the scenes that we're unaware of." He took a big bite of the stew-dipped bread, savoring the taste.

Eliam answered his daughter, "Honey, we have to face the fact that His Majesty isn't as young as he used to be. Hand-to-hand combat requires tremendous strength, skill, and stamina to survive. David was unbeatable when he was younger. I mean, he'd killed a giant when he was little more than a child. The enemy soldiers he has killed in battle number in the hundreds; some say thousands. But now he's middle-aged. He has adult sons serving in his government. Our nation needs his leadership. We can't risk his life when there are younger, stronger warriors available—men like your rugged husband, Uri, here."

Uri smiled and chuckled a little. "Thanks for praising me to my wife! Yes, spears and arrows are one thing, but hand-to-hand combat is tough, brutal work. Men are highly motivated when their lives are at stake, and they will fight to the death. David knows exactly how vicious the enemies are. That's why he chose me, even though I am a foreigner, as one of his Thirty Mighty Men. I am expendable. My life can be taken by the enemy, but his as ruler cannot."

Eliam answered, "Timing is everything, Uri. A position opened when Abiezar was killed in battle. I know that David likes to keep the number at thirty, so he was open to a qualified younger man joining us. When you overcame that ambush and killed five Philistines by yourself, that surely qualified you for David's bodyguard, and he agreed."

Uri said, "Father, I'm sure that the fact that you have personally fought alongside David for years as one of his Thirty also influenced him." Then with a knowing grin on his face, he looked at Ahithophel and said, "And of course, Papa, you being the king's personal advisor may have played a small part."

The older man stroked his beard and smiled.

After a moment's delay, Uri went on to say, "I must admit, it's been good having time off this past year. It's an unusual policy the Jews have, exempting newly-married men from combat for the first year of marriage. But I'm not going to argue with it." He exchanged a warm glance with Betta, who smiled and blushed.

Papa interjected, "It's more than a custom, Uri. It's the law of Moses. God Himself has ordained it."

Uri wiped his mouth before he responded. "I'm grateful to you for taking the time to teach me about the God of Israel and the Law He gave to Moses. And it was you, Papa, who helped me to accept Him as my own."

Eliam said, "I don't think my father—or 'Papa,' as you and Betta call him, would have let you marry her if you hadn't been willing to accept our faith, Uri. Now you are one of us, and it's great having you in the family."

Betta chimed in, "Amen to that."

There was silence for a few moments as the family consumed the rest of the lamb stew. When Betta saw the men were finished, she looked at her husband and said,

"Papa is a wonderful teacher, Uri. When my mother died several years ago, I was still a young girl. Papa and I spent many evenings together, especially when Father was away at war. Papa taught me to read and write, to work with numbers and use the correct words, along with many other things. He has brought me scrolls to read about the history of our people and our law, and he taught me to memorize God's holy Scriptures. I'm so thankful for you, Papa. You have always been there for me."

Ahithophel said, "That should be even easier now, Betta. You have this nice house right outside the palace wall. Since I live and work in the palace, I can be with you often." He motioned toward the back of the small house where the palace wall could be seen through the back door beyond the small, enclosed garden that Uri and Betta had cultivated the past year.

Her father added, "And you have this house because of the generosity of His Majesty. This is the best gift I've known King David to give as a wedding present. He is very generous to those who serve him well."

Ahithophel's eyes narrowed, and he seemed to be thinking about his son's statement, but then relaxed and remained silent.

Uri added, "And besides that, Betta is a wonderful cook!"

"With Anna's help," Betta replied happily.

Uri said, "I'm back in the army now. My exemption is over, and I know my place is with my brothers when the army marches out in the morning."

Papa said, "It's going to be difficult after a long honeymoon here at home to go back to the rigors of military life."

Uri responded, "I know, but it is time. The nation needs us more than ever. How could I not, now that I have been given so many privileges? God is good to us!"

Betta smiled again and went to give her husband's arm a quick hug. She asked her grandfather, "Papa, Father makes some good points. Why do you argue that the king should be going with the army for this campaign?"

Papa answered, "Betta, that's what kings do. That is their job. The fighting men need their king, a man they know and trust as their leader. General Joab is very capable, but the men look to their ruler who is a seasoned warrior to be at the front to inspire them." Looking at his son, he said, "He doesn't need to be leading the charge into the face of the enemy, but he should be visible, encouraging them. Besides that, he is a brilliant tactician. That's why I advised him to change his mind about staying home from this battle."

Uri asked, "Doesn't King David always follow your advice? I've heard that you are the most respected advisor in the nation." He got up to wash his hands in the basin.

Eliam said, "Yes, Uri. My father does have that reputation. However, David is the king, and he makes the final decisions. And don't you forget that!"

Uri replied, "Don't worry! I know that I am now serving and protecting a living legend. I grew up hearing of David's exploits, and I consider him to be only a little lower than God Himself. He is like a god to me. I stand ready to give my life to protect my king."

Ahithophel leaned forward and looked Uri in the eye and practically shouted, "No, Uri, no! David is not a god. He is as human as you or me. In fact, while he often seems so close to God, at other times, he is almost the opposite. David is a very complex man. He loves and adores his God, but he hates God's enemies with a passion that makes him bloodthirsty and vicious. He even wrote in one of his psalms, *'Do not I hate those who hate Thee O Lord. I loathe them. I hate them with the utmost hatred: they have become my enemies.'* Yet he is a poet and a musician at the same time. He loves to worship in the tabernacle, but he accumulates wives and concubines despite

Moses' command not to. At his core, he is a passionate, ruthless warrior God has used to defeat His enemies."

"Now wait a minute," said Eliam. "Yes, we all know about David's passion, but that's who he is. You just don't want to get on his wrong side. He is a loyal friend and comrade in arms. God has blessed him more than anyone I know."

Ahithophel responded, "My son, you know he is not always loyal. What about Michal? She crossed him once, but then he put her away in his harem and forgot about her. She is like a prisoner. He even tore her from the happy home she had made with her second husband, Paltiel of Bahurim. She has lived as a widow to this day with no children and really with no husband. That's a terrible thing to do to someone because she told him something he didn't want to hear. He isn't nearly as forgiving as the God he worships."

Ahithophel continued, "I'm just making the point that you can't expect David to be like God. He may be known as God's chosen one, but that comes from his admirers. His passionate nature makes him dangerous if he gets in a corner."

Uri spoke up, "Papa, I thought you loved our king."

"Oh, I do love him...like a brother, but even brothers can have their differences. I can tell you our relationship has not always been smooth. We've clashed on a number of occasions."

At this point, Betta said, "Papa, you mentioned his concubines. I've always wondered why the king has all those concubines when he has more than a dozen wives from his treaties with other countries. What does he do with them?"

Silence reigned for a few moments, then her grandfather said, "Nothing we can discuss, my dear. Let's just say he never saw a beautiful woman he could resist. That passion we discussed carries over to his strong attraction to women. If he sees a beautiful woman he is attracted to, he takes her, no matter whose daughter she may be or even whose wife she may be."

That comment caused Uri to fidget in his chair and to hold his wife even tighter.

Eliam said, "That's enough criticism of our king. He's never taken another man's wife as far as I know. Betta, you don't have to be afraid of King David. He knows you are my daughter and Uri's wife, not to mention the granddaughter of his personal advisor. And to you, Uri, yes, David is a man of great passion, but he is still our supreme commander and the man we answer to. Let's not forget that."

Ahithophel pushed his chair back and folded his hands over his stomach as he responded, "Yes, I agree. Enough of this talk. I do admire your devotion and loyalty to the king, both of you. However, I worry when he isn't willing to discuss the issues with his personal advisor. He always has before. Lately, he hasn't asked my opinion about anything. I'm not sure what's going on."

After a pause, Eliam replied, "Well, I will always go with his decisions, whatever they are and wherever they lead."

The aging man left it at that and said, "Well, my son, we should say our goodbyes now and let this young couple enjoy their last night together before parting tomorrow morning."

"Don't say it like that, Papa," said Betta. "Uri and Father will only be gone a few weeks." She turned dark blue eyes on her father in a question.

He nodded. "I hope so, my dear. We will be going up against the last stronghold of the hated Ammonites and their god, Molech. The walled city of Rabbah will not be taken easily. It could drag on for months if we have to build a siege tower or try to starve them out. But whatever it takes, we will defeat them."

Placing a hand on her father's arm, the young woman said, "Please watch over Uri. And Uri, you watch out for Father too. Promise me? Both of you?"

"Of course," the two men said in unison. Her father pulled his robe about his throat as Betta latched the windows against the evening air that had now turned cold.

She turned to give her grandfather a kiss and begged him, "Papa, please come by whenever you can. It's going to be lonely with both my husband and father away. I'd love to hear more of your stories about growing up with the king when he was a young boy and how those times were."

"I will come by when I can, sweetheart, and you can send word to me if you need anything. Hopefully, this will be the final campaign for a long time. Now, if I can just figure out what is going on with King David."

Betta replied, "You are the wisest man I know, Papa. You will figure it out. I love you!"

"I love you too, Betta. Good night." Both men disappeared into the darkness as Uri and Betta turned to each other with a look of love tinged with sadness.

After the two older men had departed, Betta said, "Come, Uri, let's go out front, and I'll show you the roses I planted yesterday."

Uri said, "I thought I caught their scent from the window today in the breeze. They will be beautiful this summer."

Betta replied, "I can't wait until you return so we can enjoy them together."

"Let's spend a few minutes out back in the garden."

Taking his hand, the young wife clung to her husband's arm as they stepped into the beautiful patio with two palm trees at the corners of the wall and several potted plants adorning the stone walkway. The girl Anna continued to clean up the dinner meal and then left for the night.

Stepping into the brisk, twilit evening, a few stars winked above. The couple paused to admire them.

"I have a surprise for you," Uri teased, pulling Betta's hand as he led her to a few chest-high flowering shrubs that formed a small enclosure near the wall of the garden. Stepping behind the shrubs, Betta gasped.

"A pool! With clear water!"

"Yes, my darling. Now you can relax out here privately amid the flowers during the warm evenings. See, there are jugs for pouring water to refresh yourself." He pointed to a pair of ornately-carved clay jugs sitting beside the brick-lined pool. "And there's a new privy as well."

"Ari, this is wonderful! You are a talented builder—your knowledge must come from planning field maneuvers." She hugged him with excitement.

"I'm glad you like it," he grinned. "I want our home to be comfortable for years to come, especially as our family grows."

"I feel soon God will give us a child. When you return from the campaign," Betta smiled. "Thank you for this delightful gift. Now I will always remember your kindness when I relax out here."

"Don't bathe until after dark," he reminded her. "We don't want anyone spying on you. I know your father said we have nothing to fear from the king, but I still don't like the idea of a man with his passion living so close to my beautiful wife. I want you to promise that you will avoid being seen by him whenever you go out."

"I'll be careful," she said." I will wear my headscarf low to keep my face covered."

"Your beauty can also be a curse. You can't be too careful."

They walked arm in arm back to the house as the moon crested overhead.

Chapter 2:

Intrigue in the Palace

Bathsheba's grandfather, Ahithophel, was known in his official capacity in the palace as Ahithophel the Gilonite, Personal Advisor and Counselor to His Majesty, King David, Ruler of all Israel and Judah. When he left his granddaughter's home that night, he made his way around the two-story palace west wall, then along the landscaped south wall to the columnated front entrance. The entrance faced east, looking toward Mount Moriah, the site King David had selected for the building of the temple of God—the temple that God had since forbidden David to build.

When word leaked that the king would no longer erect the long-awaited temple, rumors had sprung up among the people in the city and even the outlying villages and farms. Why would their beloved King David, a man after God's own heart, not be allowed to construct the official place of worship in Jerusalem? David had certainly intended to build the temple.

He had planned, designed and had begun acquiring the materials and workers for the construction.

But then something stopped him. All of the preparations were halted. But why? Ahithophel explained to the elders and they to the people. The reason was quite simple: David is a warrior. He has blood on his hands and God made it clear through His prophets that David was disqualified because of that.

In David's servitude to Israel's first ruler, King Saul, and in his subsequent flight as a fugitive from Saul, David and his followers fought bloody battles for years. They raided remnant Canaanite and Philistine villages and settlements in the Judean wilderness, killing men, women, and children, collecting their booty and leaving no survivors. After he was crowned king of the southern tribe of Judah, David continued to wage bloody wars against the northern tribes of Israel until they surrendered and crowned him king of both Israel and Judah. After that, he continued to lead armies to defeat and subdue most of the surrounding nations. He was indeed a fierce and bloodthirsty warrior.

Before construction of the temple began, God spoke to Nathan, God's prophet, telling him to let the king know that he was not to build the temple because he was not suited for the task. The temple was to be a place of peace where the common people could come to worship God and experience God's peace in their hearts. God said through Nathan that it would not be David who would build His temple, but one of David's decendants would build God's home on earth.

Ahithophel and other counselors who served David kept an eye on the city's rumors, and some expressed concerns that there were other weaknesses that might be eating at David's character. Why he had decided not to lead the army into battle was a question on many advisors' minds. Did it have something to do with God disqualifying him from building the temple? It had also been noted that the king was not spending as much time in prayer or consulting his advisors as before. He seemed pensive or moody, but courteous when attending to palace duties. Still, questions had been raised in secret about the king's reputation and standing.

Nodding to the saluting guards, Ahithophel entered the large foyer, dimly lit by wall sconces, which served as a reception area, and passed through it. He then made his way up the stone stairs to his second-floor quarters in the north wing, his mind filled with questions and concerns about his long-time friend and comrade. Besides the issues of age and physical ability, he couldn't put his finger on whatever else might be bothering the king, but he knew David well enough to feel something was brewing.

The sage counselor decided to check with his colleague Nathan, the seer, the man of God, whose chamber was just down the hall. He tapped lightly on the door and heard the man of God answer softly,

"Who's visiting at this hour? Come in."

Ahithophel pushed the wooden door open. "It's just me, old friend. Do you have time to chat?"

Nathan, already in his long sleeping shirt, stood to greet his colleague and said,

"Of course, Ahithophel. I always have time for you, though I'm not the night owl you are. Here, take my chair. I'll sit here on the bed. What's on your mind?"

As Ahithophel made himself comfortable, he replied, "I've just come from my granddaughter's home where I was wishing Godspeed to Eliam and Uriah. They are leaving with Joab and the others early in the morning. It was hard to see Betta facing up to the fact that her new husband would be leaving with no assurance when or if he will come home again."

Nathan got up and gestured toward a clay pitcher. "May I pour some water for you?" Then he said, while filling a cup, "Yes, I'm sure it's hard for her, but wives and mothers have been doing that since the beginning of the human race. With her father and husband as proven warriors, Bathsheba will get used to these partings in time."

Ahithophel nodded, taking a sip of the cool, refreshing water. Then, as he ran his other hand through his graying hair, he responded,

"She was asking me why the king decided to stay home for this campaign." He paused, and said, "I couldn't answer her question, Nathan. I told her I had advised David to reconsider his decision. However, the king insisted he has matters to attend to here in Jerusalem. I know the men gain a lot of strength and motivation with him directing the battle. He should be with them. I mean, that's what kings do."

Nathan nodded thoughtfully.

Ahithophel continued, "I'm beginning to wonder about David's judgment. He refuses to listen to logic lately, and he seems to feel that your priestly counsel, and that of other wise courtiers, is no longer essential. Yes, he consults you on certain matters, as we have seen, but not all. You're close to him, Nathan. Have you noticed a difference in his behavior?"

Nathan didn't answer immediately. He was obviously thinking hard about his response. Stroking his white beard, he began to speak slowly, choosing his words with care.

"I have known David since he was a lad. I was there when he slew Goliath. I witnessed Saul's persecution of him, and I was amazed at David's patience and respect for Saul, even though Saul treated him like a dog and tried to kill him."

Ahithophel nodded. "Yes, he was on fire for the Lord in those days."

Nathan continued, "David was noble in all his ways. He refused to harm Saul even when he had a chance. He said that he should never lift his hand against God's chosen one. He knew it was God's place to deal with Saul in God's own time. As you know, God did judge Saul and brought him and his sons to an inglorious end at the hand of the Philistines. Yes, David was a friend of God and a man to be admired and respected for his integrity and courage, but even more so because of his faith and trust in God."

Nathan smiled as though to himself. "Do you remember, old friend, when just a few years ago, the Lord God showed his love for David by promising him that one of his descendants would always occupy the throne? God allowed me to be his spokesman on that occasion—and I was in awe. I haven't heard God speak many times, but when He does, it's a terrifying and exhilarating experience."

"I can't even imagine talking directly with God," Ahithophel said softly.

"God was commending David for wanting to build him a house, you know, a temple. But then I heard the voice of God telling me to give David his message. *'David was not to build God's house because he was a warrior, a man with much blood on his hands. No, he would have to leave that task to his descendant. But, nevertheless, God would bless him and his descendants forever. David would always have one of his descendants on the throne. Always!'* Have any of our people—past judges, rulers, or leaders—been given a God-ordained promise like that?"

Ahithophel shook his head, remembering when David's glorious youth and God's lavish gifts for his faithful service and worship turned the hearts of the Israelites to God once more.

Nathan continued, "David was grateful. His speech overflowed with praise to God. He didn't understand how or why he, a lowly shepherd in Bethlehem, should be so richly blessed. He took from God's words that the Messiah would be one of his descendants! In his loving response, David wrote many beautiful psalms of praise to God for his goodness and mercy, but the one he wrote after receiving that promise from God was inspiring. We still sing it when we worship together. In fact, I've tried to collect many of his musical compositions in the Temple for the religious feasts and celebrations."

Ahithophel smiled, savoring these delightful memories of his boyhood friend and now king.

Then Nathan said, "David continued on that high road, and God continued to bless him. He was victorious in every battle. His decrees were welcomed by the people. Everyone loved King David. Every effort he set his hand to was blessed." Nathan's smile faded. "But you know, after a while...I don't know, I think he did begin to change. Everything became so easy for him. Maybe too easy; I suppose he began to get accustomed to having whatever he wanted. Maybe...maybe God's promise that his descendants would reign forever let David sort of...relax a little, like he didn't have to work so hard at serving God or preserving the kingdom. I don't know."

Ahithophel said, "That would be understandable for normal men, but David is not a normal man. He is God's chosen one. You've said so yourself."

Nodding, Nathan continued, "Recently, he seems to forget, at times, that God is the reason for his success. He used to confer with me every time he set out on a campaign or planned a new venture; even in small things, he would seek God's guidance. I never met a more devoted man. But that has changed. He seldom seeks a word from God these days. I haven't talked to him for several days."

Ahithophel's eyes widened. "That scares me, Nathan. Our king seems distant from you and me—and likely others as well—and we are supposed to be his closest advisors." He paused as this awareness sank in for both of them.

Then Ahithophel said, "There's another issue on my mind, so I may as well mention it. He has added several more wives in recent years. I realize most of these unions are treaty wives, cementing relations with other nations, but now he picks up a new slave girl, a concubine, almost every time his army conquers a city or region. Someone mentioned he has at least ten concubines now, in addition to his fifteen wives. Could this seeming preoccupation with women have something to do with his decision to stay home from the war? You know Moses warned future kings about accumulating horses and wives. Maybe David feels his virility is dwindling, and he must prove himself?"

Nathan hesitated briefly before sighing as he got to his feet. "It's getting late. I must get to my bed now. Thank you for stopping by. We must keep the king in our prayers."

Ahithophel replied, "Indeed we must, and I will. By the way, this conversation never happened. Thank you for taking time with me, Nathan. Now get your beauty sleep."

As Ahithophel walked down the stone passageway thinking about the conversation, he opened the door into his quarters and found his assistant, Hesel, arranging some parchments on the desk near the archived scrolls.

"Oh, Hesel, what are you doing here this late? You should be enjoying time downstairs with the other apprentices."

Hesel blinked at the older man's words and smiled. Stretching his broad shoulders, he rubbed a short, curly beard. "That sounds like a good idea."

As he turned to leave, Ahithophel assumed the young man had been hoping to glance over the dull business scrolls to improve his reading ability. He had been in training to become a religious leader when his father died but was now forced to hold a position. Ahithophel had known Hesel's family and was impressed with the maturity and integrity of the young man. He had offered Hesel a position as his assistant and protégé, and Hesel gladly accepted, He had been faithfully serving in Ahithophel's service for three years. His sister, Hadassah, had also found favor among the servants and was now in service to King David.

Hesel replied, "Things were pretty quiet down there, so I thought I would tackle these old scrolls and maps in the archive bin. I've wanted to get them organized for some time, but I can only work on them while you are out. How was your evening, sir?"

"I had some time with my son and his family. It was kind of a goodbye dinner, you know, with the army heading out in the morning. And you can read the scrolls anytime, boring as they are," he chuckled.

"Thank you, sir. Yes, I can imagine your granddaughter's concerns for her father and husband both leaving at the same time."

"For all of her life, she has watched her father go off to war every year about this time. But she and Uri have had a year-long honeymoon, and it had to end eventually. I think Uri is excited about taking his place among the Thirty. He wants to prove to His Majesty that he made the right decision by putting him in the group."

"From what I've heard, he will do fine."

"Yes, well, Hesel, I do need to wash up for bed, so we'd better say good night."

"Of course, sir. Goodnight." With a bow, the young man left the chamber.

As Ahithophel climbed into bed moments later, he pushed the nagging worry from his mind. Maybe the king was dealing with a major issue that could impact the kingdom. Maybe David would ride out with the troops the next morning after all, or soon provide a rationale for not doing so. With that thought, he closed his eyes and turned on his side to sleep.

Chapter 3:

Seeds of Discontent

T he next morning just after sunrise, the troops gathered at the city gates. Some had been summoned from the outlying areas while others were quartered in Jerusalem. Camels were packed with military provisions, and mules were harnessed to carts loaded with weapons and supplies. Though some could be heard talking with the occasional shout of a commander's order, the men were unusually quiet and reserved, going about the business of preparing to march out of the gates in a few moments.

Older men, the palace staff, and some women looked on from windows and balconies near the main gates. Others stood back to watch the company assemble, many with tears in their eyes as they waved good-bye. The king came out of the palace and stood on the steps to watch the preparations. Betta and Anna had walked around to the front of the palace where the young wife stood glancing around for her husband among the troops falling into rank. Although the area was relatively crowded, she felt someone looking at her and turned to catch the admiring glance of the king. Abruptly, she turned away to search for Uri as King David's eyes reluctantly returned to his troops.

General Joab stepped forward and bowed to the king. "The troops are ready to depart. Do you have any final orders, sire?"

"We have thoroughly studied the battle plan, and you have been given my final instructions in the scroll delivered to your quarters yesterday. I trust you've read them and have no questions?"

"No questions, Your Majesty. We are ready for the battle."

"Good." Raising his voice to be heard among the troops, including those at the back, David said, "May God bless the campaign and make you victorious. Remember, you are fighting for God, home, and your king."

The men cheered loudly as Joab motioned for the squadron leaders to direct the men out of the city.

Betta had caught a glimpse of Uri, who seemed to be quickly scanning the crowd in her direction. For a brief moment, their eyes met and locked. She blew him a small kiss, and Uri smiled warmly before resuming his duties and leading his squadron of foot soldiers through the gates on the road to Rabbah. Feeling a cold chill, although the morning was bright, Betta returned to her home and entered the house, closing the door behind her.

A few weeks later, Ahithophel returned from the market square where he had bought a few supplies. He dropped off the purchases in his room, then stopped by the office of the court secretary, a good friend and colleague, Seraiah.

Answering his knock, Seraiah opened the wooden door and greeted the king's adviser with an embrace and clasping of hands. "I'm glad you stopped by before the meeting with His Majesty this morning. We need to talk."

Seraiah was younger than his friend but old enough to have experienced the king's wrath in days past. David had berated him in front of a meeting of court officials over an innocent omission in his report of some remarks made by the king. The secretary mistakenly assumed the words were only side comments not intended for the official records. David had sternly warned him with an ultimatum that he would be discharged if it happened again, an embarrassing scenario for a respected official. Seraiah was proud of his work and was hurt deeply by the public scolding. The secretary was still smarting these many weeks later.

Taking a seat where indicated by his friend, Ahithophel said, "I agree. We do need to talk. I invited some senior elders to the meeting, and depending on how it goes, we may want to bring them up afterward to give them an idea of our plan."

"Do you think that's a good idea? They could object, you know." Seraiah scratched his dark beard with a worried look on his face.

"I would be surprised if they don't. However, I think it would be better to bring them in on it now rather than spring it on them later. Now, is there something further we should discuss before the meeting?" Ahithophel glanced shrewdly at his friend, sensing another matter was weighing on him.

"Prince Amnon wants me to submit any new documents I generate for his approval before I give them to His Majesty. I don't appreciate his lack of confidence in my work. Nor am I sure that his father will approve."

"Well, I'm not too surprised. Amnon is always trying to exert his influence. David is aware of it and will put him in his place if it goes too far. Don't worry about it."

"That's easy for you to say. He's a conniving one. I would rather work under Absalom if I had to choose between the two sons. Fortunately, I don't have to make that choice, at least not now. What do you think?"

Ahithophel considered the question briefly. "Amnon is the brighter of the two, and he is the Crown Prince. He also has his father's passion for women, adventure, and success. But Absalom is the natural politician. He's unusually handsome, and that head of curly hair wins the hearts of the women wherever he goes. The townspeople everywhere he goes are naturally drawn to his sensitivity and good nature. If he should decide to recruit a good adviser, I think he might do well. So, if anything happens to David, or if his position were to weaken appreciably, either of the sons would be ready to step up and take David's throne. Absalom would be there if Amnon didn't work out for some reason. But I strongly doubt Amnon would give up his right to rule for any reason. That's a discussion for later, one that hopefully will never be needed. Right now, we have a meeting to attend."

Gathering up some documents, Seraiah said, "We better get down there. I don't want to risk another rebuke."

The king had called a staff meeting in the main level public room. The subject of this meeting was the status of the flow of supplies to Joab's army. David wanted to be sure that Joab had all the support needed to win this campaign. Ahithophel acted as the convening authority, but David himself usually ran the meetings. Also attending these sessions were David's sons Amnon and Absalom, along with Seraiah and Jehoshaphat, the purser. The three senior elders invited at Ahithophel's request were already seated together on the other side of the chamber when the two friends arrived. In fact, everyone was present except King David.

Several minutes passed as the advisers and elders exchanged greetings and made small talk. Silence fell as some began to appear uncomfortable. One of the elders, Shimon, said, "How long does His Majesty expect us to wait for his esteemed presence?"

Ahithophel looked down his nose at the elder disapprovingly, then responded, "Until he arrives or sends a message."

Through the window, the sun could be seen rising toward its midday zenith. Finally, Amnon said, "I will see what is keeping him."

He stood, a man of good height and solid build, and left the room. Curbing his annoyance, he walked down the corridor and up a short flight of stone steps to the door of David's living quarters. At his knock, David's servant, Mani, opened the door and looked sheepishly at the king's son. "Can I be of service, Prince Amnon?"

"Do you know the king's whereabouts? He has not joined his advisors at the scheduled meeting downstairs, nor has he sent word."

Mani replied, "I'm not sure I can be of help, sir. I could make inquiries..."

"Well, find out."

Mani turned and started to pass through the connecting corridor and steps leading to the harem. Pausing, he looked over his shoulder at Amnon. "I know there was some kind of disturbance in the wives' quarters earlier, and His Majesty went up to tend to it. He hasn't returned."

Shaking his head, Amnon grimaced and left David's area to return to the waiting group to announce, "His Majesty is indisposed. I suggest we adjourn and await his summons to resume. My apologies to all."

The group rose to leave amid grumbling from the elders. One was heard to murmur, "This isn't the first time he hasn't shown up for a meeting. Our king shows greater interest in his domestic interests than in his government."

Seraiah sidled up to Ahithophel and whispered, "Can you come to my office now?"

"Of course. Should I invite the elders?"

Seraiah paused, looked into Ahithophel's eyes, then said, "Why not?"

Ahithophel caught up with the elders as they headed down the corridor. "Excuse me, gentlemen. If you have time, would you join Seraiah and me for a short meeting in the secretary's office upstairs?"

"What's it about?" asked their leader, adjusting his head covering.

Ahithophel lowered his voice, and stepping closer, said, "We want to discuss these private distractions that keep His Majesty from public duties."

The three elders conferred in whispers. Finally, the leader said, "We are concerned, as well. We will come."

"Follow me," the adviser said.

When Ahithophel and the elders arrived at Seraiah's office, the secretary moved some things around in the relatively small but comfortable room to arrange seating for his guests. Piles of scrolls were moved to the floor to free up a wooden bench, and he smoothed the covers on his cot to provide more space to sit.

As the men settled themselves, Seraiah said, "Thank you for agreeing to this impromptu meeting. What I want to talk about is very sensitive, even dangerous. If you want to leave after my introduction, I won't blame you. But if you decide to stay, you could be a help to us and to the kingdom."

One of the elders said, "With those comments, you have aroused our curiosity. What could be so dangerous?"

"Well, while David is an absolute monarch and rules with confidence, he is seemingly inspired and led by God through Nathan and the other prophets. He also values the advice of the elders. Since Ahithophel has been acting as your go-between and he asked to have you present, I am glad you agreed to come. However, I would ask you to keep anything said here today to yourselves. It would be better not to share our discussion with the other elders. Please speak to no one of what we discuss here today. So, can we have your agreement to keep our meeting private?"

The three elders nodded in agreement. Their leader, Ben-Oni, said, "Since we elders only have access to the king through Ahithophel, we appreciate the invitation we received for today's meeting. Usually, we can only meet periodically with Ahithophel and share our concerns and opinions with him. Unfortunately, today's meeting ended like others recently. In fact, lately, every time we meet with Ahithophel, he has little or nothing to share because King David is seldom available for meetings or private counseling."

"So, what is so sensitive that we must be sworn to secrecy?" another elder asked.

The scribe looked away, fiddled with some things on his desk, and didn't answer immediately. Finally, he glanced up and said, "Ahithophel and I have taken it upon ourselves to prepare a confidential record of the recent actions of His Majesty. We think they need to be preserved in a private journal in case he is ever brought to account."

Ahithophel said, "You know we all respect King David, but some of us are concerned that he has been drifting from the Lord and the city in the past few months. He is becoming arrogant and distant in his dealings with the officials he works with, as well as with the local people, often appearing distracted and uninterested."

Seraiah added, "I've talked to Nathan about it. He thinks these changes began sometime after the king was so richly blessed a few years ago. David was always faithful to God in his earlier years. I don't know what's happened, except it almost seems as if he has lost his way or somehow gotten disconnected from God. It's been a while since he has held one of his open court sessions where anyone can bring their problems to him. Now, I'm afraid this decision to stay home from the war isn't sitting well with the people. The public has seen little of him in recent months, and when he does appear, he does not seem to be truly engaged with them."

The chief elder spoke sharply. "I acknowledge there are some issues with our king, but I won't be party to treason. Where do you think you are going with this "private journal"? You can't call the king before the council. In fact, if he knew we were having this meeting, he would be within his rights to have us all imprisoned, executed, or at least, banished for life."

"Of course, you are right," said Ahithophel. But do you have a better idea of what we could or should do? We are his counselors—his advisers. He depends on us—the people depend on us. We can't let him or them down; we must do our duty and not fail our God, who has allowed us to be appointed to protect the monarchy and kingdom."

"Do nothing," said Ben-Omi, ". . . but pray for God to deal with him. He is God's anointed one. It is our responsibility to follow the king's lead, and it is your job, Ahithophel, to give good counsel and use your position to support him in carrying out his ruling duties."

Ahithophel nodded. "That's exactly what I have been trying to do all the years we have worked together. David and I have always had a solid relationship built on mutual trust and respect. But now, something is different. He has changed. Have you noticed that he has not been playing his music as before, nor has he introduced a new psalm since last summer? That may indicate that the Lord has stopped communing with him."

Seraiah spoke up. "Or maybe David has stopped listening."

"Right," Ahithophel agreed. "He doesn't seek my opinion or advice as he always did before. In fact, I feel he avoids me, maybe shuns me. As far as I know, I haven't offended him. And it's not just me—Nathan says David avoids him as well. Something is wrong. I'm not sure what to do about it."

"God knows what's going on with him," said the elder with long white hair. "He knows all, and He will do what needs to be done. The king serves God directly, and we serve the king. Have patience, Ahithophel, and you too, Seraiah. That is my counsel. What do you other elders say?"

The two men nodded. Jahem said, "I can't think of anything else we could legitimately or spiritually do."

Ben-Oni spoke. "The king may be distracted with a personal matter that must remain private. In time, his former nature will return."

"I hope you are right," said Seraiah. I'm concerned that having proven his valor on the battlefield, our king may now be turning to incidental interests to pass the time. Perhaps warfare is too tame for his spirit."

Jahem said as everyone got up to leave. "I doubt that is the case. But if he does not return his attention to kingdom matters, King David may soon have to fight the biggest battle of his life. We must trust God for the outcome."

Ahithophel looked to Seraiah, who nodded assent. He said, "Very well. We will take your advice for now, but I feel a strong sense of dread building in the palace that will soon transcend its walls. I hope we don't regret doing nothing."

Chapter 4:

David's Desire

Following Seraiah's meeting with Ahithophel and the elders, the secretary signaled to Ahithophel to remain until the elders were gone. When the others were out of sight, the secretary said, "If you're not opposed, I want to go ahead and keep a brief journal of David's conduct. What do you think?"

Ahithophel nodded and said, "Yes, but be sure to keep it hidden. I don't like misleading the elders, but I think it is the prudent thing to do. We should document his distractions with the harem. I think our leader has something on his mind besides his age, something that is involved with his staying home from the war."

With that, he exited the room and left Seraiah to handle the matter.

Seraiah sat down at his work table, took out a fresh pen and blank scroll of papyrus, and began to write.

"On the 15th day of Nisan in the 19th year of David's reign as king over all Israel and Judah, His Majesty dispatched

General Joab and his army to do battle against Rabbah, the last stronghold of the children of Ammon. His Majesty did not accompany the army as he always has in times past. Today marks the third time in as many weeks that His Majesty has called a meeting to discuss matters of state, but has not attended, and has given no reason for canceling the meeting. His personal servant, Maniel, has carefully hinted that the king is sometimes distracted by domestic issues with families of his extensive harem."

Seraiah's pen paused briefly, but then he quickly began writing again.

"The palace staff is reduced to a small number of guards plus servants of His Majesty and the royal family. Nathan, Ahithophel the Gilonite, and the king's two oldest sons make up the staff here, with a few administrative assistants on the second floor in the north wing of the palace. King David made his sons Amnon and Absalom ministers in his government about a year ago. Following this introduction, entries will be added as appropriate."

Seraiah put down the writing utensil and reread the entry. He rolled up the parchment and placed it carefully behind his bed where it couldn't be seen, rather than on a shelf with the others.

When Ahithophel returned to his room after the meeting with Seraiah and the elders, he found Hesel waiting for him. Hesel was obviously uncomfortable, pacing as much as he could in the cramped quarters. He was lightly perspiring, and when his mentor appeared, he ushered him into the room then shut the door so quickly that Ahithophel knew something was amiss. "Hesel, what's the matter?"

The young man answered, "Sir, I've just learned some terrible news from David's manservant, Maniel. I hate to be the one to tell you, but I think you should know."

"Well, what is it man? What did you hear?" Ahithophel said, alarm growing within.

"After breakfast this morning, Mani called me to follow him outside to the courtyard where we couldn't be overheard. He said, 'King David was unable to sleep yesterday afternoon at his usual time. He got up, and Mani brought him a cup of warm wine to help the king relax. Then the king went out on the roof and strolled its perimeter while looking over the city. When he reached the west end of the roof, something caught his attention below in a nearby garden.' Mani explained that the king seemed transfixed by what he saw in the neighboring property, but Mani couldn't see it because he remained inside the king's parlor."

Hesel paused as though to catch his breath and gather his thoughts. "Then King David called Mani over to the parapet to join him. He said the king asked, 'Who was that woman in the garden of that house down there?' Of course, Mani knew it was Bathsheba's home and told the king, 'She is Bathsheba, the daughter of Eliam and the wife of Uriah the Hittite.' I'm sure Mani identified her as a daughter and a wife to remind the king of the woman's connections to his loyal military subjects—two of his elite body guards—his Thirty Mighty Men. Mani admitted that everyone knows the house in question is the home of your granddaughter, Bathsheba, and her husband Uriah the Hittite."

With rising blood pressure, Ahithophel said, "Eliam and Uriah are on the battlefield. Why did David even notice my granddaughter?"

"Mani knows that your family has been part of David's inner circle for decades. At first, he thought the king might feel sympathy for the woman living alone without a husband or father. But he must have remembered she is also your granddaughter and that you would provide for her if needed. Mani also knew that David had attended Uriah and Bathsheba's wedding and presented the couple with that very house adjacent to the palace wall where they now live. For some reason, the king seemed to have forgotten who Bathsheba is."

Ahithophel was feeling more and more uncomfortable. He said, "I'm afraid I know where this is going," adding to himself, *But please, God, no. Not my Betta.*

Hesel continued, "As we all know, the king has an appetite for beautiful women. Well, David's countenance brightened, and he told Mani to send a couple of servant girls over to bring Bathsheba to him. Mani was hoping he just wanted to compliment Uriah's wife on her husband's loyalty to the king or possibly offer assistance with her male relatives away in battle. Maybe he would present an award for their valor."

Ahithophel listened patiently as his heartbeat quickened.

Hesel paused and wiped his brow. "Mani said, 'When Bathsheba was brought to David, he told all of us servants to leave and see that they weren't interrupted, then closed the door behind them.' Then Mani said, 'David didn't come out for over three hours. When he did, he called in the two female servants to help Bathsheba with her personal needs. One of those girls was my sister, Hadassah. I just talked to her, and she confirmed that the king and Bathsheba did not appear to have had a business meeting.'"

Ahithophel groaned and buried his head in his hands. He muttered, "Oh Lord. How could he? God, how could you let him do this? Oh, my poor Betta. No wonder he didn't show up for the meeting this morning. He couldn't face me." He paused as he began to understand David's strange behavior. With the army gone to the battlefield, he must have felt extraordinarily free to do as he wished without censure. Besides violating a helpless subject—a woman alone in her garden, he had betrayed one of his closest friends and colleagues. How could he? How could he?" Ahithophel wept, hurt for his granddaughter and himself as her failed protector.

Seraiah's next journal post contained a sobering account.

The following record begins with an alarming report received from Ahithophel himself, and has since been corroborated by Nathan the Seer. The events that follow will surely be recorded in history as one of the most dramatic and intriguing eras in the life of King David and all Israel.

Ahithophel had come to the secretary's office, clearly shaken. He was normally a stoic figure about the palace, not a man without humor but a man with the weight of the kingdom on his shoulders, normally a serious man. But when he arrived that day, he appeared extremely angry. His face was ashen, and his hands were shaking; it was all he could do to keep his composure. His first words were, "The king has sunk to the depths of depravity."

The secretary asked in alarm, "What's wrong, man? What happened?"

Ahithophel got control of his emotions and wiped his forehead. "As all of the palace staff is aware, the king is spending most days alone, except when with his harem. However, something is bothering him. Yesterday afternoon, he was restless and went out on the palace roof to relax in the evening air. I've heard that he sometimes watches the city settling down for the night as the lights in nearby homes are lit." He paused as his throat constricted.

"Somehow, my granddaughter Bathsheba, wife of Uriah, as you know, was using the new bath pool that her husband installed in their garden, which sits beneath the west wall of the palace. It was nearly dark, I'm told, which is why my granddaughter felt safe in bathing herself outdoors. Uriah had fashioned a small pool in a corner of the garden surrounded by shrubs. But somehow, the king saw her, and after confirming her name and identity, he sent servants to bring her to the palace."

"Whatever for?" Seraiah asked, his face crinkled in curiosity

Without saying anything, Ahithophel threw him a knowing glance.

"No! The king wouldn't take another man's wife—especially one related to one of his friends and officials. It cannot be."

With a deep groan, Ahithophel said, "He just took her, then sent her home with servants." After a short pause, he added, "My close friend from childhood, my master and my king, has violated my granddaughter—my own blood! She is the precious only child of my son. How could he do this to her, and how could he betray me by doing such a thing?"

Seraiah's eyes widened. "I'm so sorry, Ahithophel. This is shocking! I would never have believed the king capable of such an act. He has plenty of women already—and his pick of others in the city if he wanted. Why take someone's wife—a young girl of noble character, and a member of your family?"

Ahithophel said, "I have to do something, but what? If I confront him in his present state of mind, David could strike me down—me, his lifelong friend and confidant. But now I must go to Betta and try to comfort her. She has no mother or sisters to care for her."

Ahithophel left the secretary's office and started down the hall toward the steps to the front entrance. In a moment, another door opened into the hallway, and Prince Amnon stepped into his path. Ahithophel stopped abruptly to avoid colliding with the prince. Amnon paused and said, "Oh, Ahithophel, excuse me."

"My apologies. My mind is elsewhere. I must see my granddaughter."

"Seeing the look on your face, I suspect I know why," said the prince. "I heard the news about Father's dalliance with Uriah's wife."

Ahithophel said, "But I only learned about it myself a few minutes ago. How could you have known?"

"I have sources who keep me informed. Your granddaughter supposedly offered herself to my father, but then, many women do."

Ahithophel shouted, "I don't care if you are a prince—no one can talk about my granddaughter like that!"

"Easy, old man." Amnon folded his arms and leaned back against the corridor wall. I'm just telling you what my father said when I asked about the rumors. He said Bathsheba was bathing in her garden when he happened to walk by on the roof. He said it looked like an open invitation."

"I don't believe that! I'm going to talk to her right now."

"Fine. But remember who we're talking about. As the king, my father can do anything he wants; that includes reaching out to take anything...or anyone. You can't do anything about it. You'd best calm down before you talk to her."

Without another word, Ahithophel brushed by the prince and hurried down the steps. Reaching the street, he quickly walked around the palace walls, approaching the home of Uriah and Betta with trepidation. He knocked quietly, and hearing no response, he opened the door slightly.

"Betta? It's Papa." Hearing no response, he entered the home and looked around but didn't see her. Stepping slowly to the door of her bedroom, he saw Betta lying face down on her bed. Anna was braiding her hair but nodded and left as Ahithophel entered the room. He could hear Betta sobbing softly, so he stood quietly. Then he said, "Betta, my dear, I know what happened. I'm so sorry. How can I help you?"

There was no response at first, then Betta rolled over, and with visible effort, she struggled to a sitting position. Glancing up at him, he noted her eyes swollen from tears and her usual smiling face replaced by a sorrowful countenance. She tried to speak but broke down and began sobbing again.

Ahithophel felt tears gathering in his eyes. He went over to his granddaughter and helped her to stand, embracing her gently for several moments as she struggled to get herself together. He remembered picking her up as a toddler when she fell down in the meadows where they took walks to enjoy the wildflowers. He remembered brushing away her tears after she got stung by a bee. He wished comforting her now would be as easy, but it was difficult, even impossible. *My beloved grand-child, you should have nothing but God's love and kindness shine upon you. You do not deserve this. The physical humiliation is only the beginning...it may last a very long time.*

Finally, the young woman was able to speak. "Oh, Papa, the king took me, and I didn't know what to do. How do you say 'no' to the king? I must not have taken enough care to conceal myself. I felt uneasy about bathing outdoors. Uri had told me to be careful, and I thought I was. But the king saw me—he told me he did, and said he could not resist my beauty—Uri warned me and told me to be careful" she broke off, weeping harder.

Ahithophel held her again without speaking, letting her emotions run their course.

After a long moment, Betta eased away and drew her grandfather over to the divan where they could sit together, face to face.

Looking down, she began, "Last evening was so warm and peaceful in the garden that I decided to quickly take my ritual bath outdoors. It was beginning to get dark, and I only took a few moments and then hurried inside before the air turned chilly. But soon, there was a knock at the door, and two servant women stood there. I recognized their palace attire, and Anna knew them from the marketplace. The older one said very seriously, 'His Majesty, the king, requests your presence. Please come with us.' I could not imagine why he would summon me. Did he have news of Uriah? I grabbed my head cover and went with them, but when I motioned for Anna to come with me, the older female said that she must wait here." Betta was breathing faster now, and Ahithophel placed his hand over hers in a calming gesture.

Betta gave him a grateful nod. "When we arrived at His Majesty's chambers, the women ushered me inside, then turned and left, closing the door behind them. I stood there alone for a while, uneasy, as night had fallen by then. The king came in from the other room, talking to his manservant, who carried a lantern and set it down inside the chamber. I heard King David say that he was not to be disturbed. My anxiety grew. After the servant left, His Majesty was very kind. He offered me a seat and wine to drink, which I refused. I sat down on a divan near the door, but he came and sat beside me. Glancing up at his face, I then knew what he was planning."

A sob escaped her throat, followed by a gush of tears as the young wife buried her face in her grandfather's shoulder. She choked out a few words. "Oh, Papa, he took me by the arm and led me into his bedchamber. I couldn't do anything. He is so strong, and he's the king! I cried out, 'No. Please. Don't do this to your servant.' But he was determined."

For several minutes, Betta released the pent-up emotion in her soul to her grief-stricken grandfather. Ahithophel put an arm around her shoulders and drew her close, wishing he could have protected her against the king's assault.

She regained control and pulled away. With hands in her lap, she whispered a few moments later, "Papa, I feel so dirty and used. When he was finished with me, he directed the female servants to come and help me clean up and adjust my clothing and hair. They took me out by a back passageway so no one would see us, and escorted me home."

The aging man rose to his feet and said with venom in his voice, "He will not get away with this. The Lord God will surely strike him down. And, if the Lord doesn't, then I will." He thought, *How could God have allowed this? Isn't David a 'man after God's own heart'?*

Ahithophel asked softly, "Betta, have you ever had a conversation with the king, or in any way given him reason to think you find him attractive or interesting?"

Betta thought quietly for a couple of moments, then said slowly, "I've never exchanged more than a few words with him. He was at our wedding last summer as a guest of honor, so I thanked him for coming." She thought about the morning when the troops left and she had caught the king's eyes on her briefly. "I saw him looking at me the day Uri and Father left with the troops. But we didn't speak, and I went right home afterward."

Treading carefully, her grandfather said, "Betta, David told one of his sons that he had seen you from his roof. He said he saw you bathing in the garden and thought you were essentially inviting him to send for you."

Betta stormed, "I would never do that. Yes, I needed my monthly ritual bathing, and the pool Uriah made for me sounded so inviting; also, I wouldn't get the kitchen all wet. I thought the walls around our property would hide me."

Ahithophel said thoughtfully, "That should be true. Unfortunately, the king happened to be restless and took a walk on the palace roof just as you were bathing."

"He told me, but I tried to explain that Uri built the bathing pool near shrubs for protection. The king...changed the subject. He didn't want to hear anything about Uri or privacy." The pair fell silent again.

Betta asked quietly, "What will Uriah say when he finds out?"

Ahithophel paused. "I'm not sure you should tell him. He loves you deeply and is fiercely protective."

She replied, "Well, you found out. It must be common knowledge among the palace staff."

He nodded. "You're probably right."

Betta took a deep breath. "Well, no one can do anything about it. But I despise the man."

"Your sorrow will heal in time, Betta. We can pray that the Lord will deal with David in His own way."

"I don't want to hear the man's name again."

Ahithophel knew that would be nearly impossible with the family's connection to David's court. "I must get back to the palace, my dear. Will you be alright? Can I bring you anything?"

"No, Papa, but thank you. Anna will stay with me."

Her grandfather nodded. "I'll be back soon, my dear. Be strong."

"Thank you, Papa."

Six weeks passed without further mention of the assault. Ahithophel again appeared at the secretary's door. He looked much the same as he had when he first brought the news of David's crime, with a worried look in his eyes.

Seeing his friend's agitated face, Seraiah asked, "What's happened now?"

The adviser walked across the room and sat down on the edge of the bed, shaking his head and looking at the floor. Then, he said, "My granddaughter is pregnant."

The secretary asked, "How could you know that?"

He replied, "Betta and Anna were shopping in the market this morning and ran into one of the servant girls who had brought her to David. Betta drew the girl aside and whispered to her the news I just gave you. She asked the girl to take the message to David. That servant's brother is my assistant, Hesel. His sister's name is Hadassah. That's how I know."

Ahithophel fidgeted nervously as he spoke. "She must be keeping the news from me until she sees how the king will react. This could become a public scandal. If someone happens to see Bathsheba with child, the word will get out—people know her husband is away with the army. Some of the palace staff heard that David was with Bathsheba alone in his quarters a few weeks ago. Everyone will know who the father is. David can't let that happen. His public image is already shaky."

Seraiah sighed. "Sleeping with the daughter and grand-daughter of his closest official and friend, the wife of one of his best warriors—such betrayal would be unforgivable. According to Moses, if Bathsheba is found to be complicit, both David and she could be stoned for adultery."

Ahithophel grimaced and his eyes shot fire. "There's no way Betta was complicit. It was just David. The law of Moses also condemns the act of rape." He paused and then added, "David will think of a way out of this. He is dangerous when cornered. Who knows what he will do? At this point, I worry about Betta's safety."

Chapter 5:

Uriah's Fears

It had been weeks since Joab's army had marched out of Jerusalem that chilly spring morning. Uriah was glad he had been able to spot his bride near the front of the palace subtly waving at him. That warmed his heart as he marched with the army out the city gates and up the Mount of Olives to reach the Jericho road leading to the Jordan valley below. Other contingents of David's troops from various regions of the country rendevoused there at the Jordan with Joab's army. Once the full army was assembled, it took almost a full week to get all the men and supplies across the spring-swollen river. Then it took more days to get organized for the advance on Rabbah.

As the army marched into the Ammonite hills, their advance patrols observed small bands of Ammonite soldiers, apparently out on surveillance missions, withdrawing and racing back to Rabbah to report that a major Israelite army was heading their way. Uriah felt a rush of adrenalin as their objective drew near.

The army of experienced and able Israelite warriors quickly set up their camp across the valley from Rabbah, intentionally in full view of the Ammonite army holding the walled city. It took several days for Joab to get his equipment unpacked and assembled for the assault. During that time, the officers and men took the positions that had been planned ahead of time by Joab and his chief officers in the meetings with King David. Although their king was not accompanying them on the assault, he had been eager to help Joab draw up the detailed plan. It was left to Joab and his officers to scout the area around Rabbah and decide where the best approaches would be for setting up their war machines.

Within a few days, Joab was able to dispatch couriers back to Jerusalem to advise David and his counselors on what they would need in the way of specialized equipment and materials for a successful campaign. David's people in Jerusalem would set up logistic support lines from Israelite cities and all of the vassal nations under David's control. The army was large, and the campaign was going to be a long one. It might take most of a full year to take Rabbah because of their strategic location.

The city of Rabbah was built around large springs, providing the inhabitants with an unlimited supply of water. In fact, the city was known in the region as "Water City." It was built on two levels. The lower level was where the springs were located, and the citadel above was nestled in a steep canyon. The only access to the citadel was through the walled lower city. The layout utilized the natural terrain to limit approaches to the high walls. It was rumored that the walls were ten feet thick in places, with multiple stations for archers to shoot their arrows from behind shielded ramparts. The Ammonites were dug in and had amassed supplies for a long campaign.

The fighting for the first few weeks mostly involved brief thrusts and sorties to test the defenses. Joab also had to defend against occasional night raids by the Ammonites as they sought to hamper the work on the shielded siege towers and catapults which were mounted on wheeled platforms. Joab's siege towers were movable and were high enough to look over the walls and down into the interior. They could thus discover the thinner parts of the walls and shoot flaming arrows at the interior structures.

The next phase began with serious assaults on the weakest part of the walls. Joab's men found that if they tested an isolated section of wall with a small squad of men, the Ammonites might open a gate, allowing a sizable number of warriors to come out and attack their group. Man-to-man fighting would ensue until the raiding party withdrew far enough that the Ammonites would return to the safety of their walls. Uriah led some of those incursions and became adept at drawing the enemy out far enough that he could have an ambush waiting to fall on the Ammonites, destroying them before they could return to safety.

One evening after Uriah's squad returned to camp, he found a messenger from Joab waiting for him. He was instructed to come to the general's command tent immediately. When he arrived, Joab asked for a quick report on his team's action, then said,

"His Majesty has sent for you. Get your things together and head for Jerusalem as soon as you can."

Uriah asked, "Why does he want me?"

Joab replied, "I don't know. Just grab a mount and get going. You should be able to get there sometime tomorrow evening."

"But...why?"

"Uriah, he didn't say. Go now."

"Yes, sir."

As Uriah set out on Joab's horse, the strongest horse available, he followed the road down to the Jordan, his mind and emotions in turmoil. Try as he would, he could not remember anything he could have done that would result in a sudden summons to the royal palace. Uriah rehearsed in his mind everything that had happened over the past several weeks, both before the army left and since. Nothing out of the ordinary had occurred while he was still at home. Neither had Joab, nor any of his officers confronted him with wrongdoing since they had arrived at Rabbah. In fact, he had been commended for his courage and ability to draw out the enemy and destroy them, but that was not extraordinary; that was his job.

There was nothing he could think of that would cause him to be called home. Home...home? Could it be about something that happened at home? Had something happened to Betta? Or to Papa? No, if something had happened to Papa, it would have been Eliam who would have been called home. That would just leave Betta. As he focused his thoughts on his young wife, the words of Papa came to his mind. "Make sure you hold your beautiful wife close. Our king hungers for beautiful women."

Oh, please, God. Don't let anything happen to my wife. But, he thought, *What could happen to her that would warrant calling me home from the war? And if the king harmed her in any way, why would he summon me?*

As Uriah rode through the night, he prodded his mount to a faster pace, all while worrying about what could have happened. The longer he rode, the more he imagined things that might have happened. He decided in his mind that it was one of two things: either Bathsheba had been badly hurt or killed, or the king was involved with her somehow. But how? If David had forced her to his bed, he wouldn't have called her husband home to tell him about it. Would he? Then what else could it be?

As Uriah continued through the night, he was thankful for the full moon. The road up to Jerusalem was hazardous enough in the daytime. He tried to keep his attention on the trail as he began the ascent to Jerusalem, but he couldn't stop thinking about his young, vulnerable wife. *Papa is there to protect her. The king wouldn't do anything to his personal advisor's granddaughter. Would he?*

As he drew closer to Jerusalem, he decided that he must have a plan when he went in to confront David. *If the king doesn't have something important to tell me about my performance or what he needs my help with, then I will assume it has something to do with Betta. Lord, please give me the strength to face whatever is going to happen, and give me wisdom to know what to do. If it is something to do with Bathsheba, please watch over her and take care of her. Lord, I leave it all in your hands.*

Chapter 6:

The King and Uriah

As Seraiah was writing at his desk in the palace, he heard murmuring voices and footsteps rushing down the corridor. Opening his chamber door, he caught a couple of servants whispering near the stairs.

"Jehu, go see what is happening. Something is afoot."

The servant looked up in surprise from sweeping the inner rooms. "Yes, sir," Jehu said as he set the broom aside and walked down the corridor.

Seraiah sat down again but could not concentrate on the report he was writing. Within minutes Jehu returned to the chamber and gently closed the door behind him.

Wide-eyed, he said, "Uriah's back. He's in with His Majesty now."

Seraiah said, "Oh my, go quickly and tell Ahithophel; he needs to know."

In a few minutes, Jehu returned with Ahithophel, who said, "Jehu says Uriah is here. I'm sure David has summoned him home because of Bathsheba. I must know what his plan is. I'm going down to wait for Uri to come out and see if I can bring him up here to talk." Ahithophel opened the door and left naturally as though he and the secretary had been discussing business. A servant passed, carrying a pitcher of water, and gave him a brief nod.

Ahithophel found a position around the corner from the entrance to the king's chambers. In the stone-built corridor, he waited for his grandson-in-law to emerge from the king's council chamber. Minutes ticked by as Ahithophel's uneasiness grew. Whatever the two men were discussing, there could be no good outcome for anyone, especially Betta.

The door opened suddenly, and Ahithophel flattened his back along the wall, hoping Uri would come this way without the king. Sure enough, the warrior rounded the corner and stopped in surprise before Ahithophel.

"Papa. I was just coming up to see you. Are you waiting for the king?"

"No, no, Uri. I've been meeting with Seraiah. Come on up to his office where we can talk."

Uriah glanced at his dusty legs and the dried perspiration on his uniform from the long ride back from the battlefield. "I'm hardly fit for a meeting, Papa. Can we meet later after I clean up?"

Seraiah appeared at the bottom of the stairs and came to join them.

"Uri, welcome home. I assume you're here on military business with the king?" His question was cautious so as not to betray anything.

As they began walking, Ahithophel added, "Yes, Uri. I was just about to ask—why are you here?"

The younger man shrugged. "All I know is that I was in the field with Eliam and the other officers when a messenger came and said that Joab wanted to see me. When I got to Joab's command tent, he said, 'The king has called you home, so head for Jerusalem...now!' I asked why. 'Some matter or another. Just go!'"

Uriah rubbed his unshaven chin. "I asked if I could take his horse since only camels and mules were available in the corral. He said, 'Yes, just hurry.'

"When I rode out, I wondered what I had done wrong. I couldn't think of anything, and then I feared something had happened to Betta." He continued, "I had plenty of time to think as I made the ride back to Jerusalem. I thought about being out of combat for a year after getting married, but surely the king wouldn't censure me for that, not after sending me into battle with the troops. So, I had no idea why he sent for me. It was worrisome, but I trusted God that it would be nothing too serious."

As they entered Seraiah's office, Ahithophel asked, "But what did David say when you reported in?"

Uriah shook his head. "When I walked into his council room, David casually said, 'Welcome, Uriah. Tell me how the battle for Rabbah is going.' I was astounded. I thought, *for this purpose David has summoned a key warrior from the heated battle?* David could have directed the messenger who carried the summons to Joab to bring back a report. I was even more confused. What is the king doing? What's really going on here? Do you know?"

Ahithophel and Seraiah exchanged a worried look.

Before they could speak, Uriah went on to explain. "The king asked about the battle and the general's strategies, then dismissed me and told me to go home and 'wash my feet.' I knew that meant to spend the night at home with my wife before heading back to Rabbah. I wanted to. Everything in me wanted to go home and see Betta. But I couldn't."

"What? Why not?" Ahithophel asked, his heart beating faster.

Uriah looked down at the floor for a moment and said,

"Something is wrong, Papa. Nothing about the king calling me makes sense. I keep thinking about your words the night before we marched out. You said our king hungers for beautiful women, and I'd better hold my Betta close. So, now I'm suspicious. I'm worried that something may have happened to her. I was coming up to ask you if Betta is all right and to see what you think I should do."

Seraiah spoke up quickly. "Do you think that's for the best, Uriah? To disobey the king's order?"

"I don't know. I didn't think he was actually ordering me to go home. I thought he was just telling me I could," Uri said, rubbing the back of his neck.

Ahithophel paused, trying to find the words and wondering if he should speak at all. Was it his place—or the king's? Or should he let God handle this terribly complicated situation?

After a moment, he said, "Uri, I admire your devotion to the king, but you should know that when a higher up lets you know that something would please them, you take that as an order, no matter how they say it."

"I don't know, Papa...if he has hurt Betta in any way, I will not only disobey his order, I will make him wish he had never seen her."

"Uri, get a hold of yourself. Here, sit down in Seraiah's chair. I have to tell you something."

Uriah stiffened and searched Papa's face, looking for a clue.

Ahithophel circled Uri's chair, then looked him in the eye. He said, "I hate to be the one to tell you Uri, but you are right. David did have Betta brought to him. And now, brace yourself...she is carrying his child."

With glazed eyes, Uriah slumped in the chair. His muscled shoulders shook as he sobbed silently. He choked out words to Ahithophel,

"How could God let this happen? I prayed for her, just like you taught me. What have I done that God would let her be hurt...by that man? I should have listened when you told me he couldn't be trusted around a beautiful woman. Maybe we could have sent her away somewhere."

Ahithophel didn't respond immediately. Finally, he said, "Uri, you have done nothing to deserve what happened. The king has sinned against God and against all of us, but especially against you and Betta. I believe God will punish him for this, worse than anything you or I could do to him. But right now, you are not in a position to do anything. You will have to wait and let God take care of it."

Uriah paused to consider the advisor's words. "But Papa, what can I do? I must see Betta. She needs me."

"I'm sorry, Uri. I can't let you do that. If you go home now, you are playing right into his hands. Don't you see that he wants you to be with your wife so that he can say the child is yours, not his? That will absolve him of any blame."

"But I don't know what else to do. You said that he ordered me to go home. How can I disobey?"

"That's a good question. We need to think about that."

Ahithophel sat down on the edge of Seraiah's desk and stroked his greying beard. After a few moments, he stood up in front of Uriah and said, "Here's what I want you to do. Spend the night here in the palace. Hesel will see that you get everything you need, including a comfortable place to sleep.

"In the morning you must present yourself to His Majesty without letting him know that you are aware of what he has done to Betta. This will take some acting on your part, but you can do it. This is your motivation. What David has done to you and your family is unforgivable. You hate him, and that anger will carry you through whatever he is inclined to do to you.

"But here is what you must tell him. Now remember this. Say to him when he asks you why you didn't go home, 'The ark and Israel and Judah are staying in tents, and my lord Joab and the servants of my lord are camping in the open field. Shall I then go to my house to eat and to drink and to lie with my wife? By your life and the life of your soul, I will not do this thing.' Can you remember that?"

Uriah stared at the floor, but then nodded his head slowly. Ahithophel continued, "I think David will accept your explanation and may even be impressed with your character. But I'm not sure what he will do next. He may just send you back to Joab, but I think he will probably come up with another ploy. Whatever he does, you must stay firm. Remember the terrible things he has done. Whatever you do, don't let him convince you to go home."

Ahithophel looked over to Seraiah, who nodded approvingly. "Now Uri, Hesel will take you downstairs and see to your needs. Be strong, Uri."

"A good night's rest will prepare you to leave tomorrow," Seraiah chimed in.

The two men watched as the young man headed toward the steps and descended to the foyer below. Ahithophel motioned to Hesel to go with him and help with whatever he needed.

"You know," Seraiah said thoughtfully, "whatever comes of this, it will put Uriah in an impossible situation."

"His life will be changed," Ahithophel muttered.

"More than that," Seraiah said, "what can Uri do next? Denounce the king in public? Challenge him privately? Kill him secretly? Flee with Bathsheba—where would they go? I can't think of a single option for him to resolve the issue. The knowledge of his wife's pregnancy will heap sorrow upon sorrow on the man's soul. Will he be able to return to the battlefield? Would he consider taking his own life?"

"No!" Ahithophel raised his voice, then quickly lowered it after glancing around to be sure he wasn't heard. His eyes glistened with emotion. "He and Betta will be challenged —in reputation and spirit. Their life will never be the same, but they will have each other."

"What if..." Seraiah paused to consider further. "What if Uriah were to challenge the king through Prince Amnon? Amnon will not take sides, but he knows his father better than anyone. Maybe he would..."

"I don't see that happening," Ahithophel said, shaking his head. "I think this is one of those very important times when we can do nothing but trust God. I will try to provide any help they need in whatever course they choose. David has assaulted my granddaughter and deceived Uriah. He has betrayed me, his close friend and advisor, and Eliam, his brother-in-arms for many years. He has betrayed Uriah, his faithful warrior who would have died for him. He will try to deceive the people of our nation. His crime is intolerable—he should be stoned."

Catching his breath, he waited a few seconds before speaking. "But maybe your idea has merit. Amnon—or Absalom for that matter—will not go up against their father for Uriah or Bathsheba, or me. But they have other grievances. A coup might not be as far-fetched as it seems. I think either one would like to wear the crown, and the sooner, the better."

Seraiah said, "Do you mean you would urge them to topple the king by staging a coup? You'd better get that idea out of your head. David is much too strong to be taken down by a little scandal or either of his sons."

Ahithophel replied, "You may be right, but when the scandal involves your own family, it's not so little."

"I'm sorry," the other man said, "I just meant that David is not going to let personal matters overshadow his rule."

"Maybe he won't have a choice," Ahithophel retorted. "Well, for now, please pray for Betta and Uri. I hope Uri can find the right words to say to David that will not cause even more trouble."

The next morning, Ahithophel came by Seraiah's office to say, "David has Uriah in his chambers now. It sounds like David is pretty angry. Hesel is waiting in the area, watching for Uriah to come out, but he can't make out what they're saying. You know, I don't see what other alibi David can come up with if Uri and Betta don't spend time together. When he does come out, Hesel will bring him up to us."

It wasn't long before Hesel showed up, but he was alone. Ahithophel asked, "Where is Uriah?"

Hesel replied, "He came out for just a few minutes. He said the king told him to wait there while he took care of some pressing issues with his sons. But while Uriah was waiting, he told me that David seemed to accept his reason for not going home last night, although he was obviously displeased. Uriah slept with the servants, and the king was not happy to hear that. Uriah said David told him to stay here another day, and he would send him back to Joab. Amnon arrived and went in to see his father, but came out a few minutes later, and David called Uriah back in. It looks like they may be in there for a while because David called for food and wine to be brought."

Seraiah said, "What is King David up to, entertaining a soldier—even if he is one of the Thirty?"

Ahithophel said, "Maybe David's going to try and break down Uriah's resistance by getting him drunk. That sometimes works with fighting men. Then he'll probably have a guard escort him home to be sure things play out as David intends."

Several hours later, Hesel sent word by his sister Hadassah that Uriah had left David's chamber, with David smiling at the door. A guard had been summoned and was helping Uriah down the stairs, as he had obviously been served more wine with the meal than he could handle.

"Thank you, Hadassah," Ahithophel said. He and Seraiah hurried down to the front of the palace to watch Uriah in case he lost his will in opposing David. However, there was no sign of him there, so they headed for the servant's quarters on the main level. There they found Hesel had laid Uriah on a pallet where he was passed out.

Standing nearby, Hesel whispered, "The guard was given orders by King David to let Uriah sleep it off here. I offered to help Uriah home, but the king said there was no need. Uriah could barely talk. The wine was strong."

"Hesel, continue to keep watch nearby. If Uriah rouses, make sure he doesn't try to go to his house."

"Yes, sir."

With heavy hearts, Ahithophel and Seraiah headed for their chambers.

The next morning, a tap at the door awakened Ahithophel, who got up and quickly answered it, expecting to see Hesel.

"Morning, Papa," said Uri. "I decided that I should let you know how it went with the king and me when he wined and dined me yesterday."

Seraiah came down the corridor and joined them. "You haven't been home, have you, Uriah?"

Uriah looked from one man to the other and continued. "The first day after I said to David what you told me to tell him, he asked how I could be so noble when I am just a foot soldier. He said, 'Go home and relax, Uriah. You've earned it. I hear good things about you on the battlefield. Now that you have come in person with an encouraging report of our success, you need a good rest before heading back.'

"But I whispered a quick prayer to God asking for words I could say. Then I remembered. 'Your Majesty,' I told him, 'Do you recall many years ago being under siege by the Philistines on a very hot day as you and your men hid in caves in the wilderness?'

"The king looked puzzled and then half-smiled. 'Yes, it was fearfully hot that day. Two of the older soldiers passed out from the heat, and the rest of us took refuge in the caves where there was a little water. I made the men drink first, thinking of the cool and refreshing springs at Bethlehem that I had so much enjoyed as a boy.'

"I reminded him, 'The story is well-known, Your Majesty, how you murmured, 'O, that someone would get me a drink of water from the well near the gate of Bethlehem!'"

The older men nodded, remembering the oft-told tale.

Uriah continued, "So three of your mighty warriors broke through the Philistine lines, drew water from the well near the gate of Bethlehem, and carried it back to you, sire. But you refused to drink it; instead, you poured it out before the LORD.'

'Ah, yes,' the king said thoughtfully. 'Maybe I should have drunk it—the water was a precious gift from loyal guardsmen who risked their lives for me.'

"'Yes, my king, and can I—now one of your Thirty special guards—do less than you did? I cannot accept your generous offer of a comfortable bed at home, with the ark of the covenant and my lord Joab and his servants sleeping in the open field. Shall I then sleep in my home when my fellow soldiers are fighting and dying on the war front?' The king had nothing to say after that."

No one spoke. Ahithophel marveled at his grand-son-in-law's strength of character. Not every soldier would have been able to carry out the ruse.

Uriah continued, "Finally, the king spoke. He said, 'You are an honorable man, Uriah, much more than most of us. Your valor humbles me. Take your rest wherever it pleases you.' Then King David invited me to dine with him, and he kept pushing more wine on me. I drank too much. So, I didn't go home last night either, but I think the king accepted my reasoning and respected my view. I told him again that if the king could pass up the cooling water of Bethlehem in the heat of battle, I could pass up the night at home, especially after just completing a honeymoon year. Papa, please tell Betta how much I love her, and that I will come to her when the battle is won, which we hope will be soon."

With a heavy heart Ahithophel embraced the young warrior. "I will, Uri. And no matter what has happened, she loves you with all of her heart. God be with you, and safe travel," he said kindly.

True to his word, King David released Uriah to return to his unit. As the king sent him off, he handed the warrior a sealed packet. "Give this to Joab and no one else. I know I can trust you."

"Yes, sir," Uriah said.

Hesel carried Uriah's leather pouch and walked with him to the waiting horse. As they walked, Uriah carefully showed him the sealed envelope before he mounted.

"The king has entrusted me to deliver a letter to Joab," Uriah smirked. "So now I'm a courier instead of a soldier." He quickly climbed into the saddle, and with a gentle kick, he spurred his mount forward through the open city gate as Ahithophel stood at the palace and waved farewell, his heart in pieces.

Chapter 7:

Ahithophel and Absalom

A few days after Uriah's departure, Ahithophel happened to be attending a meeting in the royal chambers with Absalom and David. Their meeting was disrupted when a messenger arrived from Joab with important news for the king. When the guard ushered the messenger in, he said to David, "The messenger says he is bringing news of a setback in the battle for Rabbah."

When the dusty messenger came in, he brought a battle report from Joab. David sat up eagerly, immediately interested. Absalom appeared bored. Ahithophel kept his eyes down, but he, too, was keen to know what was happening at the battle front. So far, David had not mentioned seeing Uriah when he had returned to Jerusalem. Ahithophel wondered what the king was thinking and what his next move would be to address the news of Bathsheba's pregnancy.

"What is your message?" David asked the messenger, sitting up straighter. The man bowed and then replied, "My Lord Joab regrets to report that during a battle against the city, the men of the city came out in great numbers against Joab, and while fighting near the city wall, some of the people among David's servants fell."

David's eyes widened as he said, "Why did you go so near the city to fight? Did you not know that they would shoot from the wall? Why did you go so close to the wall?"

The messenger said sheepishly, "The men prevailed against us and came out against us into the field, but we pressed them as far as the entrance of the gate. Moreover, the archers shot at your servants from the wall; so, some of the king's servants are dead, and Uriah the Hittite is also dead. General Joab asked me to inform you of that fact specifically."

Ahithophel flinched, causing David to cast a curious glance in his direction. Catching his eye, Ahithophel gasped, "Bathsheba's husband."

David nodded, then said to the messenger, "Thus you shall say to Joab, 'Do not let this thing displease you, for the sword devours one as well as another.' Tell Joab to make his battle against the city stronger and overthrow it, and so encourage him."

Shocked, Ahithophel realized immediately what David had done. He had sent Uriah's death sentence in that sealed envelope. He glanced at David, but the king would not meet his eyes. Overcome with emotion, Ahithophel rose to excuse himself. He said to David, "I must go to my granddaughter. This is terrible news."

"Yes, of course," David said, with no evidence of concern in his voice. "Tell Uriah's wife the king regrets her loss, and we shall ensure that her material needs are provided for."

Restraining his fury, Ahithophel said between clenched teeth as he rushed from the room, "I will surely tell her."

Ahithophel first had to go to his chamber to collect himself. His head was spinning, and his heart beat in his chest until he thought it would burst. *I never imagined David was capable of murdering a close friend and one of his Mighty Men. How could he stoop so low? Doesn't the man have a conscience? He has now added murder to his growing list of sins that already includes adultery or rape.*

Then the realization dawned on him that Uriah was dead because of the advice he had given the warrior, and his anger burned toward himself. *If I hadn't been so set on thwarting David's plan, Uriah would still be alive. I killed him! I killed Betta's husband! Joab was complicit, David gave the order, the Ammonites struck him down, but it was me who caused him to die.* Ahithophel's head hurt, and he thought he was going to be sick. Then David became the focus of his rage that boiled over until he crumpled to the floor, sobbing in horror and despair.

Ahithophel didn't know how long he had lain there when he heard a soft tapping on his door. He got up and quickly composed himself, rinsed his face in water from the morning basin, then dried himself with a towel. He took a deep breath as he opened the door to see David's son, Prince Absalom, standing there.

"Oh, my lord, forgive my delay in opening the door. I was washing up before leaving, as you can see. Please come in. What can I do for you?" Ahithophel stammered.

Absalom stepped inside quickly and closing the door said, "I need your wise counsel, Ahithophel. I saw what happened downstairs, and I know why you left in such a hurry. You said you were going to your granddaughter, but you didn't. You came here instead. May I ask why?"

Ahithophel looked into Absalom's grey-blue eyes and saw in that handsome face a look of compassion. He remembered the legend that was sung by the people about Absalom. "*In all Israel, there is no one as handsome as Absalom, so highly praised; from the sole of his foot to the crown of his head there is no defect in him. When the young prince cut the hair of his head at the end of every year, for it was heavy upon him, he weighed the hair of his head at 200 shekels.*" He was indeed an attractive young man whose mother Maacah was born a princess, the daughter of a neighboring ruler. With his good looks and noble bearing, he readily caught people's attention and drew their admiration."

Ahithophel thought, *How true these words of praise are. God surely wouldn't gift one of His chosen ones so wonderfully if he wasn't special to Him. I feel that I can trust this young man. Perhaps he will in some measure rectify his father's wrongdoing.*

He said to the prince, "I needed a few minutes to collect my thoughts before I went to tell my granddaughter the tragic news. Did you hear that Uriah was killed in the fighting?"

"Yes, and I think I know why."

"What are you thinking?"

Absalom turned and sat on the edge of Ahithophel's work desk and said seriously, "You are not the only one who has informants in the palace. I think everyone in the citadel knows about my father and your granddaughter. I also know she is expecting a child, and it isn't Uriah's. It is my father's. Uriah must not know."

Ahithophel was shocked but remained silent, wondering how the news had traveled so quickly.

Absalom continued, "I'm certain my father has something to do with Uriah's misfortune. There is nothing more dangerous than the king when he's cornered. You should remember that when you cross paths with him in the future. He and Joab seem to have an uncanny ability to communicate without words. I don't know how, but somehow, Joab knew when Uriah returned that my father wanted him gone. Joab knows David better than anyone does, unless it's you."

Ahithophel kept quiet about the death warrant that Uriah had taken to Joab.

Absalom continued, "When David summoned Uriah, Joab wouldn't have to be a mind reader to figure out that it had to be about Bathsheba. With her beauty and proximity, my father would have noticed her whether or not she returned his admiration. In fact, I confronted my father about that."

"You did?" Ahithophel gasped. "What did he say?"

Absalom said, "He didn't deny it. He said she practically invited him into her arms."

"That's a lie," Ahithophel snapped. "I asked her about that. There was no doubt that her denial was genuine. Why would she risk her reputation and marital happiness with Uriah for a brief fling with the king? He's old enough to be her father."

Absalom put his hand on the older man's shoulder and said, "Calm down, man. You know my father. He said he was walking around the roof of the palace when he couldn't sleep and saw her bathing in her back garden. In admitting it to me, he said, 'What red-blooded man could resist such a beautiful woman, especially when bathing in her garden? She was almost like Eve in the Garden of Eden, so innocent and beautiful.' The king said he sent an invitation, and she came. That's all I know."

Ahithophel was fuming inside but remained quiet to hear the rest of Absalom's account.

The prince continued, "I didn't tell him that I heard recently she is expecting a child. I didn't want to get on his bad side. You know how he is these days; usually in a vile mood without much patience, at least not with me. He'd better be careful, though, because his popularity is fading fast, even with the common folk of the city."

Ahithophel asked cautiously, "But what do you think about Uriah's death?"

Absalom replied, "Uriah surprised David when he refused to go home and sleep with his wife. In fact, as I see you standing here, I'll wager that you had something to do with that. Am I right?"

"You give me too much credit, my lord. I'm just a simple old man concerned about his granddaughter's safety and happiness."

Absalom almost smiled but restrained himself, given the solemnity of their meeting. He said, "I know very little gets past you, and I respect that. In fact, one of these days, I may be calling on you for personal advice on a serious matter."

"Me?"

"Well, we never know what the future holds, do we?" said Absalom with a shrug.

Ahithophel was squirming inside, concerned that their conversation might border on sedition. Even so, he said, "If it would please you, Prince Absalom, I would be honored to serve you in any capacity I can. But just now, I must go to Bathsheba. My heart is breaking for her, and I'll have to own up to my part in her husband's death. It will be a double loss for her—losing her husband and losing trust in her grandfather who she loves."

"Of course," the prince replied respectfully. "I'm glad we talked." With that, he turned and swept out of the room, a prince with a plan, a plan that might, at some point, include Ahithophel.

When the aging advisor knocked at the door of his granddaughter's home, he hoped briefly that she wouldn't be there. But where else would she be? A moment later, Bathsheba opened the door, and seeing her dear Papa, she rushed into his arms and buried her face in his shoulder. "Oh, Papa, I'm so glad you're here. I need to talk to you, but I wouldn't dare come to your office at the palace."

His heart sinking, Ahithophel tried to delay the awful news by asking, "Why were you wanting to see me?"

"Oh Papa, something terrible has happened, and I don't know what to do."

She went to sit down on the divan, and he took a seat near her.

Betta began to sob quietly, then looked up at him and said, "I think I'm with child, and it is David's baby."

Feeling his granddaughter's pain, her Papa gathered her in his arms and said over and over, "It's all right, my dear. Somehow, this must be in God's will. He wouldn't let my innocent granddaughter suffer needlessly."

"I need my husband. I wish there was a way to bring him home from the battlefield. Could you send a messenger to say I need him?"

"Sadly, you know the soldiers never come home during active fighting on the battlefield. Only David himself could issue such an order, and I've never known him to do it for any personal reason." He thought, *Lord, forgive me.*

She began to weep as she sobbed, "Oh, Uri. My dear sweet husband. I'm so sorry."

Ahithophel let her cry quietly for several minutes, then said, "My Betta, now I have something very difficult to tell you."

She looked up, her eyes open wide and a look of dread on her face. "What could be worse than what has already happened? Having this baby will affect all of us for the rest of our lives."

"I have news about Uri."

"What do you know about him?" Her eyes widened in a tear-stained face.

"Uri was here, Betta. Just last week, he was here in Jerusalem."

"That's impossible. He would have come home to me."

"Yes, indeed, he wanted to come to you. But I stopped him. I'm sorry I did; you'll never know how sorry I am. I will regret it to my dying day."

"But why? Why, Papa? Why did you stop him? You know how much I love him and need my husband now after all that has happened."

Collecting his thoughts, Ahithophel spoke carefully. "I stopped him because I knew what King David was doing. I realized that he called your husband home because he knew that you are with child, and he couldn't let anyone know it was his baby. The exposure of his actions would lead to severe criticism and weaken his authority. There might even be calls for him to step down from the throne. His popularity is waning already."

Betta looked incredulous as she struggled desperately to comprehend her grandfather's words.

"The king planned to send Uriah home to you, so when your pregnancy becomes apparent, everyone would believe that the child is Uri's."

She teared up again. "That may have been the only way out of this mess without everyone being ruined."

Her Papa sighed deeply. "Yes, I agree. That's why I should have stayed out of it. But at the time, I couldn't bear to see the king get away with what he had done to you. Truthfully, at this point, I wish he could be forced out of his position. In fact, I hope the Lord God strikes him dead."

The young woman stared at her grandfather. "Did Uri know about the baby? What happened when you told him? What did he say?"

"Oh, Betta, he wanted to come to you immediately. He was ready to confront the king on the spot. It took Seraiah and me to hold him back. Uri wanted so much to come and comfort you. After what had happened, he was desperate to see you and reassure you of his love and devotion. But I told him he couldn't because that would be playing into David's scheme."

"But why? Why did you have to stop him? Uri and I could have figured something out."

"I had to. It was the only way to stop David's plan. I couldn't let him get away with it."

His granddaughter got up and backed away from him, obviously hurt and in shock because of what her grandfather had done.

He continued, "I advised Uri to stay at the palace and sleep in the servants' quarters. I suggested that he tell King David his conscience wouldn't let him come home to you while his comrades were fighting and dying on the field of combat. David bought that, but he tried again the next day; he even tried to get Uri drunk, but Uri stayed true to what we agreed to. Finally, David gave up and sent him back to Joab."

"Oh, my brave, loyal Uri."

"I realize now it would have been better for me to stay out of it. As a result of my interference, something worse has happened."

"Oh no, Papa. Did something happen to Uri?"

Ahithophel cleared his throat and swallowed hard. "Uri returned to Joab and...Oh, Betta, I hate to tell you this. Uri was killed in battle the first day back. I'm so sorry, Betta. I'm so sorry."

"Papa! What did you do?" Betta screamed. "You killed my husband! You wouldn't let Uriah come home to me, and now I'll never see him again." She moved further away from him and sobbed uncontrollably.

He tried to go to her and comfort her, but she avoided him, crying, "Oh, Uri, my love, Uri, I've lost you forever..."

She looked at her grandfather with pain and disgust. Then she wheeled around, ran into her bedroom, and threw herself on her pallet, sobbing. Ahithophel stood in the doorway, waiting to speak, but she sobbed, "Just go away. Please. I don't want to see you anymore."

He said, "Betta, I can't just leave you here like this. You've just learned that you've lost your husband."

Between sobs, she said, "Anna will be back from the market shortly. Just go." After a few moments, she managed to add, "I never want to see you again."

The old man's shoulders sagged, and he began to weep as he made his way out of her home and into the dark street, alone and unloved, a broken man with a broken heart.

As Ahithophel walked the deserted paths of Jerusalem, the sadness in his heart and regret for Uri's death began to harden into anger—anger at himself at first, but then anger toward his king, against David. *What has happened to the man who is supposed to be God's anointed, a man after God's own heart? He has become full of pride, lust, and power. He defiled the daughter of his closest friends and associates; it is the ultimate betrayal. He has become a man without a conscience, a man who can murder a close friend who loved him and would die for him. He murdered without a second thought. And now he is the reason for turning my beloved Betta against me.*

Ahithophel's anger turned to rage as he began plotting how he could make the king regret these sinful actions. But then the wisdom for which he was known led him to calm his mind and consider his options. He needed to make David pay, but how? He needed someone to talk to, someone who could keep a cool mind and think objectively. That was something he could not do in his present circumstances. The man he was looking for came to mind, and his pace quickened as he turned back toward the palace.

Chapter 8:

Uriah's Funeral

By the time Ahithophel arrived back at the palace, it was quiet because most of the residents had retired. However, he hoped his friend Nathan would still be up. As he tapped quietly at Nathan's door, he could hear the prophet moving around inside, then he opened the door to see who could be calling at that hour.

"Ah, my old friend Ahithophel, the night owl. What brings you here this evening?" Nathan asked, stifling a yawn.

"May I come in? I need to talk to you."

"By all means. I can see you are deeply troubled, my friend. What could have happened to bring a seasoned sage like you to such a state of mind?"

"It's a long story that begs the counsel of God's holy prophet." He began to relate to Nathan the events of the past few weeks, stopping after telling of David's lustful abuse of his granddaughter.

Nathan listened closely, nodding at times. At one point, he interrupted to say quietly, "So, David has committed adultery with the daughter of his close friend Eliam and the wife of his warrior Uriah, not to mention the granddaughter of his personal adviser. The Lord God is not pleased; I can tell you that." Nathan got up and paced briefly.

Ahithophel continued, his features turning angry, "The situation worsens. I learned that Bathsheba sent word to David that she is expecting a child." He paused to let that information sink in. "How do you think King David responded to that news?"

Nathan shuffled uncomfortably. He said with sadness on his face," I know there has been talk that David has not been himself lately. I have, on a couple of occasions, tried to discuss with him my concerns. Unfortunately, he has not been receptive. He insists he is fine, just busy and a little overworked. I thought perhaps he stayed home from the fighting for that reason. Or, possibly, he may have finally had enough shedding of blood."

Ahithophel responded with contempt in his voice, "Ha! He has no compunction about shedding blood. I wonder now if even his gift to Bathsheba and Uri of the house next to the palace wall was part of his plan. He must not get away with it. He must be punished."

"Oh, not so fast, my friend. Your anger is causing you to say terrible things without proof. You are speaking about the king of Israel and Judah. You could be imprisoned for that kind of talk, even if you are, or were, a friend of his."

"I don't care. You haven't heard the worst of it yet. Last week, David called Bathsheba's husband, Uriah, home on the pretense of asking how the battle was going. He urged Uriah to stay overnight with his wife and thus convince the world that she is carrying her husband's baby. But Uriah refused to go home while his brothers were fighting and dying for God and country."

Nathan mused, "I wouldn't have guessed that a foreigner like Uriah would be that noble."

"Well," replied Ahithophel, "I had something to do with that. I couldn't bear to see David get away with his plan, so I coached Uriah, although the plan was essentially his anyway. After a day or two, David gave up trying to manipulate Uriah and sent him back to Joab."

"Well then, you should be glad you foiled his plan."

"I was until I found out what David did next."

"What?" the prophet asked.

"David sent a sealed letter to Joab with Uriah. He told Joab to see that Uriah died in battle. Joab obeyed, and now Bathsheba's husband is dead. David murdered him to cover up his crime against Bathsheba."

"How do you know David did that? You said the letter was sealed," Nathan asked intently, always cautious and prudent.

"I saw the sealed envelope in Uriah's hand as he was leaving, and I heard the message that was later brought to David from Joab. The message stated specifically that Uriah the Hittite is dead. Why else would Joab have sent that message?"

"Uriah was one of David's Thirty Mighty Men, albeit the most recent addition. It wouldn't be unusual for Joab to report when one of them died in battle."

"You know I'm right, Nathan. It all fits together like one of David's clever plans."

"I shudder to think that. But supposing you are right. How is that going to help David get away with getting Bathsheba pregnant?"

"I'm not sure what he will do now. He could just get rid of her somehow. I worry about that. But with Eliam and me still around, maybe he will bring Bathsheba into the palace and add her to his harem."

"But she will be grieving for her husband."

Ahithophel reasoned, "I can see David doing this to publicly demonstrate his compassion. He brings in the grieving widow of a national hero and gives her a safe home in his palace. Then when she has her baby, the kingdom will rejoice at the new arrival. But he will have to do it quickly. She will be showing soon,"

Nathan pondered this and then asked, "Would Bathsheba go along with that?"

"What choice does she have? As she told me this evening, 'He's the king. Who's going to stop him?' Even if she refused his offer and tried to live alone in the city with her servant, David will not want his royal child being brought up fatherless."

Nathan paced back and forth in the small room, deep in thought. He said. "These accusations are very serious. Adultery. betrayal, murder, coveting, plus deceit and lying—all serious transgressions of God's law. However, I'm not as convinced that David is as guilty as you have said; all his life, he has had a heart for the Lord, and he has asked me time and again, to be honest with him when he goes astray. I must spend time with the Lord and seek His counsel."

Turning to look his friend in the eye, Nathan said, "As for you, my friend, be very careful. You are angry and want to strike out at God's anointed one. But that is not for you to do.

The Lord God will deal with His man. You must stand back and bide your time."

"Hmph, that's easier said than done when it's your own flesh and blood." With nothing more to discuss, he said, "I'll leave you to your prayers. Perhaps you can convince God to hurry up and take care of David before he does any more damage. Good night."

Meanwhile, a hundred miles away, the battle for Rabbah continued full force. It was late one evening during a lull in the action when Eliam, Bathsheba's father, sat in the command center of the Israeli encampment. Joab paced in the semi-darkness of the large tent, lit only by two oil lamps burning over the central table where battle plans were drawn.

Joab said, "Eliam, before I get to the reason I called you in, I'm sure you want to know why I ordered Uriah to attack the south wall of the city when we all knew it was the strongest section of the defenses."

"Yes," said Eliam. "My officers and I have been discussing that."

Joab said, "I sympathize with you over the death of your son-in-law. And let's not forget the brave warriors who died with him in that raid. Here's why I gave that order. When Uriah returned from Jerusalem, he carried with him a sealed letter from His Majesty. In that letter, our king gave me specific instructions about Uriah. He was very complimentary of your son-in-law and said he had prepared a royal commendation based on his earlier bravery. You see, I had taken the opportunity during a lull in the fighting to send a message to David, recommending Uriah and a few others for royal commendations."

"So, what was in the letter?" Eliam asked, brows knit.

"David wanted Uriah to lead a group of our best warriors to brave all odds and break through a strong section of the wall. When he had done that, David planned to promote him to the rank of Commander of Hundreds. The king knew there were risks involved, but he was confident Uriah could do the job."

Eliam was dubious and asked, "That doesn't sound like the king to suggest such a dangerous attack. Are you sure the letter was from His Majesty?"

"Of course I'm sure the letter was from His Majesty. I'm sure he had his reasons, and he is our commander-in-chief. I had no choice but to give Uriah the assignment. Now he is dead, as are several more of my best soldiers. That is unfortunate for all of us, but especially for you as his father-in-law; we counted on his bravery and leadership to win this battle."

Now we will transport Uriah's body to Jerusalem for burial with military honors. I want you to take a few of your men who knew Uriah well and lead the honor guard carrying Uriah's remains."

Eliam's eyes brightened. "I will be honored. However, are you sure you can spare us? The final outcome of the battle isn't clear yet."

"I can stall for a few days until you and your men return. His Majesty also plans to promote you. Upon my recommendation, you will be promoted to Commander of Thousands, reporting directly to me."

Eliam could barely speak. "Oh, General, our king is so generous, and so are you. Thank you, my lord."

Joab continued, "His Majesty is asking you to attend the ceremony for Uriah and deliver the eulogy. Your daughter will be there to share in the honors, as well as your father, Ahithophel. King David has made a magnanimous offer to your family. Your father already resides in the palace, but our king wishes to expand his quarters to include a full suite of rooms. He wants your family to move into the palace, to live there and dine at David's table. This is all in honor of what you have done, and for your brave kinsman, Uriah. What do you say to that?"

Eliam slightly inclined his head in a bow and replied, "I'm overwhelmed. It will be so wonderful to recognize Uriah in this way; it will also be a tremendous honor for us to be invited to eat at the king's table."

While the battle for Rabbah continued, Eliam was dispatched with a small bodyguard to transport Uriah's body back to Jerusalem. King David had prepared a royal welcome for the entourage, including musical instruments and a choir. Lookouts had been placed strategically on the road approaching Jerusalem. They were to race ahead and alert the king and his retinue of their arrival. When Eliam and his small group appeared at the top of the Mount of Olives, trumpets blew to announce their arrival.

By the time the group arrived at the royal palace, a crowd of onlookers had gathered. King David waited at the front steps of the palace to greet Eliam with an embrace and to place a royal garland around his neck. Ahithophel stood with other dignitaries on the steps behind the king. At David's signal, he stepped forward to embrace his son with tears in his eyes. The crowd roared approval until David waved his hand to quiet them while he spoke.

"People of Jerusalem, hear my words. We welcome home two of our finest warriors from the battle for Rabbah. My friend and comrade for many years, Eliam, has returned to us the body of his fallen son-in-law, Uriah the Hittite, who perished while heroically attacking the enemy stronghold. Eliam fought by my side and kept me safe in the wilderness as we hid from King Saul and waged war from our base in Ziklag. We are brothers in the army of our Lord God.

"This evening when the ram's horn sounds, we will gather at the parade grounds to honor our fallen brother, Uriah. We will hear from Eliam and his father, Ahithophel, and you may also pay your respects to Uriah's wife, Bathsheba. I will tell you then of my plans to welcome their entire family to come and live here in the royal palace. We honor Uriah at the parade ground at sunset."

The large crowd of townspeople murmured their approval.

"However, right now Eliam and his men will be given time to rest from their journey and prepare for the ceremony this evening." With those words, the trumpets blew, and the orchestra began playing as the crowd applauded. David again embraced Eliam and ushered his group into the palace while servants took care of Uriah's body, preparing it for final burial.

Ahithophel stayed with Eliam as he cleaned up and had some nourishment, then he brought him to his room on the second floor of the palace. Ahithophel waited until then to speak. "My son, it is so good to see you alive and well. I have prayed for you daily, along with Uriah, of course. There is so much I want to ask you and even more I want to tell you. But first of all, tell me how Uri died, and why?"

Eliam summarized the conversation he'd had with Joab the day before. Ahithophel then said, "Did you see for yourself David's letter carried by Uriah?"

"No, of course not. Why do you ask?"

"Because it is the key to convicting David of a series of high crimes!"

Eliam stopped what he was doing. "Oh, no, Father, how could you think such a thing? What crimes are you talking about?"

"Violating your daughter, to start. Then, he arranged for Uriah's murder, although only the letter sent to Joab can prove it."

"I can't believe this!" exclaimed Eliam. "This is King David, the son of Jesse you're talking about. The man you practically grew up with. The man I have sworn to protect with my life. He's the king of Israel and Judah, God's anointed one. He would never do these things. Tell me you're not serious."

"I wish I could, but I am deadly serious. You haven't noticed as his behavior changed over the last few months. He has become remote and self-centered. Just the fact that he stayed home from the war shows he is not the same man. The old David always led the troops."

"We talked about this before. He stayed home because he is aging and he has other matters to deal with."

Ahithophel sighed, then replied, "I understand that you are loyal to your king, and normally, I would commend you for that. But now he has even turned Betta against me. She asked me to leave when I told her about Uriah. She blames me for his death."

"Why would she do that?" Eliam's eyes widened.

"Because I told Uriah not to go home to her when David wanted him to."

"Why?"

Pausing to take a deep breath, Eliam's father said, "Because she carries David's child, and I wanted everyone to know it was the king's, not Uriah's."

Eliam appeared to be confused and then stared at his father in shock.

Ahithophel continued, "David called Uriah home to have him stay overnight with Betta. Then everyone would think the baby was Uriah's, and David would get off free. I couldn't allow that to happen. So, I told Uri not to go home to Betta. As a result, David's plan was frustrated, and he sent that letter to Joab to make sure Uriah was killed in action."

Eliam said, "This is horrendous. Something tells me inside your words could be true, but my soul is bound to my friend and king. I would die for him. I cannot accept an attack on his person or his office, not even from you, Father."

Eliam quickly threw his cloak around him and said, "Right now, I need to hear Betta's version of the story and see for myself if she is with child, and if she is, who the father is." Eliam held his hand up to stop his father from speaking. "I must go to her," he said, turning to leave the room, leaving a frustrated Ahithophel with important things left unsaid.

Bathsheba had been waiting for her father to come home. Some of the local women had come to wail with her after hearing her husband had been killed in battle. One said, "Is your father coming home to be with you?"

Betta replied, "Yes, but he must stay at the palace until he can get cleaned up from the long journey. I'm confused and in so much pain from the loss of Uri." She didn't mention that the thought of having a baby without her husband was more than she could bear. The women mourned with the young wife, with many bringing food and flowers to console her.

When her father arrived, Bathsheba ran to him, sobbing on his chest as he stroked her hair. Eliam was concerned mainly for her grief at losing Uri, and waited for the women to disperse before speaking. When they were alone, Betta asked, "Have you talked to Papa?"

"Yes," Eliam said, "but I didn't like what he had to say."

She pulled back and looked into his eyes. "What did he tell you?"

"He said the king assaulted you, and you are expecting his child. Is that true?"

Bathsheba turned away in despair. "David sent for me, but I didn't know why. I was taken to his chamber. He sent the servants away, and...then...it happened. I couldn't do anything."

Eliam went to stand beside his daughter, placing an arm around her shoulders and pulling her to him. "I'm so sorry. I would never have left you in Jerusalem alone if I had thought for a moment the king was capable of such action." He paused and then said, "This will change our lives. I received a message from King David through General Joab that David plans to move us into the palace."

His daughter shook with anger. "Why? Doesn't he know I detest him and can never trust him?"

Eliam replied, "I think he wants to honor the life and sacrifice of Uri by...by taking care of your husband's responsibilities."

Tears filled her eyes as she considered this unexpected new role. "Would we, or would I, become a servant at the palace?"

"I can't believe he would dishonor you in that way. I recall how he married Abigail the widow after her husband Nabal's death. They had a child together, a son."

Bathsheba backed away with a look of disgust. "No! I don't want to marry him or live in the palace! I would gladly scrub floors for the dirtiest home in Jerusalem than to become the king's wife after he has used me this way."

Eliam shook his head sorrowfully. "I just wish Papa had not prevented Uri from coming home to you that night. If he had been here, things might have worked out. It wouldn't have been perfect, but you would have your husband, at least, and maybe there would have been no scandal outside our family's knowledge of it."

Bathsheba began to weep. "I was so upset about what Papa told me that I made him leave. I still resent him for keeping Uri from coming home to me. I didn't get to see my husband before he was killed in battle."

Eliam hugged her and said, "Well, we will know before long the king's intentions. I won't leave Jerusalem until you are safe."

His daughter tried to dry her tears on her apron. "Oh, Father, I can't think of marrying another man when I've just lost the husband I love, especially that man."

"Let us pray for God's will in this matter," her father replied. And they did.

Later, Eliam escorted his daughter to the gathering site where Uriah's body lay in state on a makeshift platform. A large crowd had assembled. Ahithophel stood on the dais with Nathan and the king's two sons. The aging man tried to catch

Bathsheba's glance, but she averted her gaze, stabbing his heart with pain.

At that moment, Ahithophel hated David even more. He searched his mind for some way to take vengeance on the man he no longer considered his king or friend. Of the two princes standing with him, he was fairly certain now that the younger son would consider thoughts of civil war. *I need to cultivate Absalom. He may be the key to my revenge.*

As King David approached the memorial stage, he spied Eliam and Bathsheba standing at the front of the crowd. He approached them and bowed slightly. Addressing the pair, he gave an eloquent speech.

"My dear Eliam and Bathsheba, I am so sorry for your loss. Uriah was a good man, a great man. Our city mourns with you. His name will not be forgotten."

The crowd's voices swelled in agreement.

The king continued, "I have tried to think how to lessen your pain. I know you will grieve Uriah's death for a time, as is proper. But when you are ready, I would like both of you to move into the palace where my staff and I can watch over you. With your grandfather assisting me with courtly duties and your father returning to battle, Bathsheba, it is not wise for you to live alone, assisted by only a servant girl."

He turned and raised his hands to the cheering crowd. "Please give the family every kind of support they may need while they try to get their lives back together."

The crowd's voices raised again to show their approval. David then motioned to Eliam to address the crowd.

Ahithophel returned to his room in the palace, infuriated, contemplating his future...if there was one. He was alienated from his family and horrified by the king's actions. Although plans were being discussed to prepare a suite of rooms for his son and granddaughter, he could not stand by while King David covered his sin and made himself look like a hero by offering Bathsheba a home at the palace.

Ahithophel knew he could not stay in King David's service. He could not sit at David's table and eat David's bread with Bathsheba in his bed and her husband in the ground. Who knew whether David would enforce his rights as the ruler to add her to the harem. No, his time in David's palace must come to an end.

I could not leave before I stand face to face with the man. I must let him know that there is at least one person he hasn't succeeded in manipulating. He needs to know that I have watched him as he flaunted his arrogance and power. He used deceit to charm everyone into believing he is the most compassionate and chivalrous of men when he is actually an adulterous murderer. How could the Lord God let His anointed one get away with these hideous crimes?

Nathan had warned Ahithophel to be careful in opposing God's man—the king. He said, "You don't want to wake up one day and realize you are opposing God Himself."

Ahithophel thought angrily, *David has gotten away with his sinful scheme, and if God wants to let him flout His laws and not punish him, then I don't know God as well as I thought I did.* But then the thought came, *On the other hand, maybe God wants to use me to confront David. I could do that. But first, I must consult with Nathan.*

Before he could act on that thought, a messenger knocked at his door. When Ahithophel answered, the servant said, "His Majesty wants to see you immediately."

The king was standing in the center of the room alone. "Come in, my friend, and have a seat."

Ahithophel said, "I'll stand if you don't mind."

David moved to face him. "I have made an offer to your family, but I haven't discussed it with my personal adviser. You haven't been around much, or I certainly would have consulted you. What do you think?"

"What do I think about what?" Ahithophel answered shortly.

"Why, about expanding your space in the palace and bringing your son and granddaughter to live here with you,"

Ahithophel countered, "Don't you really mean bringing Bathsheba to live with you?"

David looked puzzled for a moment and then said, "I have considered marrying her, but no firm plans have been made yet."

"If you require my approval, you won't get it."

David's puzzled look turned dark as he backed away from Ahithophel. His brow furrowed and his lips were pressed tightly together. He said in a tone of sarcasm, "Oh, and why would that be?"

Ahithophel said, "I know everything you have done. You forcibly took my granddaughter, and now she is expecting your child. You called her husband from the battlefield without him knowing his true enemy was the king he loved and defended. You instructed him to go home and sleep with Bathsheba so everyone would assume her baby was his. When that didn't work, you sent word to Joab to make sure he died in battle. Joab followed your order immediately."

David listened silently and then turned to stare out the window.

"Now you are posing as the chivalrous benefactor by bringing in the grieving widow and her father. Well done, Your Majesty," Ahithophel added with contempt.

David did not speak right away as Ahithophel waited to hear his death sentence.

Finally, the king turned and walked to a corner of the room where his military gear and trophies of war were displayed. He lifted a large object from a display case to reveal a sword and sheath. As he walked to Ahithophel, he drew the sword from its scabbard. David held the sword up to catch the light and asked, "Do you know what this is?"

"It is the sword of Goliath. You have shown it to me before."

"You're always correct, aren't you, oh wise sage?"

David lowered the sword and placed the point against Ahithophel's chest, pushing him backward into a chair. He said, "I told you to have a seat." The king pressed the point of the sword against Ahithophel's throat. "Yes, I used this sword to cut off Goliath's head, and I can now do the same to anyone who opposes me. One swipe of this sword, and your head will roll on the floor. My trusted adviser has become my enemy."

He held the huge blade at his adviser's throat for several seconds, then pulled it back and said, "My dear friend, Ahithophel, I'm afraid old age has damaged your good brain. You have always been my loyal comrade and counselor, but now you have gone quite mad. You accuse your king of adultery and murder to his face. I don't want to kill you...but I could have you tried for treason and thrown in prison."

Pausing, he said, "I'm not going to do that either. But you can no longer serve me in the palace. Gather your belongings and bid farewell to your friends and family. You will leave Jerusalem and never show your face here again. Ever. Be gone by sunset. If you see my face again, it will be the last thing you will ever see."

David paused to let his threat sink in. Then he said, " It's too bad our friendship has to end this way, but I can't keep someone in the palace who has no respect for his king."

With that, David put the sword away, then turned and walked into his inner chamber and closed the door. Ahithophel left the chamber in a daze.

Chapter 9:

Absalom's Proposition

A hithophel's head was spinning as he trudged to his room to pack his things. He noticed Absalom's door was slightly ajar. Not knowing why for sure, he stopped and tapped lightly.

"Yes?"

"It's Ahithophel, my lord. Do you have a moment?"

Absalom opened the door and motioned his guest inside, then closed the door behind him. "Ah, Ahithophel, what's going on with you? You look like you've lost your best friend. Sit down and tell me about it." He motioned to a cushioned chair near the window, taking care not to be seen by anyone outside.

"I have just been discharged by your father, who came within a hair of taking off my head."

"Oh, how intriguing. I didn't think the king was energized enough for such a face-to-face encounter these days." With an earnest smile the prince sat down in a facing chair that matched the other, both cushioned by linen-covered pillows.

As Ahithophel looked into Absalom's eyes, he saw in them the same concern and compassion that he had seen in the king's eyes in times gone by. The former advisor began to talk and didn't stop until he told his entire story. He paused and looked up to see how the young prince was receiving his revelations. "Now you know my situation, and I have only a few hours to gather my things and say my goodbyes."

Resting his elbow on the table beside him that was spread with parchment and a couple of burning candles, Absalom sat in deep thought for a few moments. When he finally responded to Ahithophel's shocking story, he said, sitting up straight, "This is amazing! This sort of behavior is what will bring my father down. This may shock you, but in light of what you've just told me, I can tell you that I believe it is my destiny to wear King David's crown. I'm not sure how or when that will happen, but I believe it shall, and when it does, I want you by my side. How do you feel about that?"

Ahithophel was shocked at first, but as he considered Absalom's proposition, he began to see a possible way to avenge his family's abuse. He said, "I am flattered that you would want me at your side, my prince, but if that is what you want, I am yours to command."

"Excellent! Your wisdom and experience will be invaluable in my administration. If you are willing, I will come for you when the time is right. But where will you be?"

Ahithophel nodded and then responded, "I will return to the place of my birth, the town of Giloh. It's a small village close to Hebron. You will have no problem finding me there. I would be most pleased to assist you in any way I can to attain and hold the throne. You would be an admirable leader for our people, and I will be honored to stand by your side, should that come to pass.

Absalom said as he stood up, "Splendid. Go in peace then, my friend. I will see you again."

"Umm, there's one more detail I want to ask you if I may?"

"Of course. What is it?" Absalom sat down again and stared at the older man intently.

"It's about Hesel, my assistant. I can't take him with me. I wouldn't be able to support him in Giloh. Can you possibly add him to your staff? He's a fine young man and able to do whatever you might ask of him. I've known his family for many years, and he is an honorable man. I am thinking he could possibly serve as a discreet go-between for us. He knows my home in Giloh and can be trusted to keep everything to himself."

Musing on this, Absalom murmured, "I see. Hmm...Yes, I can do that. I will need every good man I can find as I look for ways to accomplish my plans for the throne. Tell Hesel he has a place with me, but don't say anything to him about what we have just discussed. Have him report to my man, Ari. I'll take it from there."

"Thank you, sire. You won't be sorry," Ahithophel said as his face brightened.

"Very well. So, I will send Hesel with word when I decide what to do next. It won't be long. Farewell, good sir. We'll meet again. Soon, I hope."

An hour later, as Ahithophel completed packing his few belongings into a leather bag, Hesel knocked and entered, appearing agitated.

"Master, is it true? Have you been discharged by His Majesty?"

"I'm sorry to say, it is true, Hesel. When I told the king what I thought about what has transpired recently, he was not happy. So, he has given me until sundown to say my goodbyes." Ahithophel turned from his packing to fully face the young man. "Hesel, I can't take you with me right now. I wouldn't be able to pay you. I'm not even sure how I will support myself."

"But, sir, I wouldn't be any trouble for you. I could find work, maybe enough to support us both."

"Nonsense. I have something more important for you to do. I have arranged with Prince Absalom for you to be added to his staff here in the palace. He has big plans, and I need to have eyes and ears in his inner circle. I want you to monitor developments and report to me when something happens. The prince is fine with that. I will be in Giloh, or else in my sister's house in Hebron. Can you do that for me?"

"Yes, of course. But you know my first allegiance will always be to you. Should I report to the prince now?"

"No, he wants you to report to his man, Ari. There shouldn't be any major changes in your accommodations here in the palace, but Ari will provide instructions and give you any supplies for service that you might need. The prince will decide soon how to use your skills. So, goodbye for now. There are two more stops I must make before I leave. I need to let Seraiah know of these events for his journal, and I can't leave without a least saying goodbye to my granddaughter. So, shalom, my boy. Be well."

"Goodbye, sir. I hope to see you again, hopefully very soon. Shalom."

The two men parted with a firm embrace, then Ahithophel, carrying his bag of personal effects, left the service of his king, anger and resentment clouding his thoughts. A root of bitterness was growing in his soul.

Ahithophel had heard that Betta was currently living in her father's house in the city, so after briefing Seraiah, he made his way through the evening streets and knocked at the door of the family home. Eliam had returned to Joab and the battle for Rabbah, so it was just Betta who answered the door.

"Hello, Papa," she said sadly, and motioned him into the small home.

"I can't stay long, Betta. I have to be out of town before sunset."

With a look of alarm, she asked, "Why is that?"

"Because King David has discharged me and told me to never see his face again, unless I'm ready to die."

The girl looked shocked. "Oh, Papa, I had hoped you would have given up on your charges against him. Did you confront him with your accusations?"

"Yes, and when I did, he pulled out Goliath's sword and threatened to take my head off. Then he seemed to regain self-control and told me to leave Jerusalem. He never wants to see my face again. So I have been exiled—evidently, for life."

Betta turned away to process his words as emotions struggled within her—sorrow, anger, worry, pain. Finally, her shoulders slumped, she said, "I wish you could have let it go. But I suppose what's done is done. Maybe this sad outcome will put the rumors to rest and give our family a chance to recover some chance of a normal life."

"I am concerned that David isn't through making trouble for you."

After thinking for a moment, she said, "I don't know what the king will do with my husband dead, my father in battle, and my grandfather in exile. How will this affect his plan to move us into the palace? I hope he puts that plan to rest forever." Then she seemed to recall the child she was carrying and unconsciously laid her hand on her abdomen that was only barely starting to grow round.

"Unless he decides to marry you now." Ahithophel paused to see how she would take the words, but she said nothing, struggling with conflicting emotions.

Ahithophel took a chance and continued, "My dear, that would be the most decent thing he could do under the circumstances. I know it seems reprehensible, but what of the future? What will the city say when you give birth without having seen your husband since the day he marched out with the troops? The king may have selfish reasons for wanting to move you into the palace, but the life of an innocent baby hangs in the balance, and you will be protected, directly or indirectly, by the move. David can't wait very long because the pregnancy will become noticeable soon." He paused. She was quietly weeping.

"Uri," she whispered. "I need you."

Ahithophel placed a comforting hand on her arm, and she did not rebuff him. "But please understand, Betta, this is not something I approve of. Never. I'll never forgive David—my former friend and king—for the damage he has done to my family."

Betta listened carefully and then dried her tears on the edge of her long apron. "I don't know, Papa. I may have to marry him, but I could never love a man like that. And it is too soon after Uri's death. I cannot bear the thought of him coming near me."

The elder paused before responding. "I know. This is a terrible situation for you and the baby. I don't know why God has allowed it." He hugged her, and she did not pull away although she did not respond with much emotion.

He turned to leave. "Forget I said anything. I hope this difficulty can be resolved to bring honor to God in some way. I pray you will find happiness again, Betta, somehow. I know it doesn't seem possible now, but God's ways are not our ways." Turning back, he kissed the top of her head. "Betta, you know I will love you till the day I die. We may never see each other again, but you will always be in my prayers, and whatever I am able to do for you, I will make it happen. God bless you, my sweet granddaughter."

Betta looked at him with tears in her eyes and said in a low voice, "Goodbye, Papa."

Chapter 10:

Bathsheba and David

A few weeks after Ahithophel left Jerusalem, David arranged for Bathsheba to be brought to the palace to discuss her future.

"Bathsheba, I know how difficult these past weeks have been for you. I wanted you to have time to grieve for Uriah, and I am sure this has been a painful time, especially with your father away." He did not mention her grandfather.

She looked down respectfully, not wanting to encourage his romantic interest.

"Yes, my lord. Since the army marched out to battle, my life has changed very much. But I am trusting God for the future." Wanting to scream blame at the king, she held her tongue, knowing that her future and the well-being of her child depended on the king's good graces.

David studied her demeanor and understood this was not the time to press his ardor. Instead, he needed to address the practical needs of hers and the baby's security and well-being.

"Have you given thought to my offer for you and your father to make your home here in the palace? You will be safe here."

Not from you! The young widow wanted to exclaim. But again, discretion kept her silent. She had feared this confrontation, but she had decided to be frank about her feelings when the time came. She prayed silently, *I'm trusting You, Lord, to take care of me and this unborn baby. Give me the words to say.*

Looking up, she raised her eyes to address David directly. "I have grieved deeply, and I will never forget my husband Uriah. I don't know if I can ever forgive what you have done to me and my husband. But I do understand this: for the baby's sake, I must come to the palace. He or she will need a father as well as a mother, and you are responsible for this child. Perhaps you can...adopt...the baby. If you can accept us on that basis, I will agree to live here."

Although this was not exactly the answer David wanted to hear, he did not hesitate. "I accept your decision. I understand you are in mourning and reluctant to pledge more than accepting the palace as your residence." He paused and walked over to the window, staring out as though searching for inspiration within the distant Judaean hills.

"I certainly haven't earned your respect, but I promise to treat you honorably. Maybe, after some time has passed, I can try to make up your loss somehow."

She almost shook her head impatiently but again schooled herself to listen.

David came to stand before her. "Now listen to me, Bathsheba. I don't plan to just add you to the harem. I want you to be my wife. I want to be your husband. Do you believe me?"

Bathsheba paused. "Let us put the matter in God's hands for now. In the space of a few months, the child will be born.

Perhaps we can speak again. I want what's best for the child who did not ask to be born in this manner."

David nodded assent and said, "I will have someone assist you in moving into the palace. Before the next holy day feast, we will need to come to a decision about the arrangements for you in the palace. I doubt the people of Jerusalem will approve a widow living in the palace without legal protection as my wife. I do care for you deeply, more than I could have imagined, and even more now that you are carrying my child. I will arrange a comfortable place for you in the women's hall for the time being."

"Yes, sire. I will be fine in the women's hall...I think. As an outsider with an uncertain future, I'm a little fearful that I won't be accepted in their company."

"They will be informed and instructed to treat you royally. If we marry, you will become royalty, and there will be no question or doubt of your legitimacy and your elevated status. We can discuss that later."

Without smiling, Bathsheba nodded. David signaled a waiting servant to escort her back to her home and help her begin packing up her things.

When Bathsheba was shown into her room in the women's hall, she had to catch her breath. Her accommodations were luxurious. Her private chamber was fitted with velvet curtains and woven carpets. The bed was built up on a raised platform with a white silk canopy, and a basin of fresh water was kept by her bed. On a dressing table of cedar sat a polished metal mirror with an assortment of toiletries, cosmetics, and beaded combs for her hair, all purchased from faraway traders. A selection of lovely gowns and belts hung in the wardroom closet by the shaded window. The window allowed a view toward the south that encompassed the fruitful gardens adorning the Mount of Olives. Gazing around the chamber and through the window at the beautiful sunny terrain, she wondered, *This is so different from my simple home; can I ever be happy here?*

After putting her few belongings away, Bathsheba opened the door from her room and beheld a large common area where several women, some with children, were occupied with weaving, dressing their hair, or sharing gossip. The other side of the common area opened to an inner courtyard with a decorative pool in the center populated by small, active fish that made the younger children giggle. Some women were chatting with one another, and others were talking with older children, instructing them on royal protocol. Female servants moved about the room, some carrying water from the well in the courtyard and others offering dishes of figs or dates.

Glancing around at several lads of various ages, Bathsheba thought, *Each of those boys is a royal prince. They are all heirs to David's throne, although they seem younger than nine or ten. The older princes must have their quarters elsewhere.*

Suddenly, she felt several pairs of eyes on her and looked around, embarrassed. To the women of the harem, she was the interloper. They must wonder what she was doing here—so young and beautiful. Would she become the king's latest conquest?

She saw several women looking her over, probably sizing her up as competition for David's favor. The women were all attractive and of different ages. One of the more mature ladies saw Bathsheba looking uneasy and made her way over, walking like a queen.

Taking Bathsheba lightly by her shoulders, the woman bent forward and gently kissed the girl's left cheek. Pausing only slightly, she then kissed her right cheek as well, demonstrating full acceptance of the newcomer. She spoke. "I'm Abigail. We were told you have recently lost your husband in battle. I am so sorry." Some of the other women stood up and came over, murmuring condolences. Abigail said, "I came here after losing my husband too. The king graciously provided a home for me, and we have a son together. He stays in the princes' quarters.

Several women offered smiles and the usual cheek kiss of greeting.

"My name is Bathsheba. I don't expect to be here very long."

"Well Bathsheba, His Majesty paid us a special visit to inform us of your arrival. It appears you have moved into the special chamber we call the 'Lady in Waiting' room."

"Oh? What does that mean?" Bathsheba's brows knit together.

"That's the room usually occupied by His Majesty's most recent intended; betrothed, but not yet consummated. You look familiar. Are you from around here?"

"You could say that. You can see my house...well, my former home, from that window over there."

Abigail smiled thoughtfully. "Usually the king brings in wives from foreign countries. Many here are 'treaty wives.' Our marriage to King David assures peace between our nations. We have political roles but are not encouraged to express political views. But you are not a treaty wife. Are you here under his protection now that you have no husband?"

Bathsheba teared up but willed herself to remain calm. "My father and grandfather are close friends and associates of King

David. With them and with my husband, Uriah, I have been part of the crowds that participated in the public celebrations. Also, with my servant girl Anna, I sometimes shop in the marketplace, so you may have seen me there."

"That is possible, although we in the harem remain behind closed doors for the most part. I may have seen you from the window. Do you know if the king plans to marry you?"

"No, not yet. I am not sure if...there are...matters to be worked out. I am only recently a widow. My father is with Joab's army, so he cannot advise me right now."

"That is perfectly understandable, my dear," Abigail said, pushing a long, brown braid behind her back. "I don't know what other options you might be able to consider besides marriage with the king. It is quite an honor to be asked. Do you have relatives you could live with?"

"A cousin, maybe, or an aunt or grandmother?" one of the older women joined in hopefully as though eager to eliminate competition from the newcomer.

"No, I'm afraid not." Looking around at the range of faces and complexions of the women, she asked, "Do you mind if I ask, how does the harem work? I see many wives here, and I hear that His Majesty also keeps concubines. Do all of the women enjoy the king's favor?"

"Oh, you get right to the point, don't you?" Abigail smiled. "I have been with the king for several years now, and the short answer is...sometimes. As treaty wives, we are expected to provide the king with a male heir. His Majesty does his best to ensure that we fulfill our duty. Therefore, each wife knows that the king will bring her to his bed until she bears him a son. After that, he may—or may not—summon us again. With a daughter, the future is uncertain. The king may continue trying to bear sons with each wife."

"Unless she is infertile," the older woman with dark eyes hissed.

Abigail quickly continued, "But I don't know about the concubines. We suspect they are a diversion or a secondary line of political assurance with local rulers of lesser authority."

"But Abigail, you are not a treaty wife, are you?"

"No. As is widely known, my husband Nabal selfishly denied King David—before he was the king—the needed supplies to sustain his men while on the run from King Saul. He should not have refused to help the Lord's anointed. But I provided sustenance to David's followers, and he was deeply grateful. Soon after, my husband died suddenly. David heard about it and brought me to his encampment where he married me. I was his third wife. I have been with him and the other wives since then. The concubines live in a different area behind the servant's quarters, and we don't mix with them."

Bathsheba ventured, "When...my husband died...the king offered protection here at the palace for my father and me. With my father away, I feel I had no choice but to come here. Now I have to think about the future." She didn't mention her child.

Several women spoke words of sympathy, with a couple of them getting up and coming over to encourage her.

Abigail continued, "Now the king is getting older, and many of his early wives have grown children. Some have been set up with lodging in the city. The king does not visit us as a group very often. He occasionally shares news of the kingdom and answers questions or addresses our concerns. He wants to keep the peace with our home regions so that we will give our families a good report of our living situation here in Jerusalem. All in all, our lives are good, our needs are met, and the servants offer continuous support."

The dark-eyed older woman had gone back to the corner where she was spinning wool.

Abigail said, "Do you see that older lady over there?"

"Yes."

"That's Michal, His Majesty's first wife, the daughter of King Saul. She never had any children. So sad."

"So, that's Michal. I've heard her story. She is lovely still. Yes, it is sad."

"Anyway, we all feel blessed to be part of His Majesty's life. It's what we do. He treats us well. Now, if you marry the king, you will live in his quarters for a full two weeks. Then you will be moved back here into one of the regular chambers down the hall and be one of us."

"I see," Bathsheba said sadly. Although she did not love the king, she had no wish to be treated as one among many women and used when it suited him. She had been the only woman for Uri.

The women continued getting acquainted in the days that followed, and most accepted Bathsheba without a problem.

Not long afterward, David arranged to meet with Bathsheba in the extensive palace gardens. As they walked among the cultivated roses and lilies, she was reminded of the lovely garden she and Uri had planted together at home. Life was so different now. She must be stoic and pragmatic. David was the king; he offered protection to her and the child that was growing inside her.

"It is time, Bathsheba," he said. "You must decide whether to become my wife or allow me to arrange a place for you somewhere else. It would not look right for you to stay in the harem as your baby makes its presence known. As the child's father, I want to acknowledge his or her birthright. I don't want another man to raise my offspring. What do you say?"

He had turned to face her seriously and had planned their meeting outdoors rather than in the palace, an environment that might feel forceful. Here, she was not so far from her old home, and the open outdoors encouraged freedom of thought.

She didn't speak, looking around, trying to find the right words.

David added in a softer tone, "I have been calling out to the Lord, asking for guidance. This crisis has actually brought me back to the Lord after slipping away for a long time. I don't want to hurt you anymore. I regret my selfish actions. If we marry, I promise to treat you always with respect and care. Will you be my wife?"

Finally she looked him fully in the face. "My lord, I have asked for none of this. I was content to live in my simple home with the man who loved me and devoted himself to our marriage." She paused. "We had only been married a year when he was taken from me." She paused again to let David's conscience fill in the unspoken words: "*by you.*"

"Yes, I will marry you because I can see no other future for the child or me. We will remain in the palace."

"My beloved," David embraced Bathsheba, and she allowed it without responding.

He stepped back and gazed at her with affection. "I will woo you and win your love. You will never want for anything or fear danger under my roof. I will make the arrangements."

Bathsheba acquiesced and returned to the women's hall. Abigail had been watching from the window but did not tell the other women what she had observed. She was hopeful for the young widow's sake that her future was now secure.

King David called in his closest associates to announce that he and Bathsheba would be married in a small ceremony in his quarters. He said, "I have already sent word to Bathsheba's father, Eliam, to return home for the ceremony. Bathsheba has also requested that her grandfather, Ahithophel, be present for the occasion. I'm sure most of you are aware that Ahithophel has been notably absent for some time now. Several weeks ago, he submitted his resignation in a huff, then walked out. I have no idea where he is, but if anyone knows how to find him, I'd like to get word to him that all is forgiven, and his granddaughter wants very much for him to be here for the marriage celebration."

Absalom spoke up, "Father, I think I know how he can be reached. My servant, Hesel, formerly worked with Ahithophel. He has accompanied him on trips to his old home place in the village of Giloh. Why don't I send him with a personal request from Your Majesty to attend the ceremony?"

David replied, "Excellent idea, my son. Please see to it."

After the meeting, Absalom sent for Hesel, and while waiting for him to arrive, he took pen in hand and wrote this message on a small scroll of papyrus:

"My dear friend and associate, Ahithophel,

"I feel it necessary to inform you that my father has publicly announced that he and your granddaughter are to be married in a private ceremony in his quarters. When he announced that in a closed meeting, he said that we should be on the alert for Bathsheba's grandfather, Ahithophel, because he may get wind of the announcement and try to show up. The king stated, 'He has offended my royal self with degrading and disparaging comments that cannot be forgiven. He is forbidden to show his face in Jerusalem on the penalty of death.'

"My friend, I am sorry to send this news, but I want to make sure you understand my father's state of mind. I am sending this message in a sealed envelope to be delivered by your close friend and former associate, Hesel. Please do not let him know about my father's threat. I don't want him to be concerned or feel ill will toward his king. If you please, send him back to me with a message that you have received my letter. That's all he needs to know.

"I'm sorry again to send this news, but be assured that you and I are still on good terms, and I will be in contact soon regarding our previous discussion.

Signed, Prince Absalom."

Two weeks later, Eliam was summoned to Jerusalem for the wedding. King David apologized to his bride, saying that her grandfather had declined the invitation to attend. The ceremony was held in David's chambers, and Bathsheba officially became the king's wife. David whispered to his bride after the vows were made, "Although I have other wives and concubines, my love for you surpasses my feelings for them all. My devotion to you will be complete."

Bathsheba was uneasy about what would happen when the guests departed. However, she knew now that her child would have a father, and the baby's father would be the king of Israel and Judah.

Her father Eliam spoke to her following the brief wedding ceremony. "Oh dear Betta, God works in mysterious ways. Promise me that you will try your best to tolerate what God has done in your life, the king's, and that of the child. Be a good mother, and maybe, someday, you will come to care for your new husband."

She gave a small smile and said, "I will try to accept David as my husband; it won't be easy. I'm still praying for God to help me forgive what David did to Uri and me. It's getting a little better, but it will take time."

King David came to claim his bride as the celebration wound down for the night. When the first two weeks of the marriage were up, their union had not yet been consummated. She had to admit, David was trying hard to woo her, but very carefully. He was kind and caring, and his behavior was beginning to relax her hostility toward him. Dreading the return to the women's hall after the fortnight of a so-called honeymoon, Bathsheba found to her surprise and joy that she was not transferred as expected. Instead, David arranged for a separate adjoining chamber for her, and he assigned Hesel's sister, Hadassah, as her personal servant. They were already acquainted, and Hadassah was experienced in ministering to expectant mothers. And, thankfully, she was trusted for confidentiality about the "sudden" pregnancy.

Life continued on, with King David making special efforts to show patience and kindness toward the grieving widow. As the months passed and the child began to move within her, Bathsheba experienced a newfound peace she had not expected to find in her new life. David's self-control and renewed dedication to God were beginning to soften her hardened heart.

Chapter 11:

David and Nathan

The next few months crept by as spring blossomed into summer, then summer faded into autumn. Palace life maintained a slow pace with the army still away. The soft autumn breezes allowed occasional evening strolls in the palace gardens.

David had retreated into a reflective mindset of self-examination. Despite his efforts to manipulate life as he wanted it, things weren't going well. He was unhappy, depressed, and not sleeping well. Worse, Bathsheba was still in mourning for Uriah. He could understand that. But it hurt to have his wife, the bride with whom he should have enjoyed a year-long honeymoon, distance herself emotionally from him. With some effort, she was courteous and respectful, but there were no outward signs of affection.

Everyone could see that she maintained an emotional distance from the king, and because they understood her loss, no one criticized her. That did not ease David's pain, which had cast him into a pit of anguish in which he sought to return to the Lord. If only he had done so a year before, none of this would have happened. He struggled daily with guilt, shame, and fear. Although he tried to turn his heart again to God, it was so burdened with sin that he could not enjoy the once-close relationship he'd shared with the Lord.

As the winter cold began to settle on Jerusalem, covering the distant mountain peaks with the first seasonal snows, Bathsheba went into labor. Hadassah was sent to tell the king, and he hovered nearby, unable by convention to enter the birth chamber but waiting for news just outside the door. It was a difficult birth. He heard Bathsheba cry out several times, bringing tears to his eyes. He had caused this, and although the child was not his first, it was the most traumatic due to the way he had brought it about.

After a long night, Bathsheba gave birth to a healthy pink-cheeked baby boy, assisted by several midwives. Exhausted, she finally was able to open her eyes when the infant was placed in her arms. Expecting to feel nothing for the child that had been foisted on her illicitly, she was nevertheless prepared to do her duty as a mother to the innocent babe. But as she stared into its small, hungry face and dark brown eyes, Bathsheba felt the stone in her heart begin to melt. The baby had been given by God for reasons she did not understand. But the infant boy needed her care, and she would provide it. Tenderly, she kissed his forehead and nestled him close. She had lost her husband and her grandfather, and her father was far off in battle, leaving her with a husband she did not want or love. But the child—he was part of her and always would be.

According to custom, the king was permitted to see his wife and child after several hours. Stepping into the quiet chamber, David's heart was touched as he watched Bathsheba nurse their son.

"He is healthy," David said, "and you look well. Do you need anything?"

To both their surprise, she was able to turn a smiling face toward David. "I am fine. The women have provided great care. Thank you."

Relief flooded David's soul. Maybe she could forgive him. Maybe the child could heal them both and bond their union in love. He smiled in return and placed a tentative hand on her arm that was holding the child close. She did not flinch.

In the days that followed, the king lavished Bathsheba with gifts and servants, sparing nothing for her comfort and the child's well-being. Couriers had reported that things were well in all corners of the kingdom, and the battle of Rabbah was winding down. *Finally,* he thought. *Soon, Bathsheba will accept my love for her, and life will be happy once more.*

Several days later, David's spiritual advisor Nathan requested an audience with the king, and it was granted. On that chilly winter afternoon, a fire blazed in the brazier where David stood warming his hands. No one else was in the room when Nathan entered. God had given Nathan a message for King David. Although it would be challenging, Nathan knew that God would protect him if the meeting did not go well.

David welcomed him, saying, "Come in, Nathan. I trust all is well. What's on your mind?"

Nathan said somberly, "I have received a word from the Lord God for you, sire."

"Oh? I hope it is perhaps a blessing for the beautiful son Bathsheba has delivered to us?"

Nathan remained silent, glancing down before speaking. "Let me tell you a story, and you can tell me what you think."

"Of course. I enjoy a good tale." David took a seat in a large chair close by the fire.

Nathan looked up and began, "There were two men in the same city. One was rich with many flocks of sheep and vast herds of cattle. The other was a poor man. He had nothing but one little female lamb that he had raised. It grew up with him and his children as a member of the family. It ate off his plate and drank from his cup and slept on his bed. It was like a daughter. One day a traveler stopped to see the rich man. The rich man was too stingy to take an animal from his own flock to make a meal for his visitor, so he took the poor man's lamb and prepared it for his guest."

David leapt up and exploded with anger. "As surely as God lives," he said to Nathan, "the man who did this ought to be killed! He must repay four times for his crime and his stinginess!"

A long, awkward pause ensued as Nathan fixed his gaze on the king. When David collected himself and sat back down, he returned Nathan's piercing gaze.

Nathan said, "You...are the rich man!"

Stunned, David could not readily fathom the meaning of Nathan's words. Then the meaning clicked in his mind; he felt his temper rise sharply and was prepared to rebuke Nathan. But something stopped him—something internal-- something powerful. He collapsed in his chair as if a boulder had struck him.

Nathan stood silent. He looked into David's eyes and continued his message from God.

"Here is what God, the God of Israel has to say to you: 'I made you king over Israel. I freed you from the fist of Saul. I gave you your master's daughter and other wives to have and to hold. I gave you both Israel and Judah, and if that hadn't been enough, I'd have added much more. So why have you despised the word of God with brazen contempt, doing this great evil? You murdered Uriah the Hittite, then took his wife as your wife. Worse, you killed him with an Ammonite sword." Nathan paused, never taking his eyes off David. "And now, since you treated God with such contempt and took Uriah the Hittite's wife as your wife, God will bring judgment upon you."

David could hardly breathe. He couldn't speak, filled with dread. The wrath of Almighty God was upon him.

Nathan continued to stare at David with piercing eyes. He said, "Because you have despised the Lord and done this evil in his sight, The Lord is bringing down four judgments on you. The first judgment is this: the sword will never depart from your house. Violence and bloodshed will continually plague your family. Forever. This is God speaking: 'You have despised Me.'

"The second judgment is this: thus says the Lord, 'Behold, I will raise up evil against you from your own household. I will make trouble for you out of your own family. You will war against your own flesh and blood.'

"The third judgment is this: 'I'll take your wives from you. I'll give them to a man you know, and he will violate them openly. You performed your sin in secret; My judgment will be witnessed by the entire nation.'"

David could see Nathan's mouth moving, but the voice he heard was God's.

The words pierced his heart and soul. He realized suddenly that he deserved to die—more than the vilest evildoer on earth. He managed to choke out a few words, "I have sinned. Against God." There was nothing more he could say.

Nathan paused briefly. He announced, "That's not the last word. The Lord has taken away your sin. You shall not die." He paused, and David began to feel the weight being lifted from his soul.

Then Nathan revealed one last judgment. "Because by this deed you have given the enemies of God a reason to blaspheme Him, the son that is born to you will surely die."

David's breath caught in his throat. *Not the child—he's innocent. I am the guilty one!* He prayed silently, *"No, Lord. Please. Please do not bring this unbearable grief to Bathsheba."*

Nathan stepped forward and placed his hand sympathetically on David's shoulder. Then he turned and left the room. David collapsed on the floor, a sick dread flooding his soul. Images of his sins plagued his mind and spirit as he perceived them through God's eyes. He was repulsed at himself. *It seems so long ago that I was able to enjoy the blessed peace of my fellowship with the Lord. How could I have ever let that slip away? I am surprised that God would ever forgive me and let me live, but can I ever forgive myself? Why live to see the judgments pronounced upon me?*

What alarmed him most was the immediate certainty that his helpless son would die. Sorrow wracked his soul as he poured out his grief to God, begging for mercy for his wife and the baby boy, pleading for God to direct His wrath at him instead. He wept tears of repentance and remorse for his arrogance.

David lay prone on the floor until grief for his wife and infant drew him to his feet. He splashed cold water from a basin on his face and made his way to his wife's quarters. As he entered her chamber, he found Bathsheba leaning over the baby's crib where his son lay moaning quietly.

"Is he all right?" David asked in trepidation.

Bathsheba raised her concerned face. "He's burning with fever. I don't know what to do."

Trying to keep calm, he said, "Get some water and a cloth. We'll try to cool his skin while I send someone for the priest. He may have potions to make the child comfortable." He didn't want her to know that his stomach was churning.

A servant came with a pitcher and cloth over which she poured the water. Handing it to the young mother, she stood by as Bathsheba lovingly daubed her baby's quivering limbs, cooing softly. The priest arrived, and after explaining the situation, David withdrew from the small group around the baby's crib and returned to his chamber to be alone with God.

In his private prayer nook, he fell to the floor as he had always done when communing with God. He longed for that closeness to the Father; the times when the Spirit spoke to him and brought to his conscious mind the words of the psalms he had then penned over the years.

Before David could pray in spirit, he had to cleanse his soul of the arrogance and pride that had marked his life in recent years. He remembered the words Nathan had said to him,

"You have despised the Word of God, and you *despised* God, by doing the evil acts of adultery and murder." He realized with horror. "I have indeed despised Almighty God; what a worm am I."

David took a deep breath, then exhaled slowly. He cleared his mind of all thoughts as he began praying from his heart.

> "Have mercy on me, O God, according to thy lovingkindness; according unto the multitude of thy tender mercies, blot out my transgressions. Please, Lord, don't take your Holy Spirit from me. I'm sorry that I despised you. I love you, Lord. Oh, wash me, cleanse me from this guilt. Let me be pure again. I admit my awful, shameless deeds. They are haunting me; I can't stop thinking about what I've done. I sinned against you when I did these things. You saw it all and your sentence against me is completely just and honorable."

As David laid his soul bare before the Lord, he began to feel a stirring in his heart that he hadn't felt for a long time. He continued:

> "Oh God, I was shaped in iniquity. I've been a sinner all my life, and even while you were blessing me, I've had this lust in my heart. Forgive me for forcing myself on Bathsheba. Forgive me for taking all these many wives and concubines. I know that is not pleasing to you. The wives are mostly trophies to my huge ego. Having the concubines must be repugnant to you, and yet I have continued to use them to satiate my lust. I don't know why you have allowed me to have them so long. Please cleanse my selfish heart. I have had this lust in my heart as long as I can remember."

David felt a catharsis moving through his spirit and soul.

"I love Your law and will for my life, yet there is a different law within me that makes me do the opposite of what I know is right. I love You, Oh God, and I want to be in Your will, but I know I am rotten clear through as far as my human nature is concerned. When I want to do good, I don't. And when I try not to do wrong, I do it anyway.

"I love to praise You; I love to do Your will, but there is something deep within me that is at war with my mind. It has won the fight within me, and I sinned grievously against You. Oh God, please free me from this slavery to my inner lustful nature. Only You, my Lord and my God, can do that. I praise You, Oh God, for Your endless mercy and grace. Blessed be the name of the Lord."

Exhausted, mentally and physically, David drifted between sleep and prayer for hours; the hours stretched into days and nights as he kept his mind focused on God. He couldn't eat or drink.

"Lord, before You confronted me with Your words of judgment, I wouldn't admit what a sinner I was. But my dishonesty made me miserable and filled my days with frustration. For days and nights, Your hand was heavy upon me. My strength evaporated like water on a hot sunny day until You confronted me. I finally saw my sins and couldn't hide them anymore. I said to myself, I must confess them to the Lord. And, when I did, You

forgave me and spared my life from the pit. Thank You, my Lord and my God."

The cold winter days and nights continued, but David continued repenting and confessing, at once praising God, and then feeling compelled to continue purging his wayward soul. He prayed,

"Oh Lord, search me and try me and show me anything remaining in my life that isn't pleasing to you. Let me confess it that I may have the fellowship with you that we had before."

Sleep was fitful at best. Every waking moment he turned his focus to God in heaven. All of his wrong thoughts and evil deeds were brought to mind as he wept and mourned his wrongdoing. How could he have sinned against Holy God, the One who had loved him, saved him, protected, and honored him? Why had he done these terrible deeds?

"Create in me a clean heart, Oh God, and renew a right spirit within me. Cast me not away from your presence, and take not Thy Holy Spirit from me. Restore unto me the joy of your salvation and make me willing to serve you always. Then I will teach your ways to other sinners that they may repent and turn to you also."

Then, remembering the words from God delivered by Nathan, David prayed:

"*Thank you, Oh Lord, for not taking my life, which I clearly deserved. I will sing of your forgiveness—oh, how I will praise you. I see now that you don't require sacrifices, else I would give them gladly. What you do want is remorse and repentance. A broken and contrite heart Oh Lord, you will not despise. Lord, my heart is broken before you. Please restore unto me the words of praise and worship you gave me in the days before I turned away. Purge me with hyssop and I will be clean; wash me and I will be whiter than snow.*"

As he prayed, the presence of the Lord washed over him. His vitality was drained away as he fasted and confessed, baring his soul, pleading with God, praying for his infant son, and asking God to purify his body, soul, and spirit and to fill him with His peace.

The Lord brought to mind the words of Nathan:

"*Because you have given the enemies of God a reason to blaspheme Him, the baby will die.*"

David prayed, "*Because of what I did, our baby will die. Because of what I did, the enemies of God will blaspheme your name.*" David asked of the Lord, "*Please help me to understand and accept this judgment. Yet, if it be your will, please let the child live.*"

David also began to realize he had betrayed friends and colleagues, besides Bathsheba and Uriah...Ahithophel and Eliam. Now he understood how much they must been hurt by his selfish actions. And he had killed Uriah—an innocent man, one who was loyal and steadfast in service. David prayed,

> *"Lord God, help me to redeem myself in their lives. Help me to earn the love and respect they had for me before. I can't help Uriah now, but help me to provide care and protection for his wife, for the sake of his memory and legacy."*

David also took to heart the shame he had brought upon God. He sensed God speaking to him, "

> *You thought you had gotten away with your scheme with no one knowing about it. But now, so many people will hear of it that even the enemies of God will know what you've done, and they will ridicule my Name."*

David pondered, *how will others learn of my sins? I'm not going to tell anyone.*

But the Holy Spirit of God spoke to his heart, and he knew that somehow his secret sins would be revealed for the world to see. *Instead of glorifying His Name, I will be bring dishonor to the Name of God. Oh Lord, forgive me for what I've done! Please God, please don't take your Holy Spirit from me.*

Moving uneasily in and out of sleep, he always awakened to feel God's presence hovering over him. *"Help me to be a proper husband to Bathsheba; help us to grieve together and heal together as husband and wife. Is there anything I can do to change your mind and let the baby live? Yet, your will be done, oh God."*

The child held on day after day, giving his mother hope that he would survive. But he grew weaker and settled into an alarming lethargy.

God was working in other ways too. He moved in Bathsheba's heart to give her a strange peace in the midst of her pain. She hoped against hope the baby might live. Conscious of the sin that she had unwillingly shared with the king, she understood this baby might be taken in judgment. Her soul cried out, *Please Lord, no—take me, let me die. Please allow the child to live. He has done nothing wrong.*

As the servants watched from the doorway, they fell quiet, knowing what was coming. Yes, the baby died, and with a loud cry, Bathsheba collapsed, clasping her child closely in her arms.[7]

Hadassah said to the others in the corridor, "I will go to her. Someone must inform the king."

Three of them hurried to the king's chamber and the corner where he was subdued in prayer.

"Tell him," the younger one said to the middle-aged man with the group.

"I—I'm not sure how to say it," he began.

David looked up at them with a melancholic expression. "Is the child dead?" The man bowed his head. "He is dead."

So David arose, washed himself, and anointed himself with a perfumed ointment that was used for worship occasions in the temple. He changed his clothes and went into the house of the Lord and worshiped. Then he came to his own house, sat at his table, and requested food. They set it before him, and he ate.

As they watched, they did not understand the king's actions. Did he realize the infant had died?

"Sire, why did you fast and weep before when the baby was alive, but now you dress and eat although the child is no more?"

King David looked up and said, "While the child was still alive I fasted and wept because I thought who knows, the Lord may be gracious to me and let the child live. But now he has died; why should I fast now? Can I bring him back to life? I shall go to him, but he will not return to me." The servants wondered at his words.

After eating, David went to Bathsheba to comfort her.

"No," she cried out, pushing him away. "Why weren't you here with me? Why did you leave me to suffer alone while our baby was dying?" Exhausted by grief and pain, she collapsed in his arms, weeping uncontrollably.

He held her as she sobbed. Eventually she quieted down and David said, "I couldn't come to you because the Lord was dealing with me for the sinful way I have been living. I had to confess everything in my soul, repent, and rededicate my life to God. I was praying for the baby to live, and I was praying for you to be given peace."

Over the next hours, David held his young wife to comfort her. He helped her to a divan where she was able to sleep deeply, having been up several nights with the sick child. When she awoke, her eyes flew to him, and then her expression relaxed. "I could tell you were praying for me. I am grateful."

David said, "You and I will have other children, and if God allows it, I promise that one of our sons will be my heir to the throne. You will be the mother of the king of Israel."

Chapter 12:

David's Introspection

I n the days following David's repentance, he began to open up to Bathsheba. She became more willing to listen and try and understand the man who had taken advantage of her, the man who was now her husband. For a while, both found it difficult to open themselves to each other. Neither had been in this type of situation before, and although the circumstances favored David as the king in control of their lives, he felt completely humbled by God's intervention for his misdeeds. The severe judgments that had been pronounced on him and his family haunted his mind and soul. As time went by, he examined every circumstance that arose to see if it might be the beginning of one of God's judgments on his life.

Bathsheba's servant Anna had been called to the palace to serve her, and it was through her interactions with his wife that David learned of Bathsheba's nickname, Betta.

"Shall I call you that?" he asked one morning as Anna helped Bathsheba pull her hair up for the day. He wasn't sure that he wanted to. He had never been part of her family, and that name was a token of her earlier life with a different husband.

"No," Bathsheba said gently, turning to face him as Anna left the chamber. "That was my childhood name, and Uriah called me that as well as my father and grandfather. But none of them are here now. Please call me by my given name, the name that belongs to my adult years and a new life."

"Of course," David said, touched by her honesty. He began to open his heart with her more than he had ever been able to with another woman. He told her of his family, his sisters, and mentioned that even some of his nephews had been assigned military or palace positions. She allowed him to take her hand as they walked in the garden in the evenings. As they talked, he described caring for sheep in the Judean wilderness, facing a lion with his heart full of fear, but his trust anchored in God. Amazed, Bathsheba found herself fascinated by tales of the king's youth, a young boy given great responsibility for the family's livelihood by caring for their sheep.

One night after they had admired the stars in the clear dark sky, they returned indoors, and David held out his hand, which she gave him. Leading her to his chamber, the chamber that was meant to be shared when the time was right, David settled on the divan and reached out for his wife. She came over and nestled against him, finding peace at last.

"What was it like to face Goliath?" Bathsheba asked softly, looking up at his face from his chest where she lay.

He searched his memory for the right words. "I was angry—furious—that none of King Saul's warriors would take on the giant. It was as if none of them trusted God to deliver His people! There I was, a young boy having brought supplies for my brothers who were serving in the army, and everyone was afraid to face Goliath.

"I'll go—send me," I begged King Saul," David smirked.

"What?" Bathsheba asked, intrigued.

"Saul was amazed. He looked me up and down as though wondering if I were mad. Maybe my bravado came in part from being a boy not yet full-grown. But I knew God had kept me safe in the wilderness up to that point, so I was determined to kill the giant to protect Israelite honor in service to our God."

"And you did," Bathsheba said, nuzzling his beard with her lips.

Surprised, David leaned over to kiss the top of her hair that smelled of fresh lilies. "God did it through me," he murmured. "I can't take the credit for slaying Goliath. It defies logic that a boy as I was then could kill a towering, skilled warrior with a slingshot and a stone."

"May I ask you a question? It's something I've always wondered about."

"Of course, my queen. You can ask me anything."

"The legend says that when you were going to face Goliath, you stopped in the stream bed and selected five stones for your sling. Why five? You only needed one."

David smiled as he looked into her eyes and said, "I knew God would protect me, but I wasn't sure how many stones it would take. Maybe my faith was lacking. I knew it took three stones to kill a bear one time. As it turned out, I was prepared for his brothers and the armor-bearer too, if it came to that."

"You became legendary," Bathsheba whispered. "Everyone still tells the story all around Israel and Judah. Then you killed more and more enemy warriors."

David shifted uncomfortably. "Yes, I developed a reputation for bloodshed," he admitted.

"But not just that," Bathsheba said. "The beautiful songs and praises you've written for Him are wonderful; the priests sing them and teach them to us on the feast days. You have honored God with your life..." her voice trailed off.

"With most of my life, or part of it," David said in a low voice. "As wrongly as I have treated you, God has made you an instrument of my repentance."

She turned to face him intently as he gently entwined his arms around her. "What do you mean?"

"After I took advantage of you, your innocent charm and faith convicted me that the wrongdoing was all mine and helped me see how terrible I was in God's sight. I felt that conviction even before Nathan confronted me."

"I see," she said.

He added, "Bathsheba, I can't believe I let myself slide so far from God. The Lord had blessed my life so much since Samuel anointed me as a young shepherd. I know without a doubt that God has a special plan for my life, and I was completely surrendered to His will. He has blessed me more than any man has a right to be blessed. But then, I don't know what happened. I grew away from God and bored with my life. It seemed like there were no challenges left, and I had nothing left to give Him."

Bathsheba said hesitantly, "My grandfather thought everything had been too easy for you recently. He said maybe you had begun to forget all that had been given to you now that you were older and had reigned for so many years. Does that make sense?"

"Maybe. But God has spoken to me time and again to tell me I am His chosen one. He promised that I would always have one of my descendants on the throne of Israel. Maybe I did think that since the monarchy was established in my line once and for all, it wouldn't make any difference what I did. I don't know. There was no excuse for allowing myself to slide. I owe everything to God. I do love Him with all my heart."

"I believe you do," Bathsheba murmured, laying her head on his chest again.

David continued, "Do you know what Nathan said God told him? He said that I *despised* God and had contempt for the Word of God by what I said and did to you and Uriah. I feel almost physically sick to think I was that horrible—hurting you and killing Uriah. I deserve every judgment Nathan pronounced against me."

Bathsheba stiffened, and then relaxed as she asked, "What judgments did he say you would experience?"

"There are four. The last was that our child would die because of what I had done. I wouldn't blame you if you hated me forever. Our son's death has been a heavy weight on my soul."

Bathsheba mused on that thought for a few minutes, then said, "I thought maybe the baby died because he was conceived in sin, outside of marriage. But God is so wise. I think now that the death of our son was to force you to turn back from the wrong path you were following. Innocent people *were* being affected. It wasn't His punishment; it was chastisement. It was His discipline. And it was effective. You've been confronted by the truth—and you have changed. I'm grateful for that. Finally, after all this time, I have been able to work through the bitterness in my heart to forgive you. I think I can finally be free from the hate and desire for vengeance I've been carrying since the night you summoned me. God has worked in my soul too."

"I'm so sorry, Bathsheba. There's no excuse for what I did except selfishness and greed."

She looked up at him again. "I know. I understand. But you said there were four judgments. What are the other three?"

"The first was there will be violence and bloodshed in my family from now on. In other words, forever. Do you remember when God was so pleased that He said I would always have one of my descendants on the throne? That promise was also forever. So now I know my descendants will always occupy the throne, but they will also have to deal with violence and bloodshed. Forever. My sin will have eternal consequences. How would you like to have that as your legacy?"

"I can't even imagine the pain of that, if I knew..." She shuddered.

"God is merciful to let me live."

Bathsheba sighed. A moment later, she said, "Let's agree not to talk about it. What are the other two?"

"The next consequence is that one of my family would rise up against me. I assume that means that one or more of my sons will rebel to take the throne. Since God has said my descendants will rule, He may allow that to happen. I don't know. The final pronouncement is that God will allow my wives to be violated in public view. Nathan said that judgment is the direct response from God to what I did to you. God loves you and will avenge the wrongs I have done you and your family."

Neither spoke for a long moment. Finally, David cleared his throat.

"Bathsheba, I have decided that you will be my true wife and serve as queen. My former wives will be cared for in their part of the palace, but I will be devoted to you. I cannot divorce them because that would violate treaties with their tribes." He paused and then said, "I must treat all my wives with respect, as royalty. They are all expected to bear at least one male heir, or they will be disgraced. They are able to communicate with their home families, and should anything I do displease them, I will have problems with their treaty agreements.

"As for the concubines, I can't banish them. It's not their fault they are here. I have been a lustful man, and I did what I've known other rulers to do, assuming it would prove my manliness and authority. The concubines came to me through military victories. They are essentially slaves, but their children have equal rights with the children of my wives because royal blood flows through their veins."

Bathsheba asked, "Can you not release them?"

Shaking his head, he said, "The concubines must remain here in a servile role. Since their children are my children, I want them to stay close. Nathan's third judgment may apply to them as well."

Bathsheba absorbed this with some discomfort.

David continued, "You will be my wife—fully and legally— always. You are not a contractual spouse or a spoil of war. I chose you. I have fallen in love with you, Bathsheba. I hope you can come to love me too."

Her eyes widened as Bathsheba tried to understand her husband's words.

"I've accepted you as my husband. I no longer feel the anger and resentment that have troubled my heart this past year. I am overwhelmed by gratitude to see this change in you in renewing your relationship with God. If that remains firm, our relationship will grow as well."

David said, "God removed my pride and tamed my lust. I feel as though they're gone for good, again, rightly or wrongly, because of you."

Bathsheba sat up and turned to look at him as she said, "You are the same man as before. I don't know if one wife can be enough. Carnal emotions may return after a time."

He looked at her with love and compassion. "I have been brought to my senses; I promise you and God that I will never fall into those traps again."

Bathsheba smiled. "I will pray for you. For us."

David sat up beside her and said, "God's fourth judgment has already come to pass with the baby's death, but I have the other three hanging over me. I deserve these judgments, and I must allow God to do His work and not resist Him."

As the pair looked deep into each other's eyes and found honesty, humility, and love, they melted into a long embrace that began the rebuilding of their relationship.

The experiences of that week changed David profoundly. He was no longer the proud, arrogant, and self-righteous monarch he had been in recent years. He was a broken man in many ways, humbled by the Lord's chastisement and judgments. As a result, David became more passive in his kingly role. When troubles arose, his first tendency was to examine the circumstances to see if they might be part of God's judgments. Rather than challenge opposition, he would allow circumstances to unfold and suffer the consequences. Without admitting it aloud, he missed the counsel of his old friend and advisor,

Ahithophel. He was not the headstrong boy of his youth nor the lusty warrior of young adulthood. He was the meditative middle-aged ruler.

One evening as the royal couple stood on the roof at the parapet, looking out over the quiet city as the moon rose, David mused, "I'm not sure what to do about your grandfather."

"What do you mean?" Bathsheba asked.

"Oh, Bathsheba, I've often regretted sending him away. While I was fasting and praying, my mind went back to the last meeting with Ahithophel. I betrayed the trust of my friend of years past; he had the courage to confront me for my transgressions, and he was right. And what did I do? I threatened to kill him if he showed his face in Jerusalem again. I should have listened while I had a chance. Maybe I could have prevented some of the disasters that occurred. Hopefully, I will be able to make it up to him someday."

Listening patiently as she always did, Bathsheba nodded as David stopped speaking. "I hope the two of you can reconcile. He is a good man, and he cares about your well-being."

"I don't know," David said, "I had Absalom send him an invitation to our wedding, but he just sent a rude response, one that told me his hatred was permanent." Giving his wife a painful half-grin, he continued, "I will look for another opportunity to bring him home. Maybe the Lord will change his mind."

"I hope so," she said fervently. "I still love and miss him."

David said, "So do I," as he kissed the tears from her eyes.

PART II:
ABSALOM'S REBELLION

*Who can stretch out his hand against the Lord's anointed, and
be without guilt? –1 Samuel 26:10*

Chapter 13:

Amnon's Sin

Even as David and Bathsheba grieved the loss of their child, evil intentions had infiltrated the house of David. Crown Prince Amnon sent a servant to summon his cousin Jonadab to his apartment. He had been unable to eat much or sleep hardly at all lately. If anyone could help, it was his sly cousin and adviser who always seemed to know how to get things done.

When the slender young man arrived at the prince's chamber, Amnon said, "Jonadab, come in. I need to talk to you."

Jonadab came in, closed the door, then raised his brow and stroked his chin as he and took a seat. He said, "Prince Amnon, I am at your service always. You look pale, and have you lost weight? I've noticed you languishing for several days. What's wrong?"

Leaning back on his divan, Amnon crossed his arms and glanced at the ceiling as he said, "I'm in trouble."

Jonadab laughed. "That's nothing new. You're often in trouble. What's the problem now?"

"It isn't funny," Amnon snapped. "I'm in love with Tamar, Maacah's daughter."

Jonadab sobered instantly. "Absalom's sister? Couldn't you find another woman? Absalom won't let you near her. Hmm," Jonadab said thoughtfully. "What about my sister..."

"No! Tamar is the woman I want. What can I do? She's driving me insane."

With a groan, he turned away to face the back of the divan in despair.

Jonadab shook his head in mild disgust, thinking, *She's driving you insane? You're doing that to me.* He said aloud, "Ah, I see. You've been hit by the arrow of love. Who would've thought it? The Crown Prince brought to his knees by the beautiful maiden...the forbidden fruit. So close, yet so unattainable. What to do? What to do?"

Jonadab put his hand to his temple, half-closing his eyes as he searched his devious mind for a solution. Finally, he said, "It is a simple answer, actually. You, my prince, are a charming man. No woman could resist you in the right setting. So, lure her into your presence. Once she is alone with you and sees that you are enamored of her, she won't be able to resist. She will fall into your arms like a moth to the flame."

Amnon turned over again to face his cousin. "Hmm. And how do I lure her into my presence? It's not like she spends time in my chambers."

Jonadab paused and then smirked. "Ask your father to send her to see you. He's in a much better mood these days, and he'll likely grant your request."

Amnon's brows furrowed. "Why would my father do that? He would ask why."

Well, let's see...I have it. Take to your bed and let the king know you are sick. He will come to comfort you, as you are his eldest son and heir. When he asks what he can do for you, tell him that you crave some of those delicious raisin cakes your sister Tamar is famous for. If I am not mistaken, His Majesty will direct Tamar to come and bake some of her cakes fresh for you. When she gets here, send your servants away on some pretense, and turn on the charm. You will have her in your arms before you know it."

Amnon sat up, eyes wide. "Do you really think she would come to me?"

Shrugging, Jonadab said, "Why not? You are handsome and rugged. You're the prince, and you are related to her, although that could be a taboo for some. But if she is a strong-blooded woman as all our father's progeny are, how can she resist you?"

"I will give your suggestion some thought. And...not a word to anyone about this. Agreed?"

Jonadab bowed slightly. "Of course, Your Highness. I wish you well in your quest."

As he left, Amnon moaned again and settled more deeply into the divan.

Absalom and Amnon had never gotten along since boyhood. There was always tension between them, a sort of competition, despite the royal hierarchy of offspring. Amnon, as the crown prince, lorded it over the other brothers, but especially Absalom, as his closest competitor to the throne. Absalom resented his older brother and found his greedy, self-centered demeanor repugnant. He frequently dreamed about getting Amnon out of the way so he would become heir to the throne.

The first of God's judgments spoken to David was being fulfilled. God promised David that there would be violence and bloodshed; all too soon that judgment would become evident in the lives of David's two oldest sons, Amnon and Absalom.

Truly feeling unwell and making himself feel even worse by his evil desire for his half-sister, Amnon stayed home from his job in the palace that week but didn't tell anyone why. Of course, he couldn't tell anyone the truth, and besides, no one really cared or had asked. After a few days, Seraiah, the court secretary, was meeting with the king in David's throne room and asked, "Sire, may I inquire about Prince Amnon? Shouldn't he join us this morning?"

"Yes. He should be here, but I haven't seen him lately. Where is he?"

"He hasn't been into his office for a few days, so I was wondering if he is well."

David called for his servant, "Mani, do you know why Prince Amnon hasn't been seen the past few days?"

Mani responded, "No, sire, but I will find out." The two men resumed their review of the palace records. Soon Mani reported, "Sire, I have learned that the prince has not been well and is not able to leave his bed."

"I'm sorry to hear it. Please cancel my appointments for the afternoon so I can go to check on him."

A short time later David entered his son's chamber. Amnon tried to sit up, but was actually weakened from not eating. He also exaggerated his weakness, saying, "I'm sorry, Father, I am unable to bow before you."

Concerned, David responded, "Don't try, son. I can see that you're not well. How do you feel?"

"I've been weak for several days. I ache all over, but I haven't been able to eat much." Briefly, David recalled his own fast of several days when his infant son was dying. However, he was certain that Amnon was not deliberately fasting as part of a petition to God. Unfortunately, his eldest son was not demonstrably pious.

Amnon continued, "Most food doesn't sound good except for one thing. Those raisin cakes my sister Tamar makes would be light for my stomach. I could probably eat something like that if they were freshly baked."

David nodded. "I will have Tamar send some raisin cakes over for you. I'm sure she is willing to help you feel better."

Amnon said in a low voice, "Thank you, Father. That sounds good, but if it isn't too much trouble, would you ask her to come over here to prepare them. They are so much better when they are fresh from the oven."

"Not at all, my son. Rest and get better soon. Shall I send the priest to you with a potion?"

"No!" Amnon said, fearful of being found out. "It's just that, uh..., let me see if the raisin cakes help. If not, then I will see the priest."

David immediately sent word through Mani to Tamar to go to Amnon and prepare some of her cakes for him. When she arrived at the chamber, she took a small bag of flour and other ingredients to the charcoal brazier that burned low in a corner of the outer room. Setting down the bag, the lovely girl came to the door of her brother's bedroom.

Amnon heard her arrive and eagerly watched for her to appear at the entrance to his room. His heart skipped a beat when he saw her so close.

"My brother Amnon, our father has asked me to come here to prepare some of my raisin cakes for you to eat. I am sorry to hear you have not been well."

Amnon said weakly, "I'm feeling better now that you are here. Did our father really send you or was it an angel from God?"

"Well, maybe our father is an angel. He's been very caring and concerned for all of us lately. But yes, Father told me to come over and bake raisin cakes for you. Are you well enough to eat them?"

He sighed. "Your raisin cakes are like manna from heaven. They will help me feel better."

"Very well. I will stir them up and bake them over the fire in the other room. My servant Rannah will bring them to you."

"No, wait, can you please send her away? This is a family matter, and it will be awkward for her to serve me."

Surprised, since servants always helped to care for the sick family members, Tamar said, "As you wish. The cakes will be ready shortly."

"Don't take too long. I may die from hunger."

Tamar thought, *He doesn't sound that sick to me.* She said, "I'm pretty sure you will live that long, brother."

As she returned to the outer room to prepare the cakes, Amnon called his personal servant and told him, "Round up the other servants and Rannah as well, and send them away before my sister comes back. I need to talk to her about family business. You can stay close enough for me to call you if necessary, but don't be nosy."

"I understand, sir. I'll send the servants to the market, so they will be gone the rest of the afternoon. Will you be all right here without them?"

"Yes, go."

Everyone left, and minutes later, Tamar glanced into the bedchamber. "Brother, the cakes are ready. Can you join me out here to eat them?"

"I'm afraid not. Would you bring them in here for me?"

Hiding her uneasiness as she had never been in one of her older brother's bed chambers, Tamar said, "Very well. I guess I can."

Placing the fresh-made cakes on a platter, Tamar brought the plate to his bedside and offered it to her brother. In an unexpected move, Amnon grabbed her wrist and pulled her beside him, saying, "Come, lie with me my sister."

"No, no—please don't!" She tried to pull back, but he was too strong. Her voice strained as she said, "You are my brother. Stop! Please don't do this. It would be a terrible sin. Don't do this disgraceful thing. Our nation will be shamed. God will be displeased. Please Amnon—stop!"

Lust overruled the prince, and he wrestled her onto the bed and held her down firmly, kissing her face and neck while tearing at her ornate dress.

"Amnon, please—stop and listen to me. Ask Father, and he will let you marry me. Doing this evil thing will ruin me for life, and you will destroy your future if people find out."

But Amnon did not listen, blinded by greedy lust and passion. He stifled her screams, and despite her struggles, overpowered the girl as she wept.

A few moments later, sated, he relaxed his hold of her and she pulled free. Glancing at her tear-stained face, he was overcome by guilt and revulsion for what she represented—the object of his sinful desire and actions. His face twisted into a grotesque grimace as he growled, "Get out of here. I can't stand you."

"Oh no!" she sobbed. "You can't send me away now. You must go the king and get his permission to marry me."

He spat on the floor. "I would never marry you—especially now."

Weeping, she said, "Sending me away after this will be worse than what you have already done. I will be disgraced for life. Please don't do this to me."

Amnon got up from the bed and said sternly, "Get out—now!"

Tamar got to her feet and wrapped her torn garment around her as Amnon called for his servant, who entered at once.

"Get this person out of here." he said. Then to Tamar, "Go—and stay out. I never want to see you again."

The weeping girl, head bowed, went out the door as Amnon ordered the servant to clean up all evidence of the raisin cakes and supplies Tamar had brought.

Weeping quietly, Tamar pulled her head covering over her hair and finished tearing off the sleeves of her beautiful dress; the garment that had been made especially for her as the king's daughter. In a posture of grief, she put her hand on her head and made her way to her family's part of the palace as tears flowed down her cheeks.

Absalom had just been to see his mother. As he was leaving that part of the palace, he saw his sister making her way in tears toward him. He hurried to her and taking her gently in his arms he searched her face. He said, "Was it Amnon, your brother, who has done this to you?" She nodded tearfully. "Be quiet for now, my sister; he is your brother. Don't take this thing to heart." He kissed her brow as she leaned against his shoulder for support, and he led her to their mother. He said to Maacah, "Let her live in my house to heal her grief." Maacah nodded, her own eyes filled with tears as she took her daughter in her arms and led her into the inner chamber to bathe. After that day, Tamar lived in her brother Absalom's house, a desolate woman.

Absalom immediately sought an audience with his father David. When Absalom entered his father's quarters, David said, "Ah, my son Absalom. How good is it to see you. How is it with you? Is all well?"

Absalom said, "Thank you for the opportunity to serve in the palace, Father. But that's not why I'm here."

Immediately sensing a problem, David asked, "What has happened?"

"A shameful thing has happened that will make Israel the abomination of the surrounding nations."

David's heart sank. *It has begun.* He studied his son's face and said, "Tell me."

"Amnon" is all that Absalom said.

David was not surprised. He had long held concerns about Amnon's behavior and attitude. He had witnessed before Amnon looking at Tamar with lust in his eyes. "What did he do?"

"You may recall that he has been unwell recently."

"Yes," David replied, puzzled. "I went to see him. He didn't look bad, but he hadn't been eating, and I sent your sister Tamar to bake raisin cakes for him since that is what he requested. Did she go?"

Absalom struggled to control his rage. "Yes, like a lamb to slaughter. He used that as an opportunity to assault her. He took her innocence and then threw her out like a plate of garbage. She is desolate, and I can say nothing that will comfort her."

David's face contorted, and his eyes blazed fire. "Oh dear God. No. Did Amnon actually attack my daughter? Oh Lord God. It's all my fault!"

Speaking firmly, Absalom said, "My sister came home with her gown torn and ashes in her hair. Amnon used her and threw her out of his chamber. I just stopped long enough to let you know what is happening. I am going over now to take care of Amnon, and I will show him no mercy."

David's heart felt as though it would burst. "*So it begins. This—this—was from God. The judgments...*" He could never have expected it would be so cruel and so destructive...and so soon. He grasped his son by his shoulders and held him tight. "No, Absalom. You must not confront your brother. I can't risk losing you—or him. This is a terrible thing he has done, but you must not try to avenge your sister. You must let me decide how to handle it."

"But, Father, he can't be allowed to get away with this. He deserves to die!"

David's brow furrowed, and his jaw tightened as he remembered his own sinful act of lust with Bathsheba. Suddenly, he became weary, overcome by his own shame. Pulling himself together, he said, "Amnon will pay. But we can't go against what God has ordained. He is fulfilling His judgment against me. Leave this to me, my son. I will work it out."

Absalom pulled back from his father's embrace and stared at his face, doubting whether the king had enough courage or wisdom to avenge his daughter's shameful violation. He promised himself then that Amnon would not be allowed to escape punishment for his crime.

Chapter 14:

Absalom's Summons

After what Amnon did to his sister, Absalom was overcome with hatred. However, since his father refused to let him confront Amnon, Absalom grew frustrated and unsure about what to do next. He thought, *How should I seek retribution? If only Ahithophel were here, he would know what to do.*

The more he thought about it, the more certain Absalom was that he needed Ahithophel's counsel. It wasn't far to Giloh, so he could journey there and consult with the wise advisor. However, knowing how recognizable he had become throughout the country, Absalom knew that in a small village, he would stand out among the locals. It was important to keep any dealings with Ahithophel quiet. "Ah, Hesel," he remembered, "He's the answer."

To avoid stirring up any gossip by appearing in Giloh publicly, Absalom arranged to send the man who knew Ahithophel best. He quickly sent for Hesel. When the young man arrived, Absalom closed the door and tried to sound more casual than he felt. "Hesel, I want you to go to Ahithophel and work out with him a time and a place where the two of us can meet secretly. It is very important that no one sees the two of us together. As you know, he has been exiled from Jerusalem, and I don't want to be seen with him. However, he might know of an acceptable place near here where we can meet for a few hours."

With a bow, Hesel responded, "Prince Absalom, I know a perfect place. It's my old childhood home. It's not far from here, but it's away from the main road. I can make sure nobody is on the property during your meeting. Let me go to Ahithophel and arrange a time when he can meet you there."

Hesel returned in a few days to report that Ahithophel would be at Hesel's childhood home, which was only an hour's walk southeast of Jerusalem. He reported to Absalom, "It is an isolated sheep farm occupied by my uncle and a few shepherds. I have arranged to have the place vacated and ready for you and him to meet privately. After next Sabbath, Ahithophel will journey there on the first day of the week and stay for two days."

"Excellent," Absalom smiled.

'If we leave by dawn of the second day, I can lead you to the sheep farm without us being recognized. Then you will have the entire day for your meeting. I will keep guard to make sure no one comes near and you're not interrupted. We can return to the palace that evening. Would that be acceptable, sir?"

Absalom replied, "Yes, Hesel. Well done. Make the preparations; perhaps some shepherd's garb with head coverings would suffice. This hair of mine would be recognized anywhere."

In the early morning of the second day of the week, Absalom and Hesel discreetly made their way out of Jerusalem, dressed as simple shepherds. They soon found themselves walking alone down a dusty rural path to the isolated meeting place. As the two men approached the small cottage, Ahithophel stepped out of the house to meet them. The men exchanged greetings, then Ahithophel said with a small grin, "I apologize for the humble accommodations, sire, but this is all I could put together at the last moment."

Absalom responded, "This will do fine. We're not here to have a celebration. But we do have important business to discuss, and it is very important that no one see us together. Hesel, you keep watch for us near the gate."

As the two men made themselves comfortable in the modest home, Ahithophel said, "So, young prince, I want to hear why you wanted to meet, but first let me ask about Bathsheba."

Absalom hesitated before speaking. "I don't know if you have heard this yet from another source. The child from David's indiscretion was born, a son, healthy and well."

Ahithophel's face lit up. "A son—a grandson to continue our line!" But the look on Absalom's face silenced him.

Absalom glanced out the window before continuing, "Shortly after his birth, the prophet Nathan brought an ominous message to my father. Unfortunately, he hasn't shared what was said, but I get the impression it was severe. I'm sorry to have to tell you this, but somehow, right after Nathan's meeting, the baby got sick and died within a week."

Ahithophel groaned and stared down at the table where they were sitting. Controlling his emotions, he asked, "How is Bathsheba?"

Clearing his throat, Absalom answered, "Of course, she was torn with grief over the loss of her infant. She and my father seemed...distant...up until that time. The king remained closed up in his rooms for the entire week. The servants said he was praying and fasting for the child's life, and he refused to come out or eat anything. When the baby died, David came to Bathsheba and grieved with her over the baby's death."

Ahithophel shook his head sadly. "My poor girl. She's been through so much."

Absalom spoke up, "Thankfully, she has recovered from her despair. She and my father seem to have found a way to accept each other as husband and wife at last. She is expecting another baby now."

Ahithophel looked surprised, and then his features darkened. "Is David still seeking to destroy me?"

Absalom replied, "He isn't trying to hunt you down if that's what you mean. But he does have a standing order to arrest you if you enter the city. That's why I wanted to meet you in an isolated location where we can talk freely."

Ahithophel nodded and seemed to be lost in thought. "I'd like to let Bathsheba know that I am concerned about her. I can't imagine her being happy with David after all that has happened because of him. I wish I could ask you to take a message to her, but again, we don't want anyone to know you and I are meeting."

Noticing the older man's eyes growing moist, Absalom said, "I will think of a way to discreetly inform her of your concern."

Ahithophel looked up and said, "Thank you. So you don't know anything more about Nathan's message to David?"

With a shrug Absalom said, "I don't know exactly what the prophet said, but whatever it was, it has humbled my father. He has changed."

"How so?"

Absalom responded slowly, as if looking for the right words. "I think he has become more...introspective. He's more passive now. When I told him about Amnon raping my sister, Tamar—I expected him to explode in anger. She is his daughter, after all. He was angry at first, but then he became quiet and said something like, 'This is God's will.'"

"Wait—Amnon did what?"

Absalom said quickly, "Yes, he raped my sister, and afterward, he had the servant remove her from his house. He deceived our father to have him send Tamar to him. That's what brought me here. I detest my brother for what he did to Tamar, and I want him to pay. I need your counsel about what I should do."

Absalom waited to let his news sink in, then continued, "I know you were angry with my father when he banished you from Jerusalem, and you seemed agreeable to my overtures about gaining the throne. My thinking is now becoming more definite with what has happened. But I need your wisdom to guide my plans."

Ahithophel thought for a moment and asked, "So, what are you thinking? Don't tell me; I suspect you are toying with the idea that your older brother's attack on your sister may lead to a way to remove him from your pathway to the throne."

"Exactly. You grasped the situation at once. That's why I need you. So, what is the best way to disqualify Amnon from inheriting the throne? My father doesn't want to do anything in his current frame of mind. Is there any way I could make that happen?"

"Certainly. You can remove him yourself...permanently."

A long silence ensued as Absalom realized what the older man was suggesting. "What do you mean? Are you saying I should kill my brother outright?"

"Well...that's been known to happen in royal families. So...maybe, but not now, and not by your own hand. Your father is angry with Amnon, but he hesitates to take action. Assassinating a crown prince would be a capital offense, so if you openly attack your brother now, the king would have to condemn you, even though I don't think he wants to do that. In the eyes of Jerusalem, the prophets, and the law, he would have no choice."

Absalom quietly asked, "But how? What should I do?"

Ahithophel got up and walked over to the window to gaze out at the fields dotted with sheep. Hands clasped behind his back, he turned and said, "I would advise you to relax; bide your time. After a while, the memory of Amnon's crime will fade, and everyone will drop their guard. Then, in say, a year or two, you could arrange an 'accident' that would remove Amnon from the picture. If you do it skillfully, you will not be blamed for his unfortunate demise. However, if you do it now, everyone will suspect you were behind it. So, you need to wait a while."

After a long pause with no answer, Ahithophel asked, "So, what do you think?"

Absalom remained silent, thinking over this very serious proposal.

Ahithophel didn't rush him but waited patiently for his response. Finally, the prince remarked, "I've heard it said that revenge is more satisfying when it is unexpected. However, my anger is hot, and I want to strike him down now. My concern is how my father will react. So, you think King David will be less likely to arrest me if I wait for a more opportune time?"

"Oh yes, especially if you make Amnon's death look like an accident. If I know your father, his anger about Amnon's attack on Tamar will fade in a few weeks. But he won't forget it, not ever. After he has had time to think about it, he will realize that Amnon cannot be the heir to his throne; if his crime is made public, the people will rebel. Your father is faced with a complicated situation; he may even welcome something happening to Amnon so he won't have to do it himself."

Absalom mulled this over and then nodded.

Ahithophel continued, "Once Amnon is out of the way, you will become the heir. The other brother older than you is Chileab, Abigail's son, but he is unable to take care of himself. The next brother after you, Adonijah, is a possible threat; he's a few years behind you, but you need to keep an eye out for him. He may try to do the same thing to you that you want to do to Amnon. Your main problem right now is the king. You could wait him out until he dies of old age, but he could live another thirty years."

"I will never wait that long," Absalom sputtered through tightened lips.

The advisor added, "David's popularity isn't what it was, but he still has Joab and the military behind him. I could see that clearly when my son, Eliam, chose loyalty to the king over me, his own father. So, you might be thinking about how you could begin undermining your brother with the common people. You are a handsome young man, and very likable, so you might start by getting out in the public square a little more. Get to know the city leaders, the elders sitting in the gate, and the chief families. As the king has become more of a recluse, a gap has opened for someone else to become a hero to the city."

Absalom was buried in thought for a while, then said, "You've given me a lot to think about. I will take your advice about waiting to deal with Amnon. Now I must consider how to deal with my father." Absalom rationalized, more to himself, "He is my father, but this is bigger than the two of us. It is about justice for my sister and righteousness before God—as well as the survival of our nation."

Ahithophel said, "Agreed. You have much to think about. Let's ask Hesel about some lunch." Hesel was called in and set out a simple meal of bread, cheese, wine, and dried fish.

As they ate, Absalom began a new conversation. "If things work out as we have discussed, I will want to meet with you on a more extended basis. We may need to spend many days together at a time. This place is fine for a quick meeting, but a more secure location is preferable, one with plenty of amenities. Do you know of any place beyond Jerusalem's walls where we can meet without stirring rumors or gossip?"

Wiping his hands on a towel provided for the purpose, Ahithophel said, "Nothing comes to mind at the moment. You would probably be recognized anywhere. You've been thinking about this longer than I have. Do you have any places we might consider?"

"I've been thinking about Geshur," Absalom said, sipping the cup of wine and setting it down.

"Geshur? That is some miles distant. Why there?"

"I am aware that you know Geshur well. You were involved years ago in negotiations with my grandfather, Talmai, the king of Geshur. It was you who arranged to bring my mother, Maacah, to Hebron as my father's fourth wife. Hebron was where David was crowned king of Judah, and where Amnon and I were born before my father moved his headquarters to Jerusalem."

"Ah yes, I was indeed fortunate to have that assignment. Your mother was, and is, one of the most beautiful women in the kingdom. Even as a young princess, Maacah was famous for her charm and intelligence. Her father could afford to be very selective about her suitors. It was my job to convince him that even though David's kingdom of Judah was fairly small and was just getting established, his reputation was known throughout the surrounding regions, including Israel where Saul was still king."

"That must have been a challenging assignment," Absalom mused.

"My biggest obstacle was King Talmai's concern about King Saul since their kingdoms abutted each other, and Judah was essentially at war with Israel at the time. I was able to convince the king that David was a man destined for greatness; he would eventually rule Israel. I told him that he wouldn't want to be on the wrong side of history. Now he's glad he listened to me. He and your father remain on good terms."

Absalom continued, "So, you know my grandfather probably better than I do. Geshur is only a journey of two or three days to the north, and I'm sure my grandfather could arrange for a comfortable but out-of-the-way meeting place."

Ahithophel replied, "Now that I think about it, that is a splendid idea. Geshur is a beautiful country in the foothills of Mount Hermon, overlooking the Sea of Kinneret. Your grandfather, King Talmai, promised me access to his farm in Geshur any time I was in the area. It's a place he uses as a retreat when he wants to get away for a few days. We could meet there as long as we need to without being seen."

Absalom grinned, showing white, even teeth. "So, it is done. As soon as I have dealt with my brother, I will send you a message for our meeting in Geshur."

As Absalom got up and began to pack the shepherd's bag he had brought as part of his disguise, he reassured Ahithophel, saying, "As far as Bathsheba is concerned, I will make this vow to you. To the best of my ability, I will keep an eye on your granddaughter and see that she is well cared for." With that, he summoned Hesel and said to Ahithophel, "I will send word by Hesel when there are any developments. Shalom, wise counselor."

Chapter 15:

The Sheep-Shearing Plot

Absalom returned to his duties in the court of his father David, but he refused to speak to Amnon and went out of his way to avoid an encounter. He even moved his office to another part of the palace. He made no mention of his anger, and in time, the episode with Tamar was all but forgotten. Tamar seldom left the confines of the family dwelling where she, her mother Maacah, and Absalom dwelt; in fact, they did not speak of it to anyone, although some of the servants were aware. Absalom participated in regular family activities, and David saw that the animosity between his two sons was no longer an issue. In fact, after a year, Absalom moved his office back to its original location.

After two years had passed, Absalom planned a family gathering at his ranch in Baal-hazor, which was about halfway to Geshur. He organized a major festival in conjunction with the spring shearing of the sheep. Invitations were sent to his brothers and a few other young friends; Absalom mentioned it to the king and invited him to join them.

"No, my son," King David said. "My retinue and I would be a burden to you and spoil the festivities. Celebrate without me this year."

Then Absalom said, "I know Amnon is a member of your royal staff, but could you please release him so he can come with the other brothers?"

David's instincts sounded an alarm, but Absalom seemed calm with good self-control. There was no indication of animosity toward Amnon. "Very well, Absalom. As you wish."

Although David tried not to show it, Absalom had always been his favorite son. The boy was handsome, charming, and intelligent, well-liked by everyone. Until Bathsheba had entered his life David had assumed that, when the time was right, he would announce that Absalom, rather than Amnon, would inherit the throne. Now, however, he was beginning to think about a son of Bathsheba as his heir.

A few days before the event, Amnon stopped by Absalom's office. "Hello, brother. Father has given me permission to attend your sheep-shearing event. Who all is coming?"

Absalom replied, "Oh, the ten older brothers, plus a few other friends and cousins. I'm sure Jonadab will show up."

"Sounds like fun. You know, I wasn't sure you would want me there. We haven't spent much time together recently."

Absalom paused as if trying to think what his brother meant. "Oh, I'm over that. It was a long time ago."

"Well, thanks. I'm looking forward to it."

"So am I." Absalom permitted himself a small grin.

Amnon waved and went on his way.

Over dinner one evening, David said to Bathsheba, who was dining with him, "I'm glad to see the sons are getting along. It's fortunate Absalom was able to get past his anger over Tamar's situation."

Bathsheba, drinking from a goblet, gave him a speculative look.

Catching her glance, David knew that he had put his wife in a similar predicament, but Tamar's would not have a happy ending.

"Of course, I should have done something about it when Amnon took advantage of his sister. But he is the heir, and I didn't want all of the city to find out."

"Perhaps they knew anyway," Bathsheba said quietly as she set the goblet down.

"Possibly," David said, embarrassed. To change the subject, he asked, "How are you feeling, my dear? Has the baby moved yet?"

Bathsheba placed a hand on her abdomen. "He is moving now."

David got up eagerly to come and feel the child's movement as he touched her gown. "He kicked me!" he chuckled. He kissed his wife's head before returning to his seat.

"Let's hope that's the worst he will ever do to you," Bathsheba smiled.

The sheep shearing was an exciting escape from stifled palace life for the adolescent boys and young men who all loved getting away to the countryside. Watching the servants shear the sheep's winter wool, there would be fresh meat cooked over an open fire with side dishes prepared by the kitchen staff. Music and dancing were likely, leading to great merriment that would last until the early hours of morning. It was a perfect setting for Absalom's plan. Absalom had been advised to make Amnon's death look like an accident. However, he couldn't come up with a secure plan, and besides that, he wanted the satisfaction of personal revenge for Amnon's attack on his helpless sister.

He confided in his servant, Ari, "I am going to get even with Amnon for what he did to my sister. The two of us are going to surprise him while he is drunk at the barbeque. We will slay him before he knows what's happening."

Ari said, "Your Highness, may I make a suggestion?"

"Certainly, Ari. What is it?"

"Prince Amnon is a trained warrior, as are you. I am not. We have some shady rascals working at the farm who are experienced in 'personal conflicts.' Why not use them to do the dirty work?"

"Hmm, that might be better. I was trying to think of a way that I could make his demise look like an accident. But I want to see him squirm. He needs to know it is me avenging Tamar. The troublemakers can help me finish the deed."

When the day for sheep shearing arrived, the royal party arrived late in the day. While the royals and their attendants enjoyed a hot country meal, Absalom asked the foreman to send two or three hired ruffians who would be willing to help him with a "special" matter. When the prince put his hand on the dagger in his belt, the foreman understood. When the three men were sent to him, Absalom briefed them on his plan.

"Arm yourselves and be ready. When Amnon is merry with wine, watch for my signal, then attack him without mercy. He will not be an easy man to bring down. One of you get behind him and grab him in a chokehold. While he is struggling, you two attack with your weapons. Don't worry about being arrested; it is by my order that you do this act. Be courageous."

On the second day, after the wine had been flowing freely for some time, the group of young royals became boisterous with loud joking and roughhousing. There was laughing and competitions as the half-brothers wrestled and argued loudly with each other. Amnon, sitting back against the fence to watch the fun, became inebriated. Soon he got up to relieve himself in the pasture; as he was making his way out of the yard, Absalom gave the signal to his men. "Get him!"

In his drunken state, Amnon was quickly overpowered, and the men pierced him over and over. As he lay on the ground with his life bleeding away, Absalom knelt beside his dying brother and spoke into his ear. "You destroyed my sister's life. It's your turn to pay with yours. Who is the crown prince now, brother? I, Absalom, will soon rule over Israel. Now—you—die."

Amnon quickly expired from thrusts of dagger and sword.

When the younger brothers saw what was happening to Amnon, they panicked. Someone shouted, "He's going to kill us all; run for your lives!" The group of inebriated young princes rushed to their mules, and in the drunken melee, they found a mule, any mule, mounted, and galloped away. The adult monitors who were present at the celebration rushed off to Jerusalem to report to the king that all the young princes were being murdered by Absalom.

When David received the alarming news, he was torn by grief. He tore his clothes and fell on the ground, realizing the manifestation of God's judgment. Violence and bloodshed would tear his family apart. The second judgment that a member of his family would rise up against him surely referred to Absalom, the son he loved most—but the one who had committed the bloodshed.

King David's nephew, Jonadab, arrived from the murder scene and reported to David, "Do not let my lord suppose they have put to death all the young men, the king's sons, for Amnon alone is dead." Continuing, Jonadab reported what he had known all along, "Absalom has been planning this deed ever since Amnon violated his sister, Tamar. So, do not worry about the other brothers. Only Amnon is dead."

Jonadab had barely finished his report when the young princes began arriving on their mules. Soon, all were accounted for. Loud wailing and weeping from grief broke out as the survivors revealed their hair-raising accounts. King David and the servants were shocked and in mourning because the crown prince was dead by the hand of his brother. But secretely, David's heart was comforted because Prince Amnon was dead. Guilt filled his soul as he was reminded again of his negligence in not addressing the defiling of Tamar at the start.

David was grateful Absalom had survived, and his heart longed to be with him, but David could not go to him, as justice demanded a penalty for Absalom's crime. Absalom sent Hesel to advise and summon Ahithophel, then he and Ari fled to Geshur, where they were safe from David and his troops. He was sure David would seek to arrest him for the murder of the crown prince. His grandfather's country was a safe haven for Absalom. He could stay there for as long as necessary, meeting occasionally with Ahithophel, waiting for the furor to subside, and planning his next move.

Geshur was north of Jerusalem, located on the hills bordering the eastern shore of the Sea of Kinneret, which was later referred to as the Sea of Galilee. The small country lay between Israel and Syria. Absalom went first to the royal palace, the home of his grandfather, King Talmai. When the palace guards learned his identity, they ushered him into the king's chamber.

Talmai, having been advised of the new arrival, said, "Absalom, my grandson from David's court in Israel, I'm delighted you have come to see us."

Bowing, Absalom replied, "Greetings, Grandfather. I haven't seen you since I was a youth. Are you well?"

"Yes, I am doing very well. I've sent for your grandmother. She will be thrilled to see you. Oh, here she is now. Look, Lalit, it's Maacah's son, Absalom."

Absalom's grandmother came forward to greet him and embraced him vigorously. "Oh, Absalom. You are a handsome lad. And look at that head of hair. You must have the ladies after you."

Absalom said, "Grandmother, it's a joy to see you again."

She responded, "Come and sit down beside me and tell me everything. How are your mother and your sister?"

"Well," said Absalom, "I have news to share, but may we speak privately?"

"Of course," the queen stood up again and exchanged a glance with her husband. "Shall we confer with our grandson in your meeting room?"

The king got up and led the way to his private counsel room, waiting for his wife and grandson to enter before closing the door. As they were seated, the king's face became serious.

"What has happened Absalom? Does this concern Tamar?" Talmai knew his granddaughter was beautiful, and he had been uneasy about her living in a palace with a number of young princes by several different wives of the king, vying for her attention..

Absalom replied, "I'm sorry to have to tell you this, but Tamar was brutally raped by Amnon, King David's eldest son."

The queen gasped and put her hands over her mouth as tears fell down her cheeks. "She is unprotected, and now she is unmarriageable. She must return to us."

"There is no other way for her," Talmai said firmly.

"Amnon is now dead. I had him killed."

The royal couple were stunned. The king said, "This is terrible news, my son. Have you brought Tamar and Maacah with you?"

Absalom shook his head negatively. "Not yet. I fled here for my life. My father may have me arrested and executed for the murder, which just occurred last night. I hope you will give me leave to stay here until we can arrange for Mother and Tamar to come as well. King David may not let them leave."

His grandmother said, "I'm sure your grandfather will agree; do you, sire?"

"Yes, you may stay with us, unless you prefer for me to send a message to your father to try and convince him to let you come home?"

"Maybe later, Grandfather. I don't want him to know where I am right now. He may be willing to discuss it with you later. Thank you, my lord."

"I am proud of you, Absalom. Not many men would dare to do what you have done. You have preserved your sister's honor. We will also provide lodgings for any who have accompanied you."

Absalom hesitantly asked, "Grandfather, I have heard you have a country retreat not far from here. Would it be possible for us to stay there? I've only brought a couple of my men, but we may end up having to remain for an extended time."

"True," his grandfather mused. "It is a good place, secure, not far from here. You can walk it in less than an hour. On a clear day, there are places where you can see as far as the Great Sea. But don't stay away. Please come to see us here at the palace often."

After concluding their visit, Absalom and Ari followed the directions to Talmai's retreat where they arrived late in the evening. Word had been sent ahead for the staff to prepare for their arrival. There was still enough light to see a large stone house in a peaceful rural setting. The smell of livestock and barns and the bleating of sheep hung in the cool air as they approached the house. Smoke rose from the chimney promising a good home-cooked meal for the new tenants. The working farm was located in a verdant valley with a mountain stream flowing below the barn. Sheep and other livestock could be seen grazing on the hillside across from the house. This would be a good place to settle in and wait for the private meetings with Ahithophel.

With Amnon gone, Absalom nominally became the crown prince. However, since he was in exile, it was not clear to most people who would be the heir to the throne. Absalom was confident that he would wear the crown. It was just a question of when. He would stay in Geshur to wait out his father's response and confer with Ahithophel to determine his next move.

Hesel arrived in Geshur a week later and, after a welcoming meal, was directed to the farm. Bowing to Absalom, he said, "Sir, my lord Ahithophel asked me to let you know that it will be another month or so before he can meet with you for an extended time. However, he sends his congratulations on becoming the new crown prince of Israel."

Absalom bid his time and settled in for a long wait. He spent time getting acquainted with farm work and talking with the workers who managed the crops and the livestock. When Ahithophel finally arrived, the two conspirators were able to sit down privately and talk. Ahithophel asked right away, "How is my granddaughter?"

Absalom replied, "She is well and now has two sons. The first they named Shammua, and the second one, Shohab. They are handsome, healthy babies."

"And your father," Ahithophel asked, "is he still adamant about me not showing my face in Jerusalem?"

"Oh, certainly. Your name came up in a recent meeting. It was something about the advice you gave once on some subject or another. My father's face turned bright red and he shouted, 'Don't ever mention that name in my presence again! Do you all understand?' So yes, he is still adamant."

With a sigh, Ahithophel said, "Well, let's get down to business. Why did you assassinate your brother publicly? I thought we agreed you were to make it look like an accident."

"I decided that I might as well do it for all to see because I am going to move against the king soon anyway. I might as well declare my intentions now. That's why I fled here. You are going to help me design a foolproof plan to defeat David and seize the crown."

Taken aback, Ahithophel chided the young prince. "Since you decided to take care of Amnon publicly instead of making it look like an accident, your move to take the throne will have to wait, possibly for a few years."

"What do you mean! A few years? I've set the wheels in motion. I'm ready to make my move."

"And exactly what is your move? You have no army while the king has thousands of troops who are loyal to him. Do you think your father will hand the kingdom over to you for the asking? I don't think so."

"Of course, I agree, I just thought..."

"You thought for yourself instead of taking my advice. Now you'll have to wait."

The young prince flinched at the rebuke and didn't forget it. However, he knew the old man was right, so he composed himself and realized there would be no coup for the time being. The two men went to work, developing a list of knowns and unknowns that had to be considered. The main unknown was David.

Ahithophel explained, "When I left the king's service, I felt like I knew him well. But that was based on being close to him over many years. Now, based on what you have told me, David has changed. That makes him more difficult to read. You are saying that he is more introspective and seemingly more passive. But how passive?"

As Ahithophel questioned Absalom further, he said to the prince, "I am puzzled by these changes, but one thing I am sure of, I hate the man. I want him to pay for what he has done to my family, and to me. I was one of the most admired and respected people in the kingdom; now I am a recluse in exile. I can't even show my face in Jerusalem. I had a loving family around me. Now I'm not a father or grandfather anymore, nor a great-grandfather. I am even rejected by my granddaughter, who used to adore me. King David, on the other hand, has recovered from his crimes and has married my beautiful Betta, his victim, whose husband he murdered. Where is the justice in that?"

Ahithophel's anger had turned him bitter. He continued, "David must pay for his misdeeds, and now we have an avenue to make that happen. I am willing to do anything to help you gain the throne, even if it means taking your father's life."

Absalom was surprised at the depth of his mentor's anger. *Could I actually kill my father, the chosen one of Israel, God's anointed?*

As the two conspirators continued plotting, Ahithophel reasoned that they did not yet have enough information to develop a viable plan. "We need to know more about the official reaction to Amnon's assassination and David's frame of mind.

We need to have someone close to David to keep us informed. We can rule out Eliam my son, and Joab, David's general."

Absalom said, "I've never trusted Joab. He seems to be impulsive."

Shaking his head, Ahithophel said, "I'm not sure, but the time to test him is not yet."

Absalom then brought up the possibility of Jonadab, David's nephew. "Jonadab is shrewd and moves freely around the palace. He is nosy, and he loves intrigue; he's always wanted in on what we brothers were doing and wishes he was one of us. I wouldn't trust him as far as I could see him, but he might make a good spy."

"Let's send for him," Ahithophel agreed.

Absalom countered, "Who could we send? My servant may also have a warrant for his arrest."

Ahithophel pondered this and then asked, "Was Hesel known to be involved with the slaying of Prince Amnon?"

"No, he wasn't there during the attack. I don't think anyone would be looking for him."

"Good. Let's send Hesel to check the conditions in Jerusalem. He is well known around the palace, and he knows Jonadab. He can learn quickly if there is a price on your head. He may be able to gather some gossip about King David's plans. I want him to also deliver a short letter to Bathsheba, although I hesitate to have him contact her. I don't know how she will react."

It was decided. Hesel was dispatched for Jerusalem the next morning

Chapter 16:

Maacah and Tamar

As Ahithophel packed his things for the trip home to Giloh, he said to Absalom, "Well, young prince, I suggest you settle here in Geshur for now. You are safe and a welcome guest of the king, your grandfather. In fact, I will visit him before I leave. He may be willing to put you to work helping him run his country. With your experience working for your father in his larger kingdom, you may as well put that experience to work for your grandfather. You can expand your knowledge by working for King Talmai here. Use your time wisely, and it may benefit you later on. If nothing else, you and your men should find plenty to do here with the herds and fields."

"That is my expectation," Absalom said, staring across the meadows where sheep and cattle were grazing.

Ahithophel continued, "Looking to the future, time is a great healer. Problems that loom so large today usually fade in significance as time passes. We will bide our time for a couple of years. We can test the waters occasionally, and when the time is right, we will find a way to appeal to David."

Absalom said, "It's going to be difficult not having anything to do about pursuing my dream of ruling our people. I suppose serving my grandfather's realm will be a help and prepare me."

Ahithophel said, "I strongly advise you not to say anything to him about our plans. He would have to stop you because of his treaty with David."

"Of course."

"We need to get you back in Jerusalem and on good terms with your father. You must be seen as the proper heir to the throne before we can begin building your case with the common folk. I will visit every few months. So, until I see you again, relax and enjoy this time with your mother's family. Shalom, Prince Absalom."

A few weeks after Absalom went into hiding, his mother Maacah sought an audience with King David. Her concern was for their daughter, Tamar. Maacah bowed reverently and said, "I am worried about our daughter. She has been in low spirits since her unfortunate encounter with your son Amnon. I don't know how to help her."

David responded, "I know she feels her life is essentially over because of what happened, but that was not her fault. Absalom avenged his sister, and that's why he is in exile. I know it doesn't seem fair, but that's the way it is. You can't murder a crown prince in public and expect to get away with it. Nor can

I put a crown prince on trial without making all of the circumstances known to the public."

Maacah replied, "Tamar knows she can never have a husband or children in our culture. Her defilement is known widely now that Absalom has killed Amnon, so now no prince will seek her in marriage, treaty or not."

"It's true that I wouldn't be able to arrange a marriage to royalty, like a king or prince from another country. But...maybe she could find happiness with one of the men...locally."

"Do you mean a commoner? Surely there is something else she could do. Her reputation would sink further, and I don't know if she could be happy in that type of union."

"Do you not remember that I was a commoner, my dear? You grew up a princess, but a few years before you met me, I was just a fugitive living in the wilderness. The home I came from was very poor, and I tended sheep as a boy, one of the most 'common' occupations there is. I've known many good, honorable men who are regular citizens. I would have no problem if Tamar was to marry a non-royal."

"Oh, I don't know. She might not be able to bring herself to marry at all."

"I think she would have a better chance of finding happiness with a good man here in Jerusalem. As far as I am concerned, that would be better than being sent away as a ruler's wife... or living here as a lonely spinster."

Maacah inclined her head respectfully. "Very well. I'll talk to her about it. In the meantime, I was wondering, perhaps it would do her good to visit my family up north."

"You are thinking of traveling?"

"With your permission, I would like to take Tamar to Geshur."

"I see." David got up and paced for a moment before turning to face Maacah. "Isn't it true that Absalom is living with your father in Geshur?"

Maacah glanced down. "I'm not sure. I've heard rumors that he may be there. If he is there, Tamar and I would want to see him. But even if he isn't there, we would enjoy seeing my parents and other relatives. It's been years since my last visit. I know they would love to see their granddaughter."

David pondered her request briefly, then said, "Our nation is at peace with your father's kingdom, and the road north to Geshur is well-traveled. So, yes. Go and take Tamar. I think it will be good for her."

"Thank you, my lord. And if I should happen to see our son, may I give him your regards?" She tried to keep the pleading tone from her voice.

David looked at her and smiled. "Have a good trip and give my greetings to your father."

Later that day, Maacah spoke with her daughter Tamar. "I had an audience with your father today. I wanted to see if he would allow you and me to travel to Geshur to see your grandparents. Jonadab has brought me a note from Absalom asking us to visit. Here's the note if you want to read it."

Tamar took the slip of papyrus from her mother and read it: "*Mother, please see if you can convince the king to allow you to come to Geshur. Maybe Tamar could come with you. You don't have to mention me being here to Father. Tell him that you want to see your parents. Hoping to see you soon. Absalom.*"

"I wonder why he would want me to come?" asked Tamar quietly, her hazel eyes searching her mother's face.

"He cares about you deeply. You saw how he risked everything to avenge your honor with Amnon. Would you like to make the visit with me?"

The young girl leaned forward and seemed to think for a moment. "Maybe...yes. I think so. I would like to see my brother and my grandparents too. This place has been so quiet. I don't have anyone to really talk to besides you, now that Absalom is gone. When do you want to leave?"

"I will make arrangements for a carriage and servants to accompany us. Let's plan for right after the next Sabbath."

"Yes," Tamar said, looking down again, her light brown hair falling over her cheeks.

Maacah looked at her daughter with sympathy. "By the way, you may be interested in something else your father said today."

"What did he say?" she looked up with mild interest.

"He wishes you could fall in love with a nice young man and be happy with a family."

Tamar shook her head gloomily. "Has he forgotten I am no longer marriageable?"

"Of course not. You cannot marry a prince or any noble. But your father was once a common man before the Lord anointed him as the king of Judah." Maacah smiled. "Can you believe your father used to be a shepherd when he was a boy? It's an honorable trade. There are good, honest men among our people who would love you for the woman you are. You are kind, generous, and lovely. Who would not love you?" she finished.

"Are you saying he would allow me to marry a man who is not royalty?" Tamar's brow furrowed in surprise.

"We agreed that you deserve to be happy. What happened in the past was not your fault. Your life doesn't have to end because of someone else's crime against you. Go with me on this trip and be open to what the Lord may bring your way. Who knows who or what God may send into your life?"

Tamar's long-dormant imagination came to life as she began to consider the thought of marrying and having a family of her own. She said, "I will have to think about that. It had never occurred to me that marriage might be possible. Even so, I am not an innocent maiden, and my reputation would turn any man away, regardless of social status."

"My daughter, there are good men who would understand what happened and not let it prevent them from loving you."

"Thank you, Mother. I will pray and seek the Lord's will."

A few days later, the two royal women of the king's household set out for Maacah's home country of Geshur.

Tamar found the carriage ride to be refreshing to her soul. The road north followed the Jordan River with the hills of Gilead looming across the river to the east, and the hills of Israel to the west. They passed through the deep valley that carried the Jordan River from the Sea of Kinneret in the north to the Dead Sea in the south. In the coach, she could tell they were gaining altitude as they continued northward, with increasing vegetation and cooler air. The first night, they slept in a roadside inn that also served an evening meal. Tamar felt her mood begin to lift the closer to Geshur they got.

Soon the road began to lead away from the Jordan to the east when they neared the source of the river. The road began to climb, causing the travelers to admire the valley views and peak heights in the distance. The road became steeper, revealing beautiful vistas of the sea below. The sure-footed mules pulling their carriage slowed as the road steepened, twisting and turning, skirting deep gorges and canyons until the trail finally leveled off to a broad plateau. Maacah said to Tamar, "Now we are almost to Geshur. We should be there before sunset."

"Oh Mother, I love it up here! The air is so cool and invigorating. I feel like I want to get out and just run in the woods. I haven't felt like this in ages."

Maacah smiled and squeezed her daughter's hand as she breathed a prayer of thanks to her Lord.

As her mother promised, their carriage began to pass clusters of homes and farms, and soon, the king's palace became visible up ahead. "There it is—the house I grew up in."

"Oh, it's not nearly as large as our palace in Jerusalem, is it? But it is wonderful. Will we be staying there?"

"Yes, my dear. As soon as we get settled in, I will inquire about Absalom. He may be staying here too. We'll soon find out."

When the carriage pulled up in front of the palace, servants rushed out to see who the important visitors might be. Maacah thought she would recognize some of them, but she had been away so long that she had to identify herself to them. Maacah's father, King Talmai, was immediately notified and came rushing to embrace his daughter and granddaughter and welcomed them to his home. Maacah's mother Jalit followed soon after, along with other staff and relatives. But Tamar noticed that Absalom was not with them.

After the rush of greetings and introductions calmed down, Maacah quietly asked her mother, "Is Absalom here?"

Her mother replied, "Yes and no. He is staying at the farm nearby. He was here to visit a few of days ago and mentioned that he had sent a message to you by that young fellow who was visiting from Jerusalem. He was hoping that you got the message, but he had no way of knowing if you would come. And, look at Tamar. She is the prettiest girl I have ever seen. She takes after you, doesn't she?"

"Well, her father is a very handsome man," Maacah laughed and pulled her mother aside. "Tamar had some serious injuries to her soul a while back, so we are hoping this trip will be good for her. She seems to be liking it so far."

Jalit nodded vigorously. "Absalom told us about Amnon's attack. We'll see what we can do to help her along. I want to hear more later."

King Talmai ushered them into the palace and issued instructions to his staff to get the ladies' bags to their rooms and take care of the servants and the livery. Then he turned to Maacah and said, "We have already sent a messenger to Absalom at the farm to let him know you are here. I believe you will see him within a couple of hours. Meanwhile, come in and freshen up. Dinner will be served at sunset."

Absalom and his two men were occupied with sheep in a pen by the barn when the messenger arrived. Hesel was explaining the finer points of sheep breeding and grooming to Absalom and Ari, having learned as a boy from his father. Hesel, like his king, had spent many nights as a youth in the fields tending the flocks. Now he was the first to see the messenger coming down from the house. He released the lamb he was holding and wiped his hands on his tunic while saying, "That's the messenger from the palace coming."

The men turned to greet the new arrival, who was slightly panting from exertion. Absalom asked, "Is something happening at the palace?"

The messenger took a deep breath and said, "Yes, my lord. Your mother and sister have arrived from Jerusalem. The king asks if you can come to the palace for the evening meal."

"Indeed, I can," Absalom said. Then turning to his helpers, he said, "You two can come along as well. I will need you with me if we have to return after dark. Let's get cleaned up for a royal feast."

Later that evening, the royal family was served venison roast in the main dining room while Hesel and Ari ate the same meal with the staff in the servant's quarters. Ari made a point to sit by one of the palace maids he had met earlier. After his meal, Hesel made small talk with some of the male groundskeepers, then excused himself, saying, "I'm going outside for some fresh air while there is still some light."

One of the men he was speaking with said, "Take a look at the work we're doing in the gardens and tell us what you think."

"I will. Thank you." Hesel exited the back door of the palace and strolled toward the front of the building. As he rounded a corner, not watching where he was going, he barely avoided bumping into a lovely young lady who was obviously a member of the royal family. She was well dressed and carried herself gracefully. He apologized profusely, looking at the ground, saying, "Oh, please excuse me, my lady. I wasn't watching where I was walking."

The young lady responded, "Oh, that's all right. Say, I've seen you before at the palace in Jerusalem. What are you doing here?"

He gave her a closer look. "Oh. Princess Tamar, I didn't realize it was you. Yes, I am Hesel. I work for your brother. We're staying at the farm for now. He said he hoped you would be able to come for a visit." Looking around, he asked, "Did you come outside alone?"

"Yes, Mother and my brother are catching up with family news, and there weren't any younger people around. I decided to come out here for this cool mountain air." Although Tamar recognized Hesel as one of the staff at the palace in Jerusalem, she hadn't seen him up close before, and she studied his features for a moment. He had a frank expression and appeared pleasant and well-groomed. She said, "Hesel, I knew you were working for Absalom before he...left home. But didn't you work for Ahithophel before?"

"Actually, I am serving them both as their liaison. I travel back and forth, helping coordinate their plans."

"What kinds of plans?"

"It's complicated. They are working on some kind of project, but with your brother here and Ahithophel in Gihon, they need a way to communicate. I usually make the journey back and forth every few weeks. I can still visit Jerusalem, so I see my sister and pick up news or deliver messages there as well."

As the two continued talking, they found themselves strolling around the palace grounds, absorbed in conversation. Hesel asked, "How long will Your Highness be staying in Geshur?"

Tamar answered, "You don't need to be so formal with me. In a sense, I am not royalty anymore. To answer your question, I think Mother is planning to stay about two weeks."

"Will you want to visit the farm while you're here?"

"I don't know."

"It's a working farm with livestock, crops, and farmers," Hesel said. "It's a nice walk from here, past orchards and streams with good fishing spots. There are also some walking paths, including one near a lovely waterfall. You might enjoy it."

"That does sound nice. I will ask Mother."

"Please forgive me if I am speaking out of place, but I would be happy to come up and escort you down to the farm if you like. I think your brother might appreciate that."

"I expect Mother will send me down with a family member, but thank you for offering. If we do come for a visit, I will see you then." With a quick smile, she said, "I'd better get inside. Thanks for explaining things."

Unknowing that he had a bedazzled smile on his face, Hesel watched as the striking young lady went inside. She was surprisingly easy to talk to, not like a princess, but yet she carried herself like one. He could hardly catch his breath as he marveled at her beauty and grace. *Now, that is the woman I would love to marry. Except...she is far above me. But I can dream. She is a dream...*

Chapter 17:

The Geshur Years

Over the next three years, Absalom remained in King Talmai's service in Geshur. Besides Jonadab's occasional visits, Absalom would receive other visitors from Jerusalem and learn from them any news concerning his father David. Hesel would often carry sealed envelopes back and forth to Ahithophel. After the first year had passed, Ahithophel visited for several days, and Absalom filled him in on what he had heard from his various visitors.

Absalom related an especially interesting visit from his mother, Maacah. "David allowed my mother to come to Geshur to visit her parents and me, as well as her other relatives living here. My sister Tamar also accompanied Mother on the trip. It was good to see her looking well after her ordeal. She said our father had encouraged her to travel. My mother said that although the king wouldn't be able to marry her to royalty because of Amnon's assault, he would accept a suitor from among the common people. I couldn't imagine such a thing, but the more I thought about it, the better I liked the idea. She has been brought up well, and she will be an asset to any man. I don't know where she would find an acceptable husband in our family circle, though. Apparently, she's not in a hurry."

Ahithophel nodded. "Your sister is a rare blossom, much as I see my granddaughter. I hope she can find the happiness she deserves. Did your mother happen to discover anything about King David's frame of mind concerning you?"

"Yes, but first, I asked her about Bathsheba, explaining that you and I are in touch occasionally, and I expected you to be visiting soon. She said that Bathsheba had given birth to another son. The boy's name is Nathan. That makes three living sons for Bathsheba, including Shammua and Shobab. It seems that the king still appreciates his spiritual advisor Nathan even though he confronted him so directly before. He has named one of his sons after him."

Ahithophel said, "That's another confusing issue about the new David. I'm uncomfortable not knowing what to expect from him next. He has changed, and yet I expect that much in him remains the same. As you have remarked several times, he still carries a lot of bitterness towards me.

Absalom ignored the comment and as he brushed the meal's crumbs from his garment, he said, "I asked Mother to tell me what she could about father's thinking. She said that he spends much time with his new family, having more or less lost interest in the other harem wives. Of course, he enjoys all his children and plays with the little ones in the garden. He occasionally meets with the older sons to exchange news and advice. I will say that in most ways, he is a good father." Absalom's brow darkened. "But not in the matter of Amnon."

Ahithophel sighed. "That might be an example of elders learning from their offspring since you took care of the matter instead of the king handling it in a timely manner."

As if adding an afterthought, Absalom continued, "Yes, he cares for all his sons, including those of the concubines. He has reminded us that his royal blood flows through their veins, and that puts his succession in doubt, as we have seen. Those sons are royals as well, and I have no doubt the king will provide positions and perhaps even wives for them through alliances with surrounding regions."

Ahithophel frowned. "Hmm. I still struggle with the thought that my Betta is living as the wife of the man she hated when I last saw her. I can't imagine what kind of spell he has cast on her."

Absalom continued, "When I see them together, my father seems more relaxed, and he treats her as an equal more than as a wife, if you know what I mean. I think your granddaughter has become his friend and confidante while the other wives maintain an aloof royal aspect and a certain amount of reserve around the king. My mother told me that she asked David about his feelings toward me, his errant son, and he always says that he loves me and misses having me near. But when she asked if I can be allowed to come home, David stiffens and says, 'Oh, no, that would be impossible. Absalom has committed a capital offense, and I can't forgive that; nor will the citizens. He must never show his face in Jerusalem.' She said she was moved to tears, sincerely for my sake, not just to move him. But he did show compassion when he gave her leave to visit me here in Geshur. I am thankful for that. She said his heart is warm toward me, but he cannot let me come home just yet, or maybe never."

Ahithophel responded, "We can't make our move now. You seem to be doing well here. Let's test the waters again next year."

The following year, Maacah and Tamar traveled north again to spend a few weeks in Geshur. Upon their arrival, King Talmai insisted that they stay with him in the palace, but Tamar wanted very much to spend time at the farm with Absalom. Maacah managed to get her father's permission for them to stay at the farm enjoying the tranquility of rural life, with the provision that they remain at the palace for a few days first. He said, "I want to host a reception where you and Tamar can meet our local leaders and families."

Maacah said to Tamar, "That will be a nice event. You might even meet a nice young man; maybe even *the* man. Of course, he must be someone that both your grandfather here and your father back home would approve of."

"Mother, you don't need to be worrying about me getting married. I'm in no hurry. But I will attend Grandfather's reception, then we can move to the farm, if that's acceptable."

"Very well, then. I'll have our things moved to the farm after the reception."

The grand event was held the third night, and a number of local and regional dignitaries attended. Maacah looked very much like a queen; she wore a purple garment threaded with silver and her auburn hair wound with tiny silver ornaments. Rather than appearing ostentatious, she looked mature and dignified. Tamar wore a sea-blue gown with floral stitching along the sleeves and neck that looked suitable and not flashy,

185

setting off her fair hair that was braided down her back and secured with dark blue spun yarn threading.

A young man in the reception line man was immediately attracted to Tamar. She allowed him to exchange a few casual words, and before moving on he asked if she might be willing to dance with him later. She gave him a coquettish smile and a slight nod. However, Tamar didn't particularly enjoy his company. He seemed a little too pompous. She remained reserved, firmly on guard to protect her honor from gossip that might arise if people here knew about her prior disgrace.

Moments later, she noticed the young man in an animated discussion with an older woman who must have been his mother. After that conversation, he didn't seek her out again. In fact, he seemed to avoid her. The old feeling of depression settled over her again. It came on her so sudden she had trouble breathing. Tamar said to her mother, "I'm going to my room."

Maacah sensed her daughter's distress and asked, "But why, my dear? It's still early."

The look on Tamar's face revealed what her mother dreaded to see.

With a shrug, Tamar said, "I've had enough."

She turned her head to hide tears from her mother, then hurried from the room, being careful not to stir interest. Maacah made an excuse to Queen Jalit who appeared radiant in her dark purple gown, saying, "Tamar is feeling unwell, possibly from the trip. She's going up to rest now. I'm going to take her down to the farm in the morning."

Maacah went to her daughter's chamber, where the girl was changing clothes with puffy eyes and a determined expression.

"Honey, I'm sorry. What happened? Did someone say something that hurt you?"

"They didn't have to say anything. It was obvious the word has gotten around Geshur that I am unclean."

"Oh no. Please don't let whatever happened discourage you. I told the queen that we are moving to the farm in the morning. Do you still want to do that?"

"Yes! I'd go right now if I could."

"We will move right after breakfast," her mother said, hugging her daughter close.

The next morning over a quiet breakfast, Maacah reminded her parents that she and her daughter were going down to the farm cottage.

The king, having been advised by his wife, said, "I will have your things taken down this morning as soon as the men have finished their chores. Then I will have a carriage for you when you're ready."

Tamar spoke up, "Please no, Grandfather. I prefer to walk. This is such a lovely area, and I've heard the path offers pleasant views along the road. Do you mind?"

"That's fine, Tamar. Yes, it is an enjoyable walk, and while it a little chilly this morning, the day will turn warm and sunny. I can send someone with you who knows the way."

Maacah responded, "Father, have you forgotten that I grew up here? I know how to get to the farm. We will be fine."

Her father nodded, but summoned a servant and instructed him to send a couple of guards to follow behind the women for their safety.

When Tamar and her mother came out of the front doors of the palace, they stopped in their tracks. They were amazed at the sight before them. They had walked into a wonderland of blinding beauty. A heavy morning dew had collected on every blade of grass and covered the tree leaves. The chill morning air had frozen every drop of moisture, and the morning sun reflected in and through the icy crystals, projecting an astounding scene so beautiful; it was a breathtaking wonderland of diamonds before them.

"Oh Mother, are we in heaven?"

"No, my dear, I've seen this happen once or twice when I was a girl. Isn't it gorgeous?"

"The view lifts my spirit—oh, thank you, Lord. My heart is overflowing with love and joy."

Maacah responded, "Let's get started. The road is dry, so we won't have trouble walking. Yes, thank you, Lord."

As the two ladies set out for the cottage, Tamar felt a warm glow filling her body and soul. Her mind was praising God for the breathtaking beauty of the scene before her. She was sure it was a sign from Him, meant especially for her. With every step, she felt a healing taking place as she realized that God was moving in her to remove the shame and lingering bitterness she had carried for so long. She said to her mother, "Thank you for bringing me here to Geshur. My pain from the past few years is beginning to lessen. God is in me, healing me. I can feel it!"

Maacah stopped, her tear-filled eyes widening as she stared at her daughter's radiant face. She grabbed Tamar, and the women embraced, tears streaming down both of their cheeks.

"Oh Tamar, how wonderful it is to hear those words. Only God could work such a miracle in your life. Thank You, God!"

When the ladies reached the lane that led to the farm cottage, they hurried their pace, eager to see Absalom. But when they entered the house, neither he nor his men were there. The aging housekeeper welcomed the ladies, having just received their bags. Maacah said, "Let's go to our room and freshen up after our walk. Absalom will be back soon, I'm sure."

Tamar put a hand on her mother's arm, "But Mother, I want to find Absalom and tell him how much better I'm feeling. The scenery and fresh air are so invigorating. May I go look for him?"

Maacah thought about it and asked the housekeeper if there was a servant girl who could accompany Tamar around the grounds.

"Yes, my lady," the stout housekeeper bobbed her head, "my granddaughter Kita will go with her." She called the girl who was out back separating the milk to make yogurt.

Tamar said, "Remember, Mother, that Absalom's assistant Hesel is here, and he offered to show me around."

"Wait a minute. How do you know Hesel?"

"He used to be Ahithophel's servant in Jerusalem. Since Ahithophel left, Hesel has been working for Absalom. You knew that, didn't you?"

"Oh, that young man. Yes, I know him. A good servant as I remember," Maacah smiled.

"Yes, he is," Tamar agreed. Then she added as she pulled her cloak over her gown, "But Hesel is an assistant now, not a servant. We'll be back soon." Kita met Tamar at the door, and they started down the path to the barnyard, where chickens scurried for feed.

A couple of hours later, Maacah, who enjoyed helping the housekeeper clean fresh garden vegetables for the meal, began to worry about Tamar being outdoors alone in a new place. Absalom came into the house just as she was starting out to look for her daughter. Maacah greeted him, "Hello, my son, it is so good to see you." They embraced, and then she asked, "Do you know where Tamar is?"

Absalom washed his hands at a basin of water. "Yes. Hesel is showing her around the farm, and Kita is with them. They were down at the barn where he was explaining the seeding of crops and the different livestock. Tamar actually seemed to be enjoying herself, while poor Kita looked bored," he chuckled.

Soon, the two young women returned. Hesel and the other workers followed an hour later when dinner was ready, and everyone had been called to eat.

Maacah quietly noticed the shy glances and lively conversation that passed between her daughter and Hesel. Absalom caught his mother's eye for a second and winked.

The remaining days at the farm passed quickly, and all too soon, the women were stepping into the carriage that would return them to the palace. Tamar felt sad to leave this serene place as well as her new friends, Hesel and Kita. The three of them had just begun to explore the farm's pasture lands, streams, and hills. Tamar had actually gotten a little sun on her face, which made her complexion all the richer and her eyes brighter. Maybe it was not just the sun's effect.

"I'll see you in Jerusalem perhaps when I return with information for the king," Hesel suggested to Maacah and Tamar as they settled into their seats for the drive to the palace.

"Yes—" Tamar started to say, "—that would be nice," but at a glance from her mother, she changed it to "that may be possible" as her mother smiled approvingly.

Two more years passed with Absalom in exile. Near the end of the third year in Geshur, Ahithophel came to visit again and confer with the young prince. After hearing that Bathsheba had delivered another son, who was named Solomon, they went on to the other reports Absalom had received.

Finally, the elderly sage suggested, "I think it is time to see what can be done about getting you back home in Jerusalem."

The housekeeper refilled their mugs with cider and tried to smile at Ahithophel, but he didn't notice.

Absalom said, "But what can we do? My father is still adamant that I can never see his face again."

"But his heart is warm toward you, and we can appeal to that side of him. There must be a way to see if he will allow you back home in Jerusalem, if not to the royal palace. But who is there to make that appeal?"

Absalom responded, "If he couldn't be moved by my mother, I don't know who could get to him."

Ahithophel responded, "I can't appeal through my granddaughter because our relationship is still strained." He got up and paced back and forth, mumbling to himself, then stopped and exclaimed, "I've got it...Joab!"

Absalom pursed his lips. "Why Joab? He probably considers me an enemy of the king."

"Nonsense." Ahithophel sat down. "He probably hasn't given you a thought one way or the other. However, he is very close to your father, and if he can do anything to help him, I'm sure he will. The question now is how do we approach him?"

After thinking about it a few minutes, Ahithophel said, "Joab has a soft spot for the ladies. Maybe your mother would speak a cautious word on your behalf?"

"She would have to be discreet. My father would never tolerate a hint of scandal among his wives, even though they aren't with him."

Ahithophel's eyebrows rose. "Oh, it's all right for him but not other people? I'm not saying adultery is ever right. It's just that his hypocrisy infuriates me. So where do you keep your papyrus?"

Israel and Judah had established a period of peace with their neighbors. Similarly, King David was finding spiritual peace in his own soul. He was again writing psalms and composing music to praise God. Bathsheba had settled comfortably into domestic life and was kept busy with her sons. She was a good mother and tried to be a dedicated wife to the king by striking a balance of respect and harmony. Her memories of Uriah had faded enough so that she seldom thought of him. Time was indeed proving to be a healer for both.

Maacah asked to speak with David and was brought into a meeting room.

King David said, "Ah, Maacah, how are you?"

She bowed and said, "I am well, my lord. I have come to request your permission for Tamar and me to travel to Geshur again to see our relatives."

"I assume that Absalom is still there with his grandfather. Is that so?"

"Yes. I was hoping you might grant permission this time to bring him home to Jerusalem with us?"

"Maacah, I can't allow him back in Israel. He murdered his brother, the crown prince. That's a capital offense."

"But, my lord, you have shared with me before that you love our son as I do. It's been almost three years since he went into exile. Don't you want to see him again?"

"Of course I do, my dear. I love him and miss him. I'm sorry it has to be this way."

Maacah went on to say, "King Talmai has sent word there are renegade bandits in the hills south of Geshur. He says we should bring an armed escort to ensure our safety. May I have your leave to arrange an escort with General Joab since the army is not presently at war?"

David said, "I think the general is away today, but he should be in the palace tomorrow. I will talk to him."

Thank you, sire. I appreciate your making these arrangements. I believe the travel has done Tamar good. Do you agree?"

"Yes, it is definitely good for her to get away. She seems better when she returns."

"She enjoyed Geshur very much. Last time, we were blessed to see a gorgeous display of nature that moved our very souls. I believe you may recall when I mentioned after our return, that

Tamar began praying fervently and feels that God is healing her wounded spirit."

The king nodded, "Yes, I was delighted when you told me, and I'm glad her recovery continues."

Maacah said in a mild tone, "It appears that she is interested in a young man you may remember."

"Oh? Who is that?"

"The young man was an apprentice to your old advisor, Ahithophel. His name is Hesel."

David thought for a moment, then replied, "Yes, I do remember him. He had some religious training I think. A seemingly fine young man. But didn't Absalom hire him after Ahithophel...left?"

"He did. That is where Tamar met him. He was working with Absalom on my father's farm in Geshur. I have carefully monitored the situation, and it remains within acceptable boundaries. I wonder if someone like Hesel could be a good match for her?"

David mulled this over for a moment. "I will think on it. Even more, I will take it to the Lord. Who knows what God's plan may be? I wish you a good trip, and give my regards to all your family. And keep me informed about Hesel and Tamar."

"Of course, sire." She bowed and left his presence. Maacah noticed that the king had said "all your family." *That would include Absalom...*

Chapter 18:

Plots and Plans

T he day after her visit to the royal court, Maacah updated her daughter, Tamar, saying, "I have received another note from Absalom asking us to come visit, and this time, to bring General Joab along if possible. Here's the note if you want to read it."

Tamar took the slip of papyrus from her mother and read, *"Mother, please see if you can convince General Joab to escort you personally to Geshur. We want to propose a plan to him to see if he will help convince Father to allow me to come home. Hoping to see you soon. Your son, Absalom."*

"Who is 'we'?" asked Tamar, glancing up from the papyrus.

"I think your father's previous advisor, Ahithophel, is sometimes there with Absalom. Your brother likes his advice. The king will ask Joab about escorting us to Geshur. I assume you will want to make the journey too?"

Tamar's eyes brightened. "Of course! I so enjoy the farm, and I would love to see...everyone...again."

"Very well, let's start getting our things together."

Tamar got up from her window seat to accompany her mother back to their quarters. She said, "I don't think the general will hesitate to escort us. I think he enjoys your company. He is probably getting bored from inactivity here in the city with no war to fight."

Later that evening after dinner, Maacah and Tamar made their way through the palace and out into the gardens to enjoy the magnificent sunset over the Judean hills in the west. General Joab and one of his couriers were just coming in at that moment.

"Queen Maacah." The general and his staff member bowed informally to her. "King David has asked me to escort you both to Geshur. It will be a pleasure, especially this time of year." He gestured to the lovely outdoor gardens where lush flowers and shrubs were blooming.

"When would you like to depart?" Maacah asked demurely.

Joab answered, "If possible, by the day after tomorrow. Would that be soon enough?"

She smiled gratefully. "Oh yes, General. That would be most acceptable."

"Good," he replied. "If it is acceptable to Your Highness, it would be best if we depart early in the day. My men and I will wait for you and Lady Tamar after the morning meal."

Maacah was pleased that they would have a military escort on this trip. There really had been reports of travelers being robbed in the north, and now she wouldn't have to worry about safety. Besides, General Joab was an honest and devoted courtier, accomplished in cavalry skills and military warfare. She tried not to feel warm feelings toward the general, but now that King David was spending most of his time with Bathsheba and their children, Maacah had begun to feel lonely, especially now that her children were grown. Still, she understood that under no circumstances would a divorce from the king be granted, and an affair might lead to public condemnation or even the death penalty, if only to satisfy justice. She would therefore keep her feelings to herself.

Two days later, the convoy set out on schedule. Maacah and Tamar enjoyed the comfort of a horse-drawn carriage while the men rode on horseback. A couple of pack mules followed with supplies tended by servants. The journey went smoothly. Joab pointed out key locations of historical events and prior battles to the ladies, which Tamar eagerly absorbed. Always a bright girl, her mind devoured new knowledge and stored it for possible future reference.

Maacah tried not to notice Joab's tanned face under his helmet, which he removed from time to time to wipe away perspiration. His muscular arms tightened as he guided his horse through a stretch of rocky terrain. It had been a long time since Maacah had seen a valorous man physically active. The king remained largely inactive at the palace, occasionally practicing his bowshot with an assistant in the surrounding fields.

Thinking back to her youth, Maacah remembered how excited she had been to meet David, who would succeed King Saul as the ruler of Israel. Her entire village had been eager to welcome him, and her father had shown great honor and respect. Daydreaming as their carriage bumped along in the languid heat of midday, Maacah remembered David's ruddy cheeks and dark wavy hair, as well as his bright eyes full of passion and determination. They had been so close. She had even thought that she might become his favorite wife. But now there were only glimpses of that David on rare occasions. Yet, General Joab remained physically strong and agile, leading the column of travelers competently and securely. Catching Tamar's curious glance at her, she blushed humbly.

"What were you thinking of?" Tamar asked.

"Of my youth and your father," she smiled almost sadly.

Understanding more than her mother realized, Tamar turned her attention again to the window to enjoy the travel scenery.

When they arrived in Geshur, everyone freshened up and then undertook the formalities of meeting with King Talmai and his queen along with the rest of her family and local leaders.

The next morning, Maacah arranged with her father for a carriage to take Joab, Tamar, and herself to the farm to meet with Absalom. Upon arrival, Joab jumped from the cart and lent his hand to help Maacah and Tamar down. Turning to meet Absalom, he said, "Greetings, Your Highness. I hope you are well."

Absalom grinned, "Thank you, General Joab, for bringing my mother and sister to see me. I am grateful."

Absalom was thrilled to see Tamar looking happy. He took her in his arms and swung her around, saying, "Tamar, you've grown into a beautiful woman." Turning to his mother, he said, "Your rooms upstairs at the back of the house are ready for you and Tamar." The women entered the farmhouse as servants helped the women with their things.

"Come," Absalom said, motioning for Joab to enter the house.

Joab cleared his throat and said, "I am hesitant to be too friendly with you, Prince Absalom, because of David's order for you to stay away from Jerusalem. However, for your family's sake, I will speak with you."

Ahithophel stepped forward and greeted Joab like a long-lost brother. He embraced him and said, "Joab, my old friend. Shalom, and welcome."

Joab was not prepared to see Ahithophel. The two men had known each other for decades and had worked closely when developing battle strategies. They had always respected one another and had no reason to think ill of one another. Both had been devoted to their king.

Joab tried to reciprocate Ahithophel's enthusiasm, but fell short. He returned the older man's embrace while murmuring, "What brings you to Geshur, you old fox?"

Ahithophel accepted the greeting as a good-natured jest as they went inside and sat down at the wooden table where many councils had been held. "I am here at the request of Prince Absalom, and I have a long history with King Talmai's family." Then the sage took on a more sober countenance and said, "Later, the prince and I would like to get your opinion on how we might get David and his son back together."

Joab grunted. "I will hear what you have to say. But right now, I'm hungry, and I'm quite sure I detect the scent of roast lamb. Let's talk later."

Tamar emerged from upstairs and said, "Mother is resting. Kita and I are going to explore the meadows for wildflowers."

Exiting the farmhouse, she spotted Hesel with three other men down by the barn. She and Kita walked toward him casually while Kita pointed out new growth and seasonal buds along the way. Hesel glanced over and saw the pair walking in his direction. His heart skipped a beat as he excused himself from the workers and walked up to intercept them.

"Your Highness, how good to see you again. Thank you Kita, for showing her around. Are you well, my lady?"

"Hello, Hesel. This farm life seems to agree with you. Your skin has darkened, and I believe you have grown sturdier from the heavy work. I would like to see that waterfall you told me about before. Could you point us toward it? Mother told me she used to walk to it. Kita thinks it's down one of those trails." She pointed off toward a wooded section.

"Yes, it is in that direction, but you should have an escort. It's not far. We just follow the stream."

"Oh, thank you, Hesel." The three of them strolled down the lane. Soon they arrived at the waterfall that had made a swirling pool at its base, surrounded by rocks where turtles and frogs sunned themselves.

Hesel said as they looked down at the sun-kissed water from the incline, "It is beautiful to see from below. Do you want to try to make it down the path? It's steep in places."

"I think I can make it if you will help me."

"Of course. Here, take my hand."

"Please, Miss, I've climbed this hill many times," Kita smiled with a twinkle in her eye. Would it be all right if I go on down and meet you at the bottom?"

"Of course, Kita. Go ahead."

Hesel's heart leapt as he took Tamar's small hand and helped her down the steep trail. Soon they came to a level lookout about halfway to the bottom. Tamar said, "Let's stop here. This is so nice. Please help me to that large rock."

Hesel lifted her by her waist and turned to sit her down on the rock. Feeling her form so close, Hesel's head was swimming as he momentarily brushed against her hair that smelled like lilacs and marveled at her slender form. "There you are, my lady. How's that?"

Tamar looked into his eyes, so close, for too long, then smiled and said, "That's fine. Thank you, Hesel, you are indeed a gentleman. It's so good to see you again."

Hesel's heart beat against his chest as he stared at her beauty in unabashed awe.

Tamar continued to look in his eyes and grinned, "I appreciate your kindness, and you surely know that I'm not truly a princess anymore, just a simple girl who wants to enjoy the life that God has given me. However, my soul has been wounded and life is difficult much of the time."

Hesel processed this and said, "I understand. I hope that with time, you will be healed from your...misfortune, and you will be able to love a man. You need to be with someone who will accept you as you are, not as an unfortunate victim, but as a beautiful and determined young woman finding her way in the world and remaining devoted to God. You truly deserve happiness, my lady." Everything in him wanted to hold her in his arms and be her protector. She had suffered much, and yet nothing could ruin her lovely countenance and energetic spirit.

Tamar relaxed and enjoyed the sunny rock. "Come up," she shouted to Kita. It took Kita a few minutes to climb back up the path, giving Hesel a few precious minutes to look into Tamar's eyes. She didn't avert his gaze. No words were spoken, but she smiled demurely as they made room for Kita on the rock. The three of them sat in the warm sunlight, enjoying its soothing rays while watching the cascading stream. Hesel explained which crops had been planted and pointed to a distant field where the sheep were lambing.

As the sun began its gradual descent over the distant trees, reluctantly Tamar said, "We had better get back. Thank you both for being good friends. I don't really have any back home." Then turning to Hesel, she said, "I hope we are able to see more of each other while we're here, although I don't want to keep you from your work." With a twinkle in her eyes, she said, "You make me feel alive again. Thank you."

Tamar smiled warmly, showing perfect white teeth. They climbed off the rock, Tamar last, as Hesel assisted her. Hesel let his hand linger on hers as he helped her down. Words were unnecessary as their eyes spoke volumes, but he couldn't help holding her hand, and Tamar did not pull back.

That evening, the three men sat talking around a cozy fire in the hearth, each with a cup of wine. Maacah and Tamar were in the next room talking to some aunts and cousins who had come to the farm to see them.

Joab opened the conversation with Absalom and Ahithophel by stating, "I want both of you to know that I am a representative of His Majesty, King David. Anything said here will be reported to him when I return to Jerusalem."

Ahithophel responded, "Of course. The reason we wanted to talk to you is because we know you have King David's interest at heart. All we want to do is to help him reunite with his son. His Majesty loves his son dearly and would like to have him back home. But up to now, he has not permitted Absalom to return. Can you help us?"

Joab grunted as he repositioned himself, then said, "David says Absalom has committed a capital offense in murdering the crown prince, and he cannot forgive that. I am not so sure that he has any strong feeling of love for him. I haven't heard him express that."

The young prince quickly interjected, "If I may boast, I have always had a special relationship with my father. I am his favorite son. I know I am. I don't understand his reluctance to allow me to come home when we have such a strong bond. I love my father, and I know he loves me. I have even heard from my cousin Jonadab that he heard my father openly claim to love me. Also, my mother told me at supper that the king walked to the door of the palace with her as she was leaving. He said that he knew she was really coming to see me, and that he envied her because he misses me."

Joab grumbled, "That's a little hard to believe."

"I will prove it to you. I will bring my mother here so she can tell you herself," Absalom said as he jumped to his feet and called to the room where the women were talking. "Mother, can you come in here, please?"

Maacah appeared immediately in the doorway, as if she was waiting for her cue. Absalom said, "Mother, would you please tell the general what you were saying to me about what Father said to you as you were leaving?"

Maacah came over to where the men were sitting and sat down next to Joab. She said, "Yes, Joab, it's true. David almost had tears in his eyes as he spoke about our son. He said he loved him and wished he could come with me. Then I asked him why he couldn't let him come home. He said, 'I can't. I just can't. I wish I could.'"

She began to choke back sobs as she looked at him. Then, she continued, "Joab, I know David cares deeply for our son, but for some reason, he has convinced himself that he can't let him come home. It is so sad. It breaks my heart." With tears in her eyes, she looked deeply into the general's eyes and squeezed his arm tightly.

Joab was obviously uncomfortable with the intimacy she showed while the other men watched. He managed a half-smile to the adorable Maacah and said, "Thank you, my lady. We will discuss it."

Ahithophel broke the ensuing silence. He spoke up and said to Joab, "So you see, General, the greatest service you could accomplish for your master, his son here present, and for his mother, would be to reunite David with his favorite son."

After a few more moments of silence, the sage spoke again. "Joab, you are a master strategist, I'm sure you could come up with a way to accomplish that goal."

Joab shot back, "Wait just a minute; you are the highly regarded advisor to kings. You would be the one to devise the best approach. David has always sworn by your advice."

Ahithophel started to speak again, but Joab held up his hand to stop him. Then Joab said, "That brings me to the question that has been on my mind since I first saw you here. What happened between you and David? I asked him where you were when I hadn't seen you for a couple of weeks. He said, 'I don't know. He just left.' I asked him, 'Why?' He brushed me off and said he didn't want to talk about it. So, if you want me to hear what you have to say, tell me what happened between you two."

Ahithophel paused, remembering the other people in the room, then said slowly, "You should know what happened Joab, you were a part of it."

All eyes were on Joab as he rubbed his beard and looked back in time for a few minutes. Then, he finally said, "Oh, that business about Ur...about that soldier at Rabbah?"

"Yes," said Ahithophel. "That soldier at Rabbah. That business and what brought it about. After that, I couldn't work with him anymore. I had to leave. Beyond that, I do not wish to discuss it any further."

At that point, Absalom could see that his mother was intrigued by the conversation and was about to ask what they were talking about. He interrupted by lifting his mother by the arm, and saying, "Come, Mother, you have been a big help, but now I'm sure you have had enough of this man talk." As he led her to the adjoining room, she whispered in his ear, "But I want to know what they are talking about." Her son whispered back, "I'll fill you in later. It's time for you to rejoin the ladies who have come to see you."

While Absalom was helping his mother to the other room, Joab said to the older man, "All right, so you had a falling out with David over something that was none of your business. So, why are you interested now in helping David reunite with his son?"

Ahithophel leaned forward into Joab's face. "What do you mean it was none of my business? That was my granddaughter he raped and her husband you had killed."

Joab growled, "I followed orders, very specific orders from my supreme commander."

Ahithophel snarled, "But you could have reasoned with him. Uriah was one of your best officers, but you sent him to his death."

Joab stared at Ahithophel for several seconds as Absalom witnessed the exchange between the two legendary men. The general said in a calmer voice, "You can't reason with David when he gives an order like that. I didn't know what precipitated it, but it wasn't hard to figure out."

When Ahithophel didn't respond immediately, Absalom saw an opening and moved in between them. "Gentlemen, please, let's get back to why we're here."

Ahithophel got up and paced across to a table to refill his wine glass. When he returned, Absalom continued, "Joab, let me explain why Ahithophel is here. He and I became friends when we worked together in the palace. I asked him to help me when Amnon raped my sister. He gave me good advice, which I followed. Then I acted on my own and caused this situation I'm in now. So, I have asked him again, this time, to help me gain my father's approval to come home. That's why he is here. I hope the two of you can help because I don't know what else to do."

Joab nodded and said, "All right, assuming you are correct about David's desire to have you come home, what can we do about it? You can't force the king to change his mind."

Ahithophel noticed the general had said "we." *Good. Now he's with us.* Ahithophel had collected himself, and as he settled back into his seat, he said, "I do have an idea I would like your opinion on, General. I think we must get David to convince himself that Absalom should come back."

"How do we get him to do that?" Joab asked.

Leaning toward Joab, he said, "One thing is clear. David is an absolute monarch. He is fully capable of forgiving his son for taking vengeance on his brother. He could easily make a case that the public would accept. But for some reason, he hasn't taken a stand on it."

He paused briefly and continued, "We know David is more merciful and compassionate with others than he is with himself. So, my idea is to bring in a pitiful person who will plead a case and ask David's judgment. I'm thinking of an elderly widow. We would have her tell a story about having two sons who get into a fight. One kills the other. The people in her village want to execute the surviving son for his crime. But if they do that, there will be no one to carry on the family name. So, she is petitioning David to forgive her son for his crime and let him come home."

Ahithophel paused again to allow Joab time to think before stating. "I think he will grant her petition. If he does, she can confess that she wanted to help him see that he is the one who won't forgive his son. Maybe that would help him come to terms with forgiving Absalom." He looked at the other men. "So, what do you think?"

Absalom scratched his beard and said, "I like it. I'm sure my father would respond to such a plea."

Joab said, "It might work if we could find an old woman with a talent for deception. However, I don't know of anyone like that."

Ahithophel said, "I do. She lives in Tekoa."

There was silence. The crackling of flames in the hearth seemed to punctuate the thoughts going through Joab's mind as he contemplated the ways Ahithophel's plan could go wrong. The general finally cleared his throat and stated firmly, "No deal. It's too risky. The chances of success with David are less than half. Probably more like 30 percent."

Absalom and Ahithophel sat back and stared at Joab, wondering if the case was hopeless.

Chapter 19:

Joab's Persuasion

Joab rose from his chair and declared to Absalom, "Your mother has indicated that she wishes to spend some time here in Geshur. However, I cannot be away for long. I will return to Jerusalem tomorrow. I will stop by your grandfather's palace to arrange for men to escort your mother home when she is ready to return. I'm sorry I can't help you, but the thought of deceiving His Majesty is just too risky."

After a searching look from the young prince, Joab turned and walked to the adjoining room to announce his departure to Maacah. His appearance in the doorway interrupted the conversation among the ladies who looked up in unison to see what brought the general to the room. Joab said, "My apologies, ladies. May I speak with you for just a moment, Your Highness? We need to make some decisions about your travel schedule."

"Of course, General," Maacah replied as she rose to her feet and motioned to Joab to join her in the kitchen. As soon as they were out of earshot, Maacah practically growled at Joab, "I overheard you tell my son that you won't help him. Why won't you at least try?"

"Because it is too risky. I'm afraid that David would see right through the ruse, and that could be the end of my career. I don't want to take that chance."

Maacah looked into his eyes and said, "Is there anything that I, or anyone, could say...or do... to change your mind?"

The battle-hardened warrior, the man who faced and defeated countless enemies, was startled by the queen's words and their implication. Few dared to challenge his decisions, virtually none off the battlefield. The scent of her perfume paralyzed his movements. He stammered, "There is nothing...at least nothing I can think of at this moment."

"Nothing...?"

Uh well, if you put it that way...Uh, uh, maybe..."

Maacah gave him a petulant look followed by a gleaming smile. "I would come to your defense if David becomes angry with you. I can find some way to persuade him of your well-meant intentions. I know the king well. We've been husband and wife for many years."

He tried to speak as he rapidly processed her words. "I don't know..."

Then finally, she said, "If David does send you away, I will find a way to bring you back, or I will go with you."

Joab was stunned at her words. His mind was spinning, and he didn't know how to respond to her. He just looked at her in silence.

Then she said, "Absalom will help me, and he is the heir apparent. Please convince David to let my son come home."

"Madam," he began in a grave tone, "I cannot promise results, but I will try to ease Prince Absalom's way back to Jerusalem."

Maacah smiled triumphantly and turned away to rejoin the ladies. As she walked away, she said over her shoulder, "I will remain here until you come back with the king's permission to bring Absalom home. So, come for us when it is time."

A few days later when Joab returned to Jerusalem, he carefully sounded out the king's feelings toward Absalom. King David seemed surprised by General Joab's questions about his feelings for Absalom, but he assumed it was because Joab had just seen the young man in Geshur and felt moved to help him.

"Of course, I love him," David said sharply. "He is my son. Now my oldest son. I wish he were here...to help in the palace. I...admire his fierce protective love for his sister, but his rash emotions have gotten him into this trouble."

Sipping the wine David's servant had brought them, Joab asked, "Why can you not let him come home? He will benefit under your tutelage. The kingdom will no longer be divided, which will relieve the city and our nation."

"Oh, no. I couldn't do that." David shook his head firmly in the negative.

"But why not? You are the king. You can forgive anyone of anything."

David sighed and said, "That's not the problem, my friend. It's of God. That's all I can tell you."

Joab stared at the king's back as David stood up and went over to stare at his famous sword and weaponry that stood in the corner of the chamber, reminding him of his glorious past victories. He knew the king's mind was made up.

Getting up and setting down the goblet, he said, "That is the extent of my report from Geshur. All else is well. I will take my leave now."

Without turning, David gestured with his hand to acknowledge the general's departure.

Several days passed before Joab was able to contact the woman in Tekoa who had been recommended by Ahithophel. He had to get her to agree to carry out the charade, then arrange for her to come to Jerusalem. In a private room off the stable reserved for workers, he coached her carefully because he realized he could be in trouble if the situation went awry. As Ahithophel had foretold, she was calm and readily memorized the story she would tell King David. Still, Joab was uneasy and prepared himself to face David's wrath if it came to that. He knew David was smart enough to sense something amiss, but he was counting on the king's mercy and compassion as well as his great love for Absalom to carry the day.

The woman was not a simple, naïve person. She agreed with Joab's desire to return Absalom to Jerusalem, but she was concerned about angering her king and worried about getting out alive. However, Joab assured her that he would shield her from any blame and protect her from the ruler's anger. The two rehearsed, adjusted the story to be told, and rehearsed again until they were both comfortable that she could carry out the deception.

The day arrived when David was holding his personal court where he would listen to grievances and petitions from the common people. Joab advised the elderly woman to wear older mourning garb and look distraught like one who has been grieving for a long time. Anxiously but quietly, the widow waited in the courtyard while Joab stayed away to avoid anyone connecting him with her. The widow's turn came, and she was escorted in to stand before King David, who sat on a reception throne on a dais a few feet high. She bowed before him in homage and said, "Oh King, please help me."

David noticed her widow's garment and said, "How can I be of service?"

"I am a widow," she said. "I had two sons. They got into a fight out in the field, and there was no one around to step in and stop them. One struck the other and killed him. Then the whole village ganged up against me and demanded, 'Hand over your other son, the murderer, so we can kill him for his brother's death.' They want to wipe out the heir and snuff out the one spark of life left to me. And there would be nothing left of my husband—not so much as a name—on the face of the earth."

The old lady looked down and seemed to silently sob before she continued, "So, now I have dared to come to the king, my master, about all this. The townspeople are making my life miserable, and I'm afraid for my remaining son's life and my own well-being. So, I said to myself, 'I'll go to the king. Maybe he'll do something! When the king hears what's going on, he will step in and rescue me from the abuse of those who want to get rid of me and my son—and our inheritance. I decided ahead of time, the word of my master, the king will be the last word in this, for my master is like an angel of God in discerning good and evil. God be with you!"

David's heart was touched. He waved her aside and said, "Go home, and I'll take care of this for you. But wait. Send in the people who have been harassing you. I'll see to it that they will not bother you anymore." He looked sharply toward the entrance of the hall.

The woman hesitated, then said, "Will you swear by God's name you will do this?"

"As surely as God lives," he said. "Not so much as a hair on your son's head will be lost."

Then she asked one more thing, "Why then have you done this very thing against God's people? You have just convicted yourself by not bringing home your exiled son. God does not take away life. He works out a way to get his lost son back."

David fell silent. Feeling embarrassed and the stirring of anger, he realized he had been duped. He said, "Did Joab put you up to this?"

The woman said, "No one can get anything past you, my lord. Yes, General Joab put these words in my mouth because he knew you needed to get things straight with your son. I know now that you will do the right thing. You swore by God's name that you would make this right for me. The way to make it right for me is to bring your son home and make things right for our nation. I know you will do it for your own sake and the sake of God's people."

After David sent the woman home and dismissed his courtiers, he retired to his chambers and fell on his knees before God. He prayed,

"Oh God, I seek your kindness and your guidance for my soul. A day hasn't passed that I haven't heard your words of judgment on me for my sins of adultery and blood guiltiness. I wait for every word to come to pass because I am guilty, and your judgments are true and just.

"Oh God, I have already seen violence and bloodshed in my family, as you ordained. I sense in my spirit that the son I love most will be the one who will rise up against me. I know I can't escape it. I have tried to forestall this horror by refusing to let him return home after he killed his brother. But I know now that I am going to have to let him come back. How long will it be before he makes his move to rise against me? I can't escape your judgment. I can only throw myself at your feet and beg for mercy."

David felt he needed to capture this time with God. He reached for his well-worn harp and let his heart respond to the spirit within him. Taking papyrus and pen in hand he wrote,

"I love Thee, O Lord, my strength. The Lord is my rock and my fortress and my deliverer, My God, my rock, in whom I take refuge. You are my shield and the horn of my salvation, my stronghold. I call upon the Lord, who is worthy to be praised, and I am saved from my enemies. Yea, in my distress I called upon the Lord, and cried to my God for help; He heard my voice out of His temple, and my cry for help from Him came into His ears. He rescued me because He delighted in me."

David rose from his prayer and sent a servant to summon Joab. When his general arrived, he bowed before the king, not knowing what to expect after the deception had played out. King David said, "Well, you went to great lengths to trick me. What should I do about it?"

Joab paused and then replied, "Whatever Your Highness wishes. I could not think of another way to help you see that your people want your son home. Absalom is loved by the people, and they understand why he did what he did to his brother. They want him back among us, and so do you, my lord. So, however you decide to punish me, I accept it."

David let his general's words hang in the air while he fidgeted with a dagger he always kept on the table in his chamber. Finally, he said, "I admire your handiwork. It was like something my old advisor Ahithophel might have planned. Anyway, it had the desired effect. I will allow Absalom to return to Jerusalem, but with one condition. I must not see his face. He will live in his own house, not in the palace. Is that clear?"

Joab ventured, "Yes, my lord. Of course. I will journey to Geshur and bring him home."

"Very well," replied his king. "But no fanfare; no parades. Understood?"

"Of course," said Joab. "Your servant understands and expresses gratitude for your kindness and mercy. Long live the king!

After Joab left, David went back to his study and communed again with God. Afterward, he thought, *I am fairly certain that I can see Ahithophel's hand in the events of the day. That woman from Tekoa had to have been his idea. But when would Joab have been in contact with the old advisor?*

Ahithophel had been on David's mind occasionally, ever since they had parted so abruptly almost five years before.

David thought, *Ahithophel has always been available to me, sharing his wisdom and advising me at every turn. Even before I was crowned in Hebron over thirty years ago, Ahithophel was always at my side.*

Pacing a few minutes to order his thoughts, David mused, *I should have realized that Ahithophel was right when he had the courage to accuse me. But it wasn't until Nathan confronted me that I actually heard God speaking and saying some of the same things that Ahithophel did. Now Ahithophel is gone, along with his wisdom and experience. When I need him most*, thought David. *I'm lost without him. Why did I drive him away? It was a terrible mistake.*

Sitting down, David wrote these words in his journal concerning Ahithophel: *"A man mine equal, my guide, and my acquaintance. We took sweet counsel together and walked into the House of God together. We were brothers, walking arm in arm. The Lord God blessed me and directed my paths through him. He was the Urim and Thummim, a reliable guide when trouble surrounded me. I miss you, my brother. I hope and pray that one day we will be reunited. May it be so, O Lord."*

Chapter 20:

Absalom's Return

Ahithophel remained with Absalom, Hesel, Maacah and Tamar in Geshur, hoping to receive word from Joab about his attempt to sway David. After a few weeks had passed with no word, the men became discouraged, and Ahithophel began making preparations to leave. Ahithophel told Absalom, "I will pick up any news available as I pass Jerusalem, but I cannot risk being seen there. The king may have softened his stance, but I'm not going to take chances. I'll check with the locals for news from the surrounding areas."

Absalom replied, "But what should I do if Joab has no success with my father?"

"That's a good question, Prince Absalom," said the sage. "Send Hesel and let me know when you hear how it went. We will decide then what to do next."

At that moment, a servant rushed into the room and shouted excitedly, "The king's men have just brought news that an Israelite army detachment is approaching Geshur. Their leader appears to be General Joab!"

Absalom called to the next room, "Mother, come. They think Joab is coming. We are going to the palace to meet him."

Maacah called back, "You go on. We will wait here until after the arrival business has been concluded."

The two men rushed into town to greet the detachment, speculating as they hurried to King Talmai's palace, where Joab would have to report first. As they neared the reception area on the palace grounds behind the gate, Absalom saw Joab's horse and gushed, "It is Joab! This can only be good news."

The two men stood impatiently awaiting the general's reception with Talmai to finish. When it did, Joab came out of the king's chamber and approached them where they stood near the entrance. He said to Absalom without fanfare, "I've come to bring you home, young prince. Your father has approved your return."

"Oh, thank you, General. How wonderful! I am overjoyed. Come, let's go on out to the farm. Mother and Tamar are waiting to hear your news."

When the new arrivals had reached the farm. Maacah retained her queenly reserve while admiring Joab's powers of persuasion with King David. Later, the three men with Maacah and Tamar had their meal served to them while they pumped the general for details of his negotiations with David. Maacah's smiling approval made the effort especially worthwhile for the general. He briefed them on the woman from Tekoa and her skill in bringing David to see that bringing Absalom home was the right thing to do.

Absalom said, "Let's not forget that it was Ahithophel's idea. Ahithophel, your reputation is well deserved. It was your idea, but it was the general who made it work. Well done, both of you!" He raised a cup of wine to toast them, and the others followed suit.

After they had congratulated each other, Joab advised Absalom of his father's edict. Clearing his voice, he said, "There is one caveat. You cannot see the king's face. He will not receive you formally or publicly. You must stay away from the palace. There will be no fanfare and no parades or festivities. You are to quietly retire to your home where you will live with your mother and sister. That's all your father had to say."

After a few moments of stunned silence, Ahithophel whispered to Absalom, "Well, that's a start."

Joab saw the two men conferring and interjected, "And you, Ahithophel, I did not mention to the king your presence here with Absalom. However, I sensed that he may have suspected it. Now that you have accomplished your purpose in being here with the prince, you have advised him well, and he is able to return home. I suggest you do the same to avoid raising questions."

Ahithophel looked into his cup and then set it down as though relinquishing something valuable, but it was not the wine permeating his thoughts.

Joab explained, "I'm not sure how King David would feel about you being here since apparently you two parted under unfavorable circumstances. My detachment will be taking the river road back to Jerusalem, so you will want to take the overland road to Giloh. We will leave at first light in the morning." Glancing around to ensure everyone understood and would comply, Joab left to see about his men and make preparations for their return trip in the morning.

Maacah and Tamar went outdoors to admire the sunset while the two men retired to the great room with their wine glasses. When the two men were alone, Absalom asked, "So, what is our plan? Do I begin raising my army when I return to Jerusalem?"

Ahithophel replied in surprise, "Prince Absalom, are you still determined to move against your father? You said yourself that he seems to have changed since his meeting with Nathan. What exactly is driving you to revolt against him at this point, now that you can go home?"

Absalom sat up straighter and folded his arms on the table. "I believe it is my destiny to wear the crown. My father has achieved all that he has worked for. He has essentially conquered the region. He has no vision for the future as far as I can tell. Since Rabbah fell, there is nowhere for the army to go. I believe he is ready to settle permanently into family life, whether he knows it or not. My time has come. I am ready to wear the crown and protect Jerusalem while advancing her interests."

The old sage spoke quietly but firmly. "I know your father as well as anyone does. He will not willingly give up the throne to you, or to anyone else. If you want the crown, the only way you will get it is to take it from him! Even if you were to be successful in raising an army, most of our people still love David. You would have to deal with that hurdle before you can proceed. Somehow you will have to convince the citizens that your father is a changed man—changed for the worse. I am not sure they will see him the same way you do."

Absalom's visage darkened. This was not what he wanted to hear.

Ahithophel continued, "Your campaign to claim the people's loyalty will take time. You will have to win their hearts and turn them against their king. You would have to travel throughout the land, convincing all the residents of the towns, villages, and farms that you are an emissary of your father, sent to learn the needs of the people so you can work with the king to find ways to help them. They need to see you as a future ruler who will be capable of providing for their needs. When they become convinced of your abilities and see that King David has lost interest in them, then you can begin recruiting your army."

Absalom's cheeks grew red, and he started to speak, but Ahithophel continued talking.

"My young prince, I'm not sure you understand that war is not a game. Warfare is violent; many people die. You are likely to start a bloody civil war if you continue on this path. You would be fighting the most experienced and ruthless warriors ever seen. There will be great bloodshed on both sides. You will be fighting your own father. Could you kill the king if it came to that?"

Without hesitation, Absalom said, "I don't know that I could. But it doesn't have to be that way. Hopefully, I can gain enough followers that we can negotiate a peace where he will turn over the throne and retire from ruling. I am definitely going forward with my plan. I just need your wisdom and advice to ensure success. Are you with me?"

With a sigh, Ahithophel said, "Yes, Absalom. I am still with you. But for the immediate future, you must bide your time until your father welcomes you back into his presence. That may take a year or two. The people need to see you and your father getting along, at least for a while. Then you can begin your public relations campaign."

Absalom relaxed in his chair. "I see."

"In the meantime, behave as a crown prince should. Get out and move around Jerusalem to get to know people and make friends in your daily life. When David welcomes you back to the palace, that's when you begin in earnest to build your army. Send word to me when that happens, and I will be in touch with you to plan the next phase. Until then, may the Lord God bless your path." The elderly man got up and prepared for his travel home as Absalom went out to confirm travel plans with Joab.

Chapter 21:

The Sunset

While everyone was getting prepared for travel, Hesel was trying to find a way to see Tamar before they left. Absalom and his family were preparing to return to Jerusalem, but Ahithophel had arranged with Absalom to have Hesel return with him to Giloh. He needed his help with his property. Ahithophel assured Hesel that he would be able to return to Jerusalem within a few weeks. Hesel would normally have been happy to spend time with his old mentor, but now there was a new concern troubling him. He would not be able to see Tamar. He felt he had to have some time with her before their departure.

Hesel entered the back door of the house, and seeing no one, he made his way through the empty kitchen and slipped up the backstairs. Absalom and Ahithophel were deep in discussion in the living room. He wasn't sure where her room was, but he saw a door ajar and walked softly to peer inside. He was in luck. Tamar was in the room packing for her departure.

She was being assisted by one of the maids. He rapped lightly on the door.

Tamar was feeling sorrowful as she made preparations for their departure. Her mother had told her of the plans concerning Hesel, causing a heavy burden on her heart. She loved Geshur and all that had happened there, but mostly being with Hesel. When she saw him at the door, her heart leapt for joy. However, she maintained an even composure, resulting from her years of training as a royal princess.

"Oh, Hesel. What are you doing here? I'm just packing for our return to Jerusalem."

"Yes, my lady. I was hoping to have a few words with you, and I didn't want to miss the opportunity. So...uh, I was wondering if you could spare a few minutes." He could hardly keep his heart from pounding so loud that the whole house could hear him.

Tamar looked around the room, then gave the maid some instructions to continue packing. She said, "I will wear the pink dress tomorrow, so leave it out with these accessories. You may go ahead and pack the rest of the clothes. I'll be back soon to finish up. Thank you for your help." She then walked over to Hesel and said, "What did you want to talk about, Hesel?" still maintaining her cool demeanor.

Hesel said, "Actually, I was hoping you could take a walk with me. There is a special place I want to show you before you go."

"Oh, what kind of place?" she asked. "Is it as nice as the waterfall?"

"Oh, yes," he replied. "Much nicer. At least I think it is. It is special to me because it is my private place where I can be alone with God. I want you to see it."

"Oh. If it your private place, are you sure you want to take me there?

"Yes. I want to take you there very much."

"But why, Hesel?"

"Because, my lady...because you are very special to me as well. Please come with me."

"Of course, I will come with you. I'm just teasing you, Hesel. I think you know you are special to me too."

As they reached the back door, Hesel gulped, almost swallowing his tongue. Hesel could not believe the joy that threatened to burst his heart. But then he had to face reality. He said, "I know we should not be alone. Do you want to bring Kita with us?"

Tamar thought about this for a moment. "You're right; we should not be alone. But I trust you, and given my past, what more can people say about me? I don't think anyone will notice or care. But let me ask Absalom to be sure."

"Of course," Hesel said, unconsciously backing up a step in disappointment. He was sure Absalom would say no, being a protective brother.

Tamar disappeared inside, and in a moment, reappeared in the doorway with her brother.

"Where do you want to take her?" Absalom asked. "We are leaving early in the morning."

Hesel nodded his greeting to Absalom. "Just up the ridge over there, Prince Absalom." He pointed to a hilltop that shouldn't take more than a few minutes to reach by walking briskly.

Absalom jutted his chin toward his sister. "Go ahead, but don't linger. Kita can follow a little way behind for appearances." He called for the girl and briefly explained the plan.

"Thank you, brother!" Tamar exclaimed, feeling wildly happy. "Come on, Hesel, let's hurry."

He did not wait for a second invitation. They walked rapidly up the path toward the rise and a narrow goat trail that led to the hill's summit.

Absalom watched them for a couple of moments then went off to the barn to make sure Joab and the men were about ready.

Kita followed discreetly behind, picking wildflowers and pausing to watch the sun's glorious descent over the distant mountain peaks.

Tamar said, "Let's walk fast. We need to be back for the evening meal."

"I don't want to tax you, my lady. I can carry you if you wish."

"Don't be silly, Hesel. I'm quite fit. My training as a royal princess, you know."

"Oh, good. Then if I get tired, you can carry me."

"Ha ha. Very funny. Just hurry up, slow poke."

The young couple walked briskly up the winding trail for several minutes. The sky was growing dimmer though it was not yet twilight. Toward the top of the ridge, the path led them into a stand of tall pine trees. When they began to emerge from the trees, Hesel said, "Oh, Tamar, I think the Lord is waiting for us at the lookout."

"What are you talking about?" She barely finished her question when they emerged from the trees as the path opened up to a rocky promontory looking out on a view of the valley below. But the view was far overshadowed by the beauty of the sky. The couple was met with the most glorious sight imaginable. Neither of them had ever witnessed such glory. The evening sky was full, completely full of shimmering, beautiful, bright colors, from the far horizon clear up to the heavens above. The beauty filled the entire sky with a flaming kaleidoscope of color, a dynamic display as the bright clouds shifted, melting into one another, generating even more beauty than existed the moment before. It was beyond gorgeous or magnificent. It was miraculous.

The two small humans could scarcely catch their breath. They stood on the outcropping of rock where the land before them fell away steeply, all the way down to the inland sea over three thousand feet below. Even the water in the sea reflected the beauty of the scene before them. No words could begin to describe the sight that their eyes could see, but their minds couldn't comprehend. Their hearts were filled.

Tamar finally said, "Oh, how beautiful. Thank you, Hesel, for bringing me here."

But Hesel had fallen to his knees and was raising his hands to God, as he said, "Oh Lord God. We thank You. You have surely laid your hand upon us. This is too wonderful. I can't comprehend why You should bless us so. I can only praise You. The heavens do indeed declare the work of Your hands.

"Oh Lord, our God, how majestic is thy Name in all the earth. When we see your glory displayed before our eyes, what are we? You have crowned us with Your majesty and glory. How I praise you. The heavens praise You." Tears rolled down his cheeks as he unashamedly worshiped before his God.

Then Hesel saw that Tamar seemed to be lost in the glory of the moment also. She tried to speak, but something internal began to overcome her. She, too, fell to her knees as the Spirit of God seemed to fill her with His love and healing, renewing her from the inside out.

Hesel reached out and touched Tamar's hand, and when he did they were both immediately enveloped by the Holy Spirit.

It was as if both felt the Spirit of God drawing them out of their bodies, melding their spirits into one with Him. For a long moment, they remained still in communion with God under the vast evening sky.

Then, suddenly, they were back in their bodies and conscious of their surroundings. Hesel released Tamar's hand and stammered, "Oh my lady, I am so sorry. I don't know what happened."

Tamar had trouble speaking, but then said, "Don't apologize, Hesel. I felt it. It was God. He joined us together. I think He has given us a vision...of us belonging to each other. Did you feel it?"

He turned to help his living angel to her feet. "I may as well confess here because I'm not sure I could tell you anywhere else."

Curious, Tamar asked as they faced each other, "What do you need to confess?"

A shy smile spread over his face. "I've loved you since we first met three years ago. You have been in my thoughts constantly, even when we've been apart. In my dreams I know you as Tami. Is it all right for me to call you Tami now?"

"Yes", she answered. "I like that. Now that God seems to be confirming that we belong together."

Hesel said, "How else could it have worked out for us to be here in my special place—our special place," he corrected himself. "Not only alone with God, but with your brother's permission. Here we are together in this magical setting, with the sun setting on our world together."

Tamar said, "You are a poet, Hesel. You might talk to my father about composing praises of God for him."

He shook his head to disagree. "I'll never be gifted that way. But I am blessed beyond measure to be here with you and share this time that I hope will be the beginning of our lives together."

"Yes, I want that too," she said solemnly before breaking into a big smile.

Hesel could barely contain his joy and spontaneously threw his arms around her as she gave his cheek a quick kiss. "But Tami, what do we do now?"

She looked into his eyes so full of love for her and lifted her face to his as she said, "You can kiss me now. I'm no longer afraid. God has healed me." Hesel took her in his arms, and their lips met in a soft, tender kiss that sealed their union in the Lord.

Reluctantly, Tamar pulled back and said, "Kita has been very patient." She pointed at the young girl who stood uncertainly several yards below them on the hillside, arms full of flowers.

Hesel said, "We have to part now. I'm not sure when we will see each other again. Hopefully, it won't be too long." Then looking into her eyes, he said, "Tami, I consider us to be betrothed. Do you feel the same?"

"Yes, I do. God has joined us together, and He has healed me in the process. I will wait for you to come back to me."

As their joy mingled with sadness over the pending departure, they felt the Spirit of God blessing their future union. They hurried down the hill, Kita with them, until they reached the bottom and made their way to the house under the rosy streaks of sunset.

They saw Absalom talking to Joab while loading the last of their goods into the cart near the barn. He glanced their way but did not stop talking to the general.

As they approached the house where their paths would separate for a time, Hesel gave Tamar a last longing look, "Until we meet next."

"Yes, as God leads," Tamar assured him before entering the house to join her mother.

Chapter 22:

Tamar's Sorrow

L ater that evening as Tamar was getting ready for bed, she had to go back downstairs to retrieve the shawl she had left in the sitting room. She thought everyone had already retired, but as she was picking up her things, she heard men's voices in the kitchen. She stopped with the shawl in her arms to hear who was talking. The men's voices were quiet but intense. She recognized her brother's voice: "But how can I turn the people against my father? The common citizens have always loved him."

She heard Ahithophel take on a coarse, ugly tone as he answered, "You tell them the truth. You tell them he has become a loathsome criminal. You tell them that he has no regard for the common people anymore. You can tell them what he did to me and my family. He stole a young, innocent bride and then killed her husband to get him out of the way! He betrayed those closest to him."

Absalom replied in a low tone, "I don't think he is as bad as that."

"It doesn't matter what you think. It's what the people think that determines whether you can pull off a coup. If you want the crown, you will have to turn the nation against him."

"Then I will do it. I will have Hesel work with me to take care of the logistics. He's good at that sort of work."

"Yes, with him helping you, the regular people will turn against David quicker than you would expect. Hesel can take much of the detail work off your hands so you can deal with the public."

Tamar couldn't believe what she was hearing. *Hesel is mixed up with these men who are seeking to overthrow my father's government! The man I thought I loved...this could lead to civil war. People die in wars, and my family is in the middle—on opposite sides. I didn't think Hesel could do such a thing.* Her inner world came tumbling down, and Tamar felt herself falling back into the pit of despair.

On the trip back to Jerusalem from Geshur, Joab thought soberly about Absalom's quest to return to Jerusalem. His stallion rode past the carriage with Absalom, Maacah, and Tamar, and he marveled again at the young man's heavy, flowing locks that were roughly tied back. Few men had hair like that, which made the prince noticeable. That could be good or bad, depending on the situation. The other men rode mules or horses, some ahead of and some behind the carriage. Joab nodded at Absalom as he passed the carriage, and the prince nodded back.

Absalom could see that Tamar was distraught. He said, "My sister. What's wrong? I know you love being at Geshur and don't wish to leave, but there will be a feast to welcome us back, and Father will be happy to see you looking well."

Tamar didn't answer, hiding her tears with her handkerchief.

Maacah glanced at her daughter and said kindly, "Are you catching a cold, my dear?"

Tamar shook her head and turned to look out the carriage window.

Maacah said, "Are you alright? Did something happen to upset you?"

Tamar sniffled, "Don't worry about me. I'll be fine." However, she didn't speak unless spoken to for the rest of the trip home. The three sank into their own thoughts about returning to the palace. Tamar just wanted to be alone. Maacah was eager to catch up in the harem on all that had happened in their absence. Absalom was brooding about how to woo the common people's loyalty. There would be no welcoming feast for him at the palace.

Ahithophel's words motivated Absalom as he returned to Jerusalem. He took up residence at the family farm outside the city and began developing an identity among the local residents. He found an attractive, accomplished young woman who would be a suitable wife. Through a messenger, his father, King David, approved the match, but there would be no extravagant public wedding. Absalom married Elisa and started a family, chatting amicably with their neighbors and spending time at the city gates to learn from the wise and knowledgeable elders. They didn't quite understand why Absalom had not assumed a prominent place in palace life, but they were pleased to see his interest in self-improvement and shared their acquired wisdom.

Absalom spent a large portion of his time ministering to townsmen who had trouble or needs. He helped with legal matters and gave advice for planting crops from what he had learned in Geshur. Handsome and good-natured, the prince was generous with all, and his handsome features were usually pleasant and smiling. It was hard not to like him, and he played that to the hilt. Absalom *was* the consummate politician.

Hesel had been retained at Ahithophel's home in Giloh much longer than he had anticipated. It was torture because of his burning desire to see Tamar. There was no way to communicate with her. He could only cherish her in his heart and wait for the day he could be with her again. He longed to gaze at her beautiful face, to love her and be loved by her, and to plan for their eventual marriage, hoping for the king's approval.

Ahithophel wasn't sure what was going on with Hesel. He had noticed that the young man was acting differently. He seemed distracted and not really concentrating on his work. The aging man had expected Hesel to be happy working with him again, but now it didn't appear that he was. After they had been back from Geshur a few weeks, Ahithophel asked his protégé, "Hesel, you don't seem content here with me. I thought you wanted to come to Giloh. May I ask if something is bothering you?"

Hesel was silent for a few moments, then asked his mentor, "Sire, how long will you be needing me to stay here with you rather than with Prince Absalom?"

The old mentor replied, "Well, it may be for a while. I am thinking that I may be moving my residence to Hebron before long, but my property here in Giloh needs considerable work before I can sell or lease it to someone to farm. I thought you would like to spend time here with me."

"Yes, of course. But in Jerusalem, you said you wouldn't be able to support us both financially."

"Well, that's not a problem at this time. You are still officially employed by Absalom. I guess we could say we are on a remote assignment. So, finances are not a concern. Actually, we are both in the employ of the prince."

Hesel wasn't sure what to make of that, so he decided to tell the truth about why he had been so distracted. He said, "The real reason I may seem to be a little off is because..."

"Because what? What's different now?"

"I fell in love with Princess Tamar. Now she is all I can think about."

"Oh, really? Well, that answers my question. That's amazing. Absalom mentioned in Geshur that his parents had told Tamar she is free to marry outside royalty. So, has she returned your interest?" The old man lay down the parchment he had been reading and looked with interest at his young protégé.

"Yes, she has. That's what makes it hard to be away from her. In Geshur, God gave us a vision that we would be together permanently with Him. It was glorious. She told me that she loves me."

Ahithophel threw up his hands and clapped them together. "Oh my goodness, what a blessing that must be for you two. God has smiled down on you, my boy. She is a princess, and you are a noble courtier."

Hesel replied, "Do you think it might be possible...or would you need me to take a message to Prince Absalom? That would give me a chance to see her and explain what I am doing here and how long it might be before I can return to Jerusalem."

The old man answered, "Yes, of course. Things are quiet now, so there hasn't been a need to communicate with Absalom for a while. However, I can find a reason to send you to Jerusalem. You finish up the work on that shed, and I'll prepare a letter for you to take to the prince next week."

Hesel's smile as he bowed and left the room brightened Ahithophel's day.

The following week, Hesel made his way to Jerusalem, arriving late in the evening. Although his heart was beating faster as he approached the capital city, his mind told him it might not be the best time to show up unannounced at the prince's home. He should probably check in at the palace first. However, his heart won the battle, so he bypassed the king's palace and made his way across the city to Absalom's farm. He paused on a low hill across the main road running past the residence, hoping to see his love moving about in the house through the open doors and windows. Instead, he saw no movement at all. The house was dark, as were the outbuildings. It was too early in the evening for the family to have retired, yet the house appeared to be deserted.

Hesel waited a few minutes, lifting a prayer to heaven for guidance. Then while he was still praying, from the corner of his eye, he saw movement at the rear of the house. A man exited the back door carrying a lantern. As Hesel watched, the man walked a short distance to an outbuilding, which he entered and closed the door. Hesel was sure the man was Absalom's servant Ari. The small building he had entered must be his quarters. Hesel quickly made his way around the main house and knocked at the door of the building he had seen Ari enter.

After a moment the door opened, and there stood his friend Ari, looking surprised to see Hesel standing there in the darkness. "Hesel, what are you doing here this time of night?"

Hesel answered, "May I come in?"

Ari opened the door wide and motioned for him to enter.

"Where is everyone?" Hesel asked.

"I'm sure that you really mean, where is Tamar. Am I right?"

"Yes. Of course. But I expected to see the entire family. Is everyone all right?

"Have a seat, my man, and I'll get you something to drink. While I'm doing that, I can tell you that Tamar and her mother have returned to Geshur. I'm not sure when they will return."

"Geshur? Why? They were just there."

"I'm not sure of all the reasons, but I overheard enough to know that Princess Tamar has had a relapse of her depression and has been shut up in her room since they returned from Geshur. She has hardly eaten anything. She was that way all the way back from Geshur. Her mother hasn't been able to get her to talk, to explain what her problem is. However, as I see you standing here, I would wager that it has something to do with your absence. Am I right?"

Hesel's heart fell when he heard about Tami's relapse. He said, "No, Ari, I have no clue what could be bothering her. We had a wonderful time together the evening before everyone left. What could have happened?"

"I don't know, but her mother finally decided in desperation to take her back to Geshur, where she had seemed to be happy. She hoped that might help."

Hesel said, "I must go to her. However, I have a responsibility to deliver this envelope to the prince. Where is he, anyway?"

Ari responded, "Here, in the city. I don't know where he has gone this evening, but I'm sure he will return tonight. Do you want me to deliver the envelope for you?"

"Would you do that, Ari? You can explain that I was alarmed at the news of Tamar's condition and felt I needed to go to her. I'm sure the prince is aware that Tamar and I have become close...friends, and you are his trusted servant, so why not?"

Ari asked, "Did you bring a mount? It's a long walk to Geshur."

"No, I didn't. Is there a horse or mule here for me to use? I won't be gone long, just enough to see the princess and return."

Ari set the pitcher down and said, "I'm afraid the mules were all taken for their carriage, and most of the horses were taken by their servants. I'm afraid you are left with only Sybil or Berber."

"I know Sybil but who or what is Berber?"

"Oh, Berber is my donkey. You won't want to ride her to Geshur, though. That would take forever. But you will love Sybil. She is my faithful and dependable dromedary."

"Oh, Sybil will be fine." Although Hesel had walked all the way to Jerusalem the day before, there was no way he could wait until morning to make the trip to Geshur. He said, "There is a near-full moon tonight that will give me and Sybil enough light to find the roads. I don't want to travel the dangerous

Jericho road at night, so I will take the overland road north out of Jerusalem."

Before he left, Ari prepared a travel bag, including food for him and a feedbag for Sybil. The camel recognized Hesel from the three years in Geshur, but she was not impressed until Hesel took an apple from his bag and let her eat it out of his hand. Hesel was experienced with camels, and his confidence seemed to satisfy her that he would be an acceptable passenger. Hesel tapped her knee, and she knelt down to allow him to mount into the soft comfortable saddle. Then they were off.

Hesel settled in for the long ride. Sybil was in no hurry, but at Hesel's urging, she picked up her pace, and the miles rolled away. Hours later, the road Hesel was looking for branched off to the right, down to the Jordan Valley. Hesel was then able to catch some short naps. He found that as long as he talked or sang to Sybil occasionally, she was willing to keep up the pace even while he napped.

Sometime after sunrise, Hesel saw that they were approaching the junction with the river road. Hesel knew the road well, remembering the many trips he had made back and forth carrying messages for his masters. He knew there was a roadside inn there where he could allow himself a short respite. Sybil needed time to rest and graze also.

As he lay napping under a palm tree, he decided he would continue all day, then stop for a few hours' rest in the evening. He could see if Sybil could manage another night's travel. That would be pushing her, especially since most of the road from there would be uphill. But his concern for Tamar wouldn't let him wait. If they rode through the next night, that would get them to Geshur by noon the next day.

Tamar sat on the shady porch of the farm, looking out over the pastoral scene before her. Her memories were bittersweet. Being in Geshur should have brought her much comfort because of the life-changing encounter with Hesel. But sadness caused by hearing that her betrothed love was mixed up in a plot to destroy her father had forced her into the valley of depression. She prayed to God who she thought had brought them together: *Oh Lord, if that was really You there with us at the sunset, joining us as a couple, then how could You allow Hesel to be involved in something so evil? Their plot could cause a bloody civil war. My entire family could be killed. Oh God, I am so confused. Please help me to understand Your will in all this.*

Her prayer was interrupted as her mother came out on the porch to join her. As she sat down, Maacah said, "Isn't this a lovely place? So peaceful. So serene. Are you feeling better this morning?"

Tamar looked away. "No, not really." She thought, *This beautiful place should be a reminder of the wonderful feelings I found here, but instead, it is a torment of what I have lost.* "I'm sorry I have caused so much trouble for you and my father. I appreciate what you're trying to do for me, but it's all so...so sad." Then, despite her efforts not to, she broke down sobbing, burying her face in her hands.

Maacah put her arms around her daughter and said, "I wish you could explain what happened. You seemed so happy that last night we were here, but by morning, that had all changed. What changed?"

Tamar continued sobbing. Then, suddenly, she stood up and ran down toward the barn.

Maacah let her go, hoping she would be all right. She watched as Tamar disappeared behind the barn and then reappeared briefly down the trail along the stream before the path took her out of sight. Maacah knew that was a trail Tamar had walked with Hesel before. She sent a prayer heavenward, asking God to protect her daughter and help her through the terrible depression. *Oh Lord. Only You can cure her. Please, Lord, she has suffered so much.*

Chapter 23:

Tamar and God

Tamar trudged along the familiar trail in her loneliness, hardly noticing the lush greenery she had admired so much before. Arriving at the waterfall, she climbed on a rock and sat at the top. She could see the landing below where she and Hesel had ventured together, him holding her hand and guiding her gently over the rocky places on the trail. Her thoughts and feelings were a jumble of confusion. The love she had felt and the despair when she learned of her beloved's betrayal dismayed her.

She lifted her face to heaven and cried aloud, *"Where are You, God? Why did You fill me with love and admiration for a man—only to dash me on the rocks of despair? Lord, I know that Hesel is just a man, and men can hurt and disappoint even You. But You, Oh God, where is Your lovingkindness? Please don't leave me alone. I need You, or I will perish."* Releasing her emotions, she broke down in tears, crying, *"Please God... please help me."*

After her sobs slowed and finally subsided, she felt a stirring in her soul. She said meekly, "Lord, are You there?" There was only silence, yet she continued to feel something deep within her. A thought entered her mind: *Go to the sunset.*

Tamar thought, *No, not there. I couldn't stand the pain.*

But the thought wouldn't go away. *Go to the sunset.*

She said aloud. "Is that You, Lord? Are You telling me to go to the sunset, where You showed us Your majesty and Your love?"

Go to the sunset. The thought would not leave her.

Unsure of what was driving her, the young princess rose to her feet and started back along the trail to the farm house. It was midafternoon by the time she got back to the house. She walked clear through the house without seeing anyone and out through the kitchen to the trail in the back of the house. Kita was in the backyard helping the cook clean vegetables for the evening meal. Tamar spoke to her as she passed, saying, "Please tell my mother I'm going for a walk but I won't be gone long."

"Of course, my lady." Kita nodded and continued with her task, and Tamar started up the steep path to the lookout.

As Tamar entered the stand of pine trees, she began to have misgivings. *Do I really want to do this?*

She prayed aloud, "Lord, if You want me to go to this place, please give me the courage and strength. I'm trusting You, Lord." She felt her resolve build as she neared the end of the path opening to the clearing and the lookout. Emerging from the shelter of the trees, the lovely young woman stopped suddenly and caught her breath—a magnificent view.

Her previous visit here had been overwhelmed by that miraculous sunset. But this time, the sun was still above the horizon, and the air was clear, illuminating the scene below, stretching to the Great Sea on the horizon. As she soaked up the beauteous vista, the sun dropped behind a bank of clouds, briefly darkening the view. But then, as if displayed for her alone, a dazzling ray of light broke through a small opening in the clouds. A single sunbeam illuminated the place where she stood, blinding her momentarily. As her eyes adjusted to the brightness, her mind tried to rationalize what she was seeing; was God touching her soul through the glorious light?

Standing still and silent, she closed her eyes, feeling the warmth permeate her skin and reach into her depths. It was as if God was embracing her and reassuring her that all would be well.

Within moments, the ray faded as the opening in the cloud closed as quickly as it had opened. Tamar stood frozen on the rocky crag. She lifted her face to heaven and cried out, "Oh Lord, I believe! I listened to the words of men, and I believed them more than I believed the promise that You inspired in Hesel and me. I believe that You will fulfill the words You spoke to us; thank You for Your grace."

Tamar slid down onto the rock, and lay there, drained emotionally. *Oh, Hesel, I let myself believe that you would betray me and my family by joining a terrible plot to take my father's throne. Please forgive me, Hesel.* She cried aloud, "Please forgive me, Hesel, for doubting you. I'm so sorry."

In the silence that followed, she could hear the wind rustling in the pine trees behind her. Then a man's voice spoke—it was Hesel's voice—saying, "I forgive you, Tami."

The princess said aloud, "Hesel! If only you were here, I would hold you and never let you go."

To her surprise, the voice answered, "I am here with you. Look, it's me."

Confused, Tamar turned around and looked up. "Hesel... Hesel, it is you! But where did you come from?"

Hesel said, "Let me hold you for just a moment first." Hesel pulled her to her feet and wrapped his arms around her. But he didn't feel the response from her that he had expected. She pushed back from him and asked, "How did you get here? You are supposed to be at your master's home in Giloh."

Hesel stepped back and replied, "I was sent to Jerusalem with a message for your brother. But when I arrived at your house, Ari told me you had gone with your mother back to Geshur. They thought your distress might have something to do with me. Tami, the last time I saw you, we made a commitment to each other and considered ourselves betrothed. What happened? And what did you do that you want me to forgive?"

Tamar said, "Give me a minute. Let's sit down over here, and I'll tell you." When they were seated, she began. "First of all, I want you to know that I still love you. But my heart and soul have been troubled by something I heard after we parted that last night after the sunset."

"What was it?"

"Before going to bed that night, I went downstairs to get my shawl. I heard my brother and your master Ahithophel talking in the kitchen. I didn't mean to eavesdrop, but their words caught my attention."

"What were they saying that could have affected you and me?"

"They were plotting to turn the people against my father so they can take his throne. They are planning a coup—all based on lies, and they included you as one their main supporters."

Shocked, Hesel exclaimed, "They said what?"

"They said you are so good at making things happen that they couldn't do it without you. You had already done such a good job coordinating their plans that they were discussing how you would be one of their top aides when they come to power."

"Tamar, are you sure you heard right? They are planning on starting a war?"

Her face was quiet and serious. "There was no question about it. Ahithophel asked Absalom if he could kill my father if it came to that. I think Absalom was not sure he could, but said he would kill him if he had to. They discussed when Absalom would start raising his army and the part you would play. Oh, Hesel, it was terrible! Especially when they talked about how you are with them and what a valuable role you are playing already. Please, Hesel, tell me it isn't true! Tell me you are not involved in a plot that could destroy my father and cause upheaval in the kingdom."

He had to wait until his brain stopped spinning before he could answer.

"Tami, I promise you. I had no idea that they were planning this. I'm thinking back to what I've heard from them, but I have never heard talk about a coup. I have wondered at times what they were planning, but all of the messages I carried back and forth were always in sealed envelopes. I guess my esteem for both men has been so high I would never suspect a terrible thing to come from their work together. Oh Tami, I have been so naïve. I have been helping to stage an uprising against King David? What a fool I've been." His expression showed he was tormented.

Tamar threw her arms around his neck. "Oh, Hesel, you are innocent. Thank You, Lord. Forgive me for doubting you.

I doubted you, Hesel, and I doubted God, even when He had spoken to us so clearly. What a fool I have been. Now can you forgive me?"

"Of course. But what caused you to come here?"

"Oh, Hesel, I felt God's Spirit. The sun went behind the clouds—and a solitary ray of light shone on me. I felt God's love and protection more than I ever have in my life. I was crying out for God and you to forgive me. How foolish I was to have believed Ahithophel and Absalom over God's blessing of us."

Neither spoke. Instead she leaned against him as he kissed her hair, and when she turned her face to him, their lips met in a healing kiss that wiped away their hurt and anxiety. They spoke their love words between kisses as they witnessed another beautiful sunset.

Tamar looked up and asked, "When can we be married?"

He answered, "Soon. However, we must first speak to your father about what you heard. Then, maybe, we can talk to him about our marriage."

A few days later, Maacah, Tamar, and Hesel, along with a couple of Talmai's men, returned to Jerusalem, and Tamar requested an audience with King David. Her request was granted. Hesel was worrying about David's reaction to his involvement with both his son Absalom and his daughter Tamar. Finally, the guard opened the double doors to the king's public room and nodded to the couple, indicating they should enter. Tamar went first, with Hesel close behind.

David rose from the table where he had been seated and came to greet his daughter with a kiss on both cheeks. "Tamar, it's good to see you looking well. And, this is Hesel," said the king as he extended a hand to Hesel. But Hesel had fallen to his knees and bowed low.

David said, "Rise, young man. Come, both of you. Let's move to my private chamber where we can be more comfortable." David led them through a curtained doorway into a smaller room with cushioned seats and a low divan by a window. With a hand signal, the king ordered beverages to be brought.

King David turned to Hesel and said, "I remember when you were with my old advisor, Ahithophel. How did you end up working for my son, Absalom?"

Hesel cleared his throat and said, "I believe my master Ahithophel spoke to the prince and asked if he could use my services since my master was going to be leaving the palace and returning to his home in Giloh. I appreciated the prince taking me on as a general assistant. I have enjoyed serving your son."

"So Ahithophel and Absalom must have a good working relationship to make such an arrangement."

"Yes, sire, I believe they do."

"Do you know if they still have such a relationship?"

Hesel glanced at Tamar, who nodded her support. "Indeed, they do. It has been my responsibility to serve as a liaison, carrying messages between them."

"And what sort of messages do you carry?" King David unconsciously stroked his gray-streaked beard.

"I don't know, Your Majesty. They are sealed messages, and I have not inquired about the contents. However, Princess Tamar can share with you a conversation she overheard between the two men in Geshur."

Tamar fidgeted nervously, but the king tried to ease her discomfort with a smile. He said, "Yes, Tamar, tell me what you heard."

The young princess related to her father all she could remember about the conversation between her brother and Ahithophel. She said, "Father, I was so upset, not only about their conversation, but that they talked like Hesel was part of their plan."

David became very somber after hearing her tale. He looked back and forth between his daughter and Hesel, especially looking directly into Hesel's eyes. He asked Tamar, "Have you told your mother what you heard?"

"No, I haven't told anyone except Hesel."

David stood up and paced for a moment before he paused and said, "I don't want you to tell anyone what you overheard. Try to forget ever hearing it. Can you do that?"

"I don't know. I'll try. But I promise not to speak of it to anyone."

David walked over to the window and stared outside for a few minutes before he returned to his seat. He looked at Hesel for a moment, then shifted his gaze to his daughter. He spoke to Tamar, "Daughter, am I to understand that you have developed feelings for this young man?"

"Yes, Father. Strong feelings. I want to marry him."

Hesel gulped, then held his breath, waiting for the king's response.

David shifted his gaze again to the young man. "Hesel, do you feel the same about my daughter?"

"Oh, yes, sire. She is the most wonderful, most lovely, and surely the strongest woman I have ever known. I love her with all my heart and want nothing more than to be wed to her."

"Well, Hesel, are you aware of the tragedy she experienced from her brother Amnon?"

"Yes, Your Majesty. To me, she is as pure and chaste as she has always been."

"I appreciate your words, Hesel. You know that what happened to her was in no way her fault, but the fact remains that she cannot be promised to a man of royal standing. For her to be wed, her mother and I hoped she might be given to a good man of common standing that she can love. It seems she has."

David paused, "However, there is one problem."

Hesel caught his breath, tensing every muscle in his body. He stammered, "What problem is that?"

"Well young man, it appears that Prince Absalom, along with your former master, Ahithophel, are plotting to overthrow my government by force, possibly leading to the death of my family and faithful followers. I am finding it difficult to allow my son's henchman to take away my daughter."

Hesel released the breath he had been holding. "I understand completely. However, since I have only just realized what the prince is planning, I will remove myself from his service immediately. I have always held Master Ahithophel in the highest regard. When I learned of their plans, I was devastated. I am scheduled to take a message to him tomorrow. I want to confront him and demand an explanation. Maybe I can learn something from him…something that I can relay to you."

The king nodded. "But what assurance can you give me that you are not going to let them know what I have just told you?"

Tamar jumped to her feet and exclaimed, "Oh, Father, no! Hesel would not do that. He is an honest and respectful man. He loves our Lord God and lives by His Word. You can trust him."

Hesel said, "Please Tamar, let me answer for myself."

David said, "Yes, Tamar, let the man speak."

Hesel replied, "Your Majesty, I give my word that I want nothing to do with sedition against you. I swear my allegiance to you, my king, and I promise never to lift my hand against you or your family. Please believe me. I love your daughter with all my heart. We have prayed together for this meeting with you today, asking God to give you an open heart to hear our words and our appeal for your blessing."

David stared at him intently, then looked up before speaking. "I want to believe you, in great part because of my daughter. However, what would you do if I refused to allow you to marry my daughter?"

Hesel felt a sinkng pain in his stomach. "What would I do? What could I do? My heart would surely rebel and try to oppose your ruling. But I know that would be useless to try. I suppose I would grieve deeply for her and I would continue to love her to my dying day. I have just pledged my loyalty to you so I would have no choice but to accept your ruling while dying on the inside. My lord, she is my life. Please allow me to spend the rest of my life serving you and trying my best to make her happy."

David looked steadily into Hesel's eyes searching for clues to this young man's soul. Finally he said, "I believe you. I give your marriage my permission and blessing."

"Oh, Father, thank you," said Tamar as she leapt to her feet and hugged her father, and then timidly, Hesel. Somewhat embarrassed, Hesel turned and knelt before King David, his future father in-law. "Sire, you have made us both happy. I can never thank you enough. I am your loyal servant to command as long as I live."

Motioning Hesel to his feet, David said, "Don't make me sorry I believed you. Let's wait until my son's rebellion is resolved before we plan a wedding. You must realize we are dealing with a dangerous situation. There is a good chance many people will lose their lives. Do not tell anyone what you have heard."

King David paused, then said, "Hesel, I want to talk to you alone. Tamar, please inform your mother of my decision and tell her to see me if she has questions. My talk with Hesel won't take long."

Hesel squeezed Tamar's hand as she turned to leave. Their eyes met, and she formed the silent words with her lips, *I love you.*

After Tamar left, the king motioned for Hesel to be seated in the chair close to his. "Hesel, I don't want you to confront either Absalom or Ahithophel about what Tamar heard. For the time being, I want you to continue working with them as if nothing has changed. Be their liaison man, but give close attention to what's going on. I want you to be my eyes and ears. But be very careful. Very careful. What they are planning could cost many lives, and I doubt they would hesitate to eliminate you if they suspect you are onto them. Do you think you can do this?"

Hesel gulped but managed to say, "Yes, my lord. I have pledged to you that I will do anything for you, so how could I refuse?"

David responded, "I am not ordering you to do this, Hesel. I am asking you. If you err, let it be in too much caution. If you learn anything that you think I should know, get word to me through Tamar. You don't need to tell her about our arrangement, but mention something like, 'Your father would probably be interested to hear ...' — whatever it is you want me to know. If you have critical information, come directly to me and tell the guards that His Majesty sent for you."

"You want me to be your agent? I will do it. But, sire, aren't you going to stop them before they go any further?"

"No, Hesel. I'm not surprised at what you and Tamar have told me. I am disappointed, but God has told me to expect something like this. We will wait and see what they think they can do and let the Lord handle it. Whatever happens will be His will."

"Of course, Your Majesty," Hesel inclined his head respectfully.

"Now," the king said as he got up, "I promised to join Bathsheba and our sons for the evening meal. Safe travels, Hesel. And remember, be careful."

Hesel stood, bowed again, and said, "Thank you, sire. God be with you."

"And also with you," David raised his hand in a brief wave as Hesel left the chamber.

Chapter 25:

Absalom's Campaign

After two more years in Jerusalem, Absalom felt that he had accomplished everything he could. He had managed to avoid his father, as he had been instructed, but the fact that they were estranged did not escape public notice. As Ahithophel had predicted, he needed his father's acceptance to complete the public image he sought to portray.

His life was pleasant; his wife had already given him a son and a daughter. He named their daughter Tamar after his wounded sister who lived with them and helped to care for the little ones. Yet, that churning in his gut never left him. Absalom yearned to wear the crown, to sit on the throne and have the admiration and respect of the people. He coveted the power that comes with the throne and believed with all his heart that he deserved it, especially after his father's grave sins had come to light.

However, it was becoming obvious that King David was not going to reach out to his son. Therefore, Absalom would have to initiate a reconciliation. But how?

What would Ahithophel suggest? As Absalom remembered his time with the advisor, he recalled how the sage had said Joab could serve as his representative to David. *I'll try that,* he decided. Absalom sent a messenger to Joab, asking him to come and meet with him privately. However, days passed with no word from Joab. Absalom sent a second message, but like the first one, he received no response. Finally, in frustration, Absalom instructed his servants to take action: "Go, set fire to General Joab's barley fields over there next to mine," he motioned with his hand at the adjoining fields.

"But Prince Absalom, do you..." one of the farm workers asked tentatively.

"You heard me—do it now!" Absalom was filling quickly with rage.

The farmhands clandestinely set fire to the edges of the field, and the smoldering flames quickly ate up the barely. Within minutes, a cry arose from Joab's workers, and the general himself ran out of the house to stare at the smoking rows. Minutes later, Joab showed up at Absalom's door.

Escorted by a servant to Absalom's sitting room, Joab asked tightly, "What do you mean by setting my barley field on fire?"

Absalom answered quietly now that the general had appeared, "If you had responded to your crown prince's earlier summons, that wouldn't have been necessary."

Joab was not accustomed to such treatment except from the king himself. However, because of his longstanding loyalty to the kingdom, he knew he must show respect to the prince. His warrior's self-discipline prevailed as he willed himself to be calm. "How can I be of service, my lord?"

Absalom leaned forward and said, "I need you to go to the king and ask him why have I come from Geshur? I might as well have stayed there. Now let me see my father, the king's face, and if there is iniquity in me, let him put me to death."

Joab shook his head. "I can't predict how he will react."

"Nor I. But my future can no longer remain in question. I need answers."

"Very well. I will seek an audience with him."

"Good," Absalom said, "and I will look into having your barley replanted."

Hours later, Joab returned and was shown into Absalom's sitting room again, with the doors closed behind him.

"Your father is calling for you. Come now with me."

"Truly?" Absalom was overjoyed—not so much in seeing his father, but in being accepted into his presence, which would shortly become public knowledge. His plan was going to work!

Joab escorted Absalom to the royal palace and left him outside the door to the king's chamber. "Wait here," he said as he knocked softly, then entered. Joab was in with David for just a few minutes, but it seemed forever to Absalom.

Finally, Joab came out and motioned for Absalom to enter. Joab said sternly, "I'll be waiting here."

The prince understood that he was being told, "Don't try anything; I'm here to protect the Monarch."

Absalom entered the familiar room for the first time in seven years.

David stood quietly in the center of the room. As their eyes met, Absalom felt a surge of regret at their estrangement and fell to the floor at David's feet. He sobbed, "Father, forgive me for what I've done."

David didn't speak, but Absalom could hear him weeping quietly. The father reached down and helped his son to a standing position, then drew him into a strong embrace, kissing him and saying, "Absalom, my son. My son, Absalom. Welcome home."

Then David held his son at arm's length and looked into his eyes, studying his expression. "I forgive what you've done, but only God can forgive what you are planning to do."

Absalom was stunned. How could his father know? No one but Ahithophel was aware of his plans. "Father, what do you mean? My plans are to serve you, my king."

David stepped back almost sadly but said in a firm voice, "I know your plans because the Lord God told me seven years ago, 'One of your family members will rise up against you. You will have violence and bloodshed in your family forever.' He was talking about you, the son I have loved most. You are going to rise against me—so go do what you must."

"Father, I..." Absalom stuttered and then stopped speaking at the look on his father's face. With a bow, he said, "I am loyal to His Majesty," then turned and left the chamber.

Absalom's household in Jerusalem was growing. His mother and sister lived in the house, along with his wife and children. Ari continued as Absalom's man-servant. His room was in an outbuilding that housed the servants.

Hesel, on the other hand, had spent much of the two years in Giloh with his master Ahithophel. When he did return to Jerusalem permanently, his lodging was in a public hostel that provided a room and one meal each day. He continued to carry messages back and forth, but now Absalom needed him for greater things.

While in town, Hesel found occasions to visit Absalom's home. Some of those times Absalom was away on business. Tamar was still helping with the children and teaching Absalom's wife about the courtly ways of the palace to prepare for state occasions and special events with the royal family. Tamar and Hesel were able to see each other, but they were never alone to observe the decorum of courtship until their marriage could be formalized. Both were eager to be together in their own home away from the palace, but it wasn't time. Like Jacob waiting for Rachel, Hesel was patient and did not insist on trying to get her alone. He treated her with complete respect as befitted her royal status and was deserved by her noble character. Tamar felt so valued by this kind, compassionate, self-disciplined, and hardworking man that her love for him deepened in the months that followed. When seated beside each other for dinner, their hands might "accidentally" brush now and then, and on at least one occasion, Hesel bumped into Tamar in the short corridor leading out back to the garden, and the couple spontaneously exchanged a rich, warm kiss as Tamar blushed and giggled while Hesel reddened with delight. Tamar continued into the garden while Hesel had to head for the outbuildings, but they managed to share a deep smile and an airborne kiss before parting ways.

After the reunion with his father, Absalom began making plans for the next phase of his revolution. He sent word to Ahithophel in Hebron by Hesel, revealing the meeting with David and his desire to begin recruiting his army. Ahithophel's return message advised Absalom to meet him in Hebron for reasons he would explain on arrival. Absalom packed some meager provisions and in disguise departed the next morning.

Hebron was second in the kingdom only to Jerusalem in population and importance. It was Absalom's hometown, the place where he and his five brothers closest in age were born. His father David ruled the country from there for over seven years. After he was crowned king of Israel also, he moved his capital to Jerusalem. Hebron was rich in history, including Abraham and Sarah's burial site in the cave of Machpelah, where Jacob and Leah were also entombed.

It was in Hebron where Absalom found his old advisor in the public square where they had arranged to meet. Ahithophel chuckled at Absalom's disguise, but greeted him warmly, then escorted him to his sister Joanna's home where he was staying.

The old sage said to his young protégé, "The first thing I want to ask about is my granddaughter, Bathsheba. Is she well?"

"Yes, she seems content and happy, surrounded by a loving family. She and my father seem to think their youngest son, Solomon, may have the most promise for the future."

Ahithophel beamed and said, "Thank you for that news. Do you think King David is thinking of naming Solomon as his successor?"

"The king is not going to name anyone to follow him. I am the crown prince, and that is my destiny. My rule will come to fruition soon."

Ahithophel said, "Then let's get down to business. I wanted us to meet here in Hebron for a couple of reasons. After I received the written notes you sent from Jerusalem, I was happy to hear that you had finally managed to be reconciled to your father."

Absalom's lips tightened. "It wasn't much of a reconciliation. We were able to express our feelings a little, but Father revealed that he knows about my plans to take the throne from him."

"What? How could he know? I've told no one anything about what we've discussed."

"It wasn't you. He said God told him. Seven years ago. But that's not the strangest thing. He said something like it's 'fore-ordained by God,' so he won't try to stop me. It looks as though he is resigned to me taking over."

The old sage sat back and tried to process what the prince was saying. He asked, "Did you confirm that you do plan to replace him?"

"Oh, no. I just told him that all I want is to live in peace with him and loyally serve my king."

Ahithophel was lost in deep thought for a minute or two. He said aloud, "The man has certainly changed. I'm not sure what to make of it. I wonder what role his new advisor, Hushai, is playing?" After another pause, the old man stated very slowly, "We must keep his words in mind as we make plans. It's a mystery, and I don't like mysteries."

For seven days, the two conspirators huddled in a private room. Ahithophel said one morning, "Our first order of business is to build a team of leaders. Every town will have a group of elders.

They are the people who are most influential in their communities. You are going to have to travel around the country, introducing yourself as the king's envoy, sent to meet with them to prepare for the future when David retires from ruling. Build a relationship with them. Find out their most important concerns and interests for their towns and villages, and then you become their champion.

"It is important at first that you present yourself as an envoy of your father, King David. You are the crown prince, and your father is preparing you for the throne. He is sending you out among the people to learn how to best lead them."

Absalom nodded, "That makes sense.

Ahithophel added, "Cultivate the elders until you can begin to introduce your ideas about positive changes—innovations or adjustments that can improve the things they are concerned about. Build them up. With your charm and natural authority, you should have no problem building rapport with the local leaders.

"Now, let me tell you how we helped your father to become the king of Judah about twenty-five years ago. You may want to consider the same strategy now."

"Oh, what strategy was that?"

"Well, David and his small army had been raiding the towns and villages in the Negev for several years and had accumulated a large amount of booty from their raids, the spoils of war. There was livestock, iron weapons and tools, all kind of things. More than we would ever need. As we were discussing what we could do with it, I told David that I had been talking to the other advisors and senior officers about a possibility we should consider. No one opposed it, but it is scary."

"David said, 'Let's hear it'.

"I told him, 'You are very popular here in the Judean hills. People are drawn to you and your cause. This army you are leading is a group of men who gravitated to you, partly because you are from the tribe of Judah, as they are, but also because you are so obviously blessed by the Lord in everything you do. You are a charismatic leader. Let's face it.'

"David said, 'What you say is so only because the Lord has ordained it. So, what is your point?'

"I said. 'What I have been toying with in my mind is the possibility of consolidating your appeal. We could consider withdrawing from the nation of Israel and starting our own country. Your own independent nation. Think of it. We could call it the Kingdom of Judah. We've never been popular with the rest of the tribes in Israel. In fact we've been outcasts ever since Saul developed his hatred for you.

"I said to him, 'Here's my plan. Let's begin handing out gifts from our spoils of war to all the elders in the larger towns and villages of Judah. Some of us advisors and senior officers can deliver them to each community and begin talking to the elders and citizens about the possibility of banding together and establishing our own nation with you, David, son of Jesse, as our King. I think it would work. The people respect you and many of them even love you, even without the gifts.

'If we could establish a new nation, our army would grow and we wouldn't need to hide out from anyone. By giving the elders gifts from our booty, you will surely win them over. That will help you to personally develop relationships and win over the elders in each of the communities, thus leading the common people to your call.

"Well, David had to think about it and spend a lot of time in prayer, and also talk it over with his other advisors and counselors. But David accepted our plan and we began dividing the spoils and delivering them to the leading communities of Judah. In no time the elders and the citizens spread the word. It must have been favored by the Lord because with His help, it happened."

Absalom said, "I never knew that was how my father was crowned king of Judah. That's amazing. And you, my advisor, had a role in that. That's inspirational."

"Well, it's all in the records. My point is that if you win the Elders over, it's downhill from there.

"It will take time, but we have plenty of time. I'm talking about a year or so before you will be ready for the next step. You need to develop relationships with the elders in each of the tribes to lead the common people to your call. That means you will be on the road much of the time."

Later, as the two men settled in Ahithophel's room at his sister's house, Absalom leaned back and said thoughtfully, "That is going to take considerable work. It will be a sizable task just keeping organized. I'll need to have people helping me to keep track of the different communities, the names of the elders, and their concerns. Hesel might do well as my lieutenant in that regard."

"He will do a good job for you. Now, concurrently with step number one, increase your involvement with the common people in Jerusalem. One way would be to intercept people coming to ask favors of the king. Find out what they are coming for, and if you can, give them what they need. Do it humbly and without fanfare. Pour on the compassion and make them feel that you are the kind of ruler they really need."

Absalom said, "I've already been doing that, but I can do more at the city gates."

"The next step is a little risky, but let's take your father at his word. He said he would not stop you, so let's try something and see how he reacts. Here's what I want you to do. Get a horse and a fancy chariot and drive it around Jerusalem for a few days. People will notice and wonder what you are doing, and why.

"If King David does nothing, the next step is to gather a few young men to run ahead of your chariot. That will demonstrate that you are someone very important—and it will get the attention of the public. They will want to know why you are becoming a public presence. Stop at a forum-type area and speak to the people about how your father is preparing you to take over the throne. Share some ideas about how you will rule when you are in charge. But remember that you need to keep everything positive regarding your relationship to your father."

"Right. I don't think people will necessarily agree with me if I complain and criticize him," Absalom said.

"You and your father are a team, working together for the nation. You are proud of him and hope you can be loved by all as he has been. The people must see you as the beloved son of David and begin thinking of you as his successor. As time goes by, you can gradually show concern about your father's health and capabilities. But at first, keep everything positive."

"Of course," Absalom said.

"Do those things for a time and see if you hear from the king. If he does not step in to question or stop you, increase your men to a large number—twenty-five or more. Now then," Ahithophel's eyes widened, "if David doesn't send soldiers to stop you, we will assume he meant it when he said he won't fight you. If he is going to give you free rein, you can do anything you wish to be established as the coming king."

Absalom asked, "How would you suggest I do what you said about the elders? I don't have a mountain of booty to spread around."

"You can still use the same strategy. Obviously you would have to operate on a much smaller scale. However the principle is the same. People tend to be grateful when they receive a gift, even if it isn't a large one. You have access to the royal treasury and you can requisition funds to support your travels. Simply take enough on each trip to be able to wine and dine the elders and you will soon have them eating out of your hand.

Absalom listened to what his advisor had to say and couldn't wait to get started. As soon as he returned to Jerusalem, he called for Hesel to meet with him for a strategy session.

"There are a couple of things I want to talk to you about. You have become a valuable assistant. You have not only been a good liaison with Ahithophel, but you are resourceful and take the initiative to help without my having to ask. But I want to talk to you about my sister."

Hesel tensed, concerned that Absalom might forbid them to be together or try to manipulate Tamar for his own purposes. The young man said, "Sire, I am sorry if I have overstepped my bounds by seeing her sometimes in your house. I would never do anything to make her or you uncomfortable."

Absalom waved a dismissive hand. "I see you and Tamar are interested in each other. Normally, I would take offense because you are a commoner. However, because Tamar was hurt so badly by Amnon's attack, I believe she deserves happiness in unconventional yet suitable ways. My mother said the king told her that he has consented for Tamar to marry a non-royal."

Hesel replied, "Your sister and I revealed our desire to be wed—with his permission—and he has given it. I would have told you sooner, but we have held off planning the wedding due to the king's schedule."

"I see. Well, that is good news. I appreciate your seeing Tamar's true beauty, inner and outer. She is a virtuous woman and will make a good wife, as we've seen as she helps in our home."

"I have no doubt of that, Prince Absalom. I'm grateful for your approval," Hesel said.

Absalom nodded. "Now, the other thing I want to discuss with you is my public relations campaign. My father has agreed that I should be getting out among the people and letting them get to know me better. I am the crown prince, and he is getting older and beginning to think about his retirement. He is preparing me for the throne one day."

Hesel thought, *I have to pretend that I'm unaware of the secret rebellion.* "That is great news, Prince Absalom! God bless the future King Absalom!"

For a moment, Absalom's face brightened at the words 'King Absalom,' but then he quickly said, "Yes, it is truly amazing. There is much work ahead of us, and I hope you will play an important role. You have been carrying correspondence between Ahithophel and me for some time. You know we are working on a project, but we haven't told you what it is about. Well, now I can tell you that Ahithophel will become my personal advisor when I take the throne. That won't be for a while yet. My father is still quite able to fulfill the duties of the monarchy and probably will continue on the throne for a while longer. But it's not too soon for me to become better known by the people of both Israel and Judah."

"How can I help, sire?" Hesel listened attentively.

"You will continue as my liaison with Ahithophel, although I will be traveling to see him on occasion, but in disguise. We don't want to reveal that he is working with me yet for a couple of reasons. For one, he left my father's service, as you know, rather suddenly several years ago. Most people don't know why he left, but rumors fly when there is a vacuum of information. We want to avoid misinformation circulating throughout the city or even the country. Do not reveal anything about our relationship to anyone. Do you understand?"

"Of course, my lord. I assumed that was why Ahithophel came to Geshur so often."

"Yes, of course. Now, beginning right away, I will be stepping up my public attention campaign. I need you to be in charge of the logistics because I will be expanding my public appearances, not only in Jerusalem, but most likely throughout the kingdom."

"That's wonderful. What will you require, sire?"

"First, find me the most beautiful horse available in this area. Preferably choose a white stallion, but he must be broken to pull a large chariot, which I would also like you to procure for me. The chariot should be designed and decorated to represent royalty. I will be circulating around the Jerusalem area in that chariot every few days. You have my permission to recruit as much help as you need as we work to increase my presence in the nation." Absalom went on to discuss other details of Hesel's responsibility as they planned the details of the prince's campaign.

It didn't take long for Hesel to finalize preparations for Absalom's image-building. When the prince next returned to Jerusalem, he launched his plan right away. Dressed in fine clothes but nothing too extravagant, he intercepted people on their way to King David's court and impressed them with his generosity and kindness. If someone would fall to his knees before the prince, Absalom would pull him up and kiss the person's head. He would ask where they lived and sympathize, saying, "When it is my time to rule, I will make things right for you because I am a champion of justice." So, in that way, Absalom stole the hearts of the men of Israel.

Hesel was able to acquire for the prince a white stallion from a passing Arab caravan en route to Egypt. The chariot wasn't hard to find and decorate to Absalom's satisfaction. The crown prince and his retinue made quite a sight as he rode about the city in his bejeweled chariot pulled by a beautiful steed and preceded by a large group of young men dressed in white tunics. People were raising questions about him and the reason for his extravagant display. Occasionally, he would stand in front of the crowd that quickly gathered around and proclaim how King David was sending him out to prepare him for future leadership duties.

When it became obvious that Absalom would not be opposed by his father, he took his show on the road, visiting the surrounding communities as far as Hebron. He spent several months setting up in the city squares or marketplaces and speaking to the people.

His message was always the same: "Citizens of Judea (or Israel)! My name is Absalom, the eldest son of King David, who is encouraging me as the crown prince to visit the cities, towns, and villages of our prosperous nation and make myself known to the good people of Israel and Judah. Why? Because King David wants to ensure a smooth transition of authority when he retires from royal duties. My father is beginning to slow down as age takes its toll. It is necessary for me to get acquainted with the good people of (whatever village or city) and hear your ideas of how I can meet your needs when it is my time to rule."

Absalom's charm was hard to resist. His handsome face and infectious smile melted the hearts of the people everywhere. Some said he must be an angel. He excelled at making each person feel as though they were special to him, the handsome young prince. Everyone agreed that he would make a wonderful king.

Absalom would spend a few days in each place getting to know the elders and people there and taking special care to identify and cultivate men who were attracted by his message. Hesel acted as his lead organizer and accountant. The prince directed Hesel to enlist a team of men drawn from all twelve tribes of Israel and Judah. Each tribal representative was charged with keeping records of followers and leaders in the villages within his tribe. Their task was simplified since David and Joab had already established elements of the Israeli army in each of those regions. The appointed leaders were responsible for mobilizing the men of the city if a call came from the king.

Absalom spoke as if he were a messenger from the king, deceiving people into believing in his future leadership. He left local leaders with instructions to promote his ideas and indoctrinate the fighting men in military training, the first step of raising his army for the revolution.

As Hesel worked with Absalom, an opportunity to meet with King David came while Absalom was out of town. Hesel left Absalom's home to take a message to Ahithophel. After leaving the city, he waited until evening and stole back into Jerusalem, careful to avoid being seen. At the palace, he told the guards that he had been summoned by the king. A guard took his name and disappeared into the royal chambers. He returned shortly and indicated that Hesel should follow him.

The king was waiting in his private quarters where he was dining with Bathsheba and his oldest two sons. When Hesel appeared in the doorway, David said, "Ah, Hesel.

Come in." Then he said to his wife, "This is Hesel, Tamar's intended husband."

Bathsheba's eyes widened, having heard the story from Maacah. "Welcome, Hesel. Have you eaten? Please join us."

Oh, my lady, I didn't mean to interrupt your meal. I'll wait in the reception chamber if that is acceptable."

King David said, "Don't be silly. You are about to become a member of our family. The servants will bring you a plate." David motioned to the butler who nodded and went to arrange a plate of food for the new arrival.

After dining, David took Hesel into his private chamber where they could talk. The king said, "I assume you have some news for me."

Hesel nodded. "I have been asked by the prince to assist in organizing public relations activities, Your Majesty."

"Why?" David asked bluntly.

"He reports to the people that his purpose is to carry out Your Majesty's wishes to acquaint him better with our territories and citizens."

"Why would I want that, according to Absalom?"

"He claims to be carrying out your wishes in preparation for the day you retire, my king."

"And when is that day supposed to be?" the king asked, staring intently at Hesel.

"As far as I've heard, he hasn't said."

David paced a few steps. "What does he say about my ability to rule?"

"At first, he is most complimentary, sire. He says that you and he are working together. He said you are grooming him for the future of the kingdom." After a pause, he continued, "But then lately he adds you may be slowing down a little with age, citing your decision to stay home from the battle for the Ammonite capital."

"Hmm" was all David said, pondering Hesel's report.

Hesel squirmed in his seat. "I'm sorry to say this, but on the most recent trip, I heard him say unkind words about you, sire."

"Oh? What did he say?" David took a seat and crossed his legs to listen.

Hesel explained as the king's expression darkened. Finally, David said, "I see what he is trying to do. It will take time, but he will begin to turn public support from me to him. I see Ahithophel's strategy here. Absalom would never conceive of a plan this subtle."

Hesel sat up and said, "It wouldn't take much to squelch his plan. Why don't you stop him?"

David shook his head and replied, "How many times do I have to tell people that it is God's will for my son to rise up against me? I can't fight God."

Hesel said, "I admire your faith and dedication to what you see as God's will."

King David said, "You need to watch very carefully. If my son and his advisor begin actively recruiting an army, leave them. I don't want you getting caught in their web of deceit or being in the path of God's justice when it comes."

"I should be all right for a while. I'm mostly helping with logistics."

"When the time comes, I advise you to put distance between yourself and my son. If God moves me to retaliate, my warriors won't hesitate to destroy everyone around him— may it never be."

Hesel asked, "What about Tamar and Maacah?"

King David replied, "I don't think Absalom would harm his sister or mother, but you would be expendable if he suspects you of betrayal."

Hesel replied, "When the time comes, I plan to confront Ahithophel and insist that he tell me what they are up to. I hope he respects me enough to tell the truth. I don't understand why they want to do this. It's insane. They probably don't understand why you are doing nothing to stop them."

The king replied, "I'm waiting on the Lord. I will move when and if—and only if—He directs me. It's all in His hands."

Absalom's confidence was growing with his success in reaching out to the people of the land. He was emboldened to increase his Jerusalem retinue to fifty men. He also continued his outreach to the more distant tribes who didn't yet know him. It wasn't practical to take his full retinue of runners to the outlying areas, but even with a few runners, he made an amazing spectacle in the villages where such a sight had never been seen.

Soon, Absalom began speaking of his father's behavior as less benevolent. "King David seems to be changing. I'm sorry to say that he is beginning to have problems with his memory and attitude. I suppose it is age. He is becoming argumentative, more aloof to the common folks like you all."

As Absalom's insolence grew, he would report atrocities his father had committed, including adultery with Bathsheba and the murder of Uriah. In time, the entire nation learned of David's failures. His son was gradually turning the people against their beloved king and unwittingly fulfilling God's words spoken through Nathan.

In time, the entire nation knew Absalom (or thought they did) and began to look forward to him replacing David as king. Word of Absalom's activities inevitably reached the ears of King David's advisors. General Joab, his advisor Hushai, and courtiers close to the king asked David for permission to stop Absalom from patronizing the kingdom's citizenry.

"No! God will deal with Absalom," David said adamantly.

Joab was astounded that King David would not allow him to hold Absalom accountable. It was obvious that his son was attempting to set himself up to succeed David as king. Absalom's behavior was grievous to Joab, who had been instrumental in bringing Absalom back from exile and reconciling him with his father. Now, Joab could see the young prince was methodically working to turn the people against their king.

As gossip and rumors increased, Joab decided to try talking to Queen Maacah about her son. Cautiously seeking an audience with her, Joab arranged the meeting so that no one—especially the king—would suspect his motives.

Joab was ushered into Maacah's presence in Absalom's home while the prince was campaigning out in the provinces. Joab bowed briefly and said, "Queen Maacah, I am here to discuss your son, Prince Absalom."

Sitting in her reception chamber where she would receive guests and courtiers, she asked, "What are you talking about?"

She greatly admired General Joab in more ways than one, but she would never let him know.

"Surely you've seen what he is doing among the people," Joab began, taking a seat when she pointed to one nearby.

"Do you mean his riding the chariot around town?"

"Yes, and his speeches he makes to the people. He claims that King David is sending him out to become familiar with the countryside and the local residents because his father is grooming him for the crown."

Maacah's face expressed surprise. "Well, isn't David preparing my son as the future ruler?"

"Of course not. King David plans to remain an active monarch for many years."

Maacah's brow furrowed. "Absalom has mentioned none of this to me. Why doesn't the king stop him?"

Joab replied with scorn in his voice, "I don't know. He doesn't approve of what Absalom is doing, but he refuses to let me put an end to this. It has something to do with what he says God told him several years ago is foreordained." His tone grew quieter. "Is it possible that you could talk to Absalom and see what he is up to?"

Looking perplexed, the queen said, "I suppose. I'll talk to him when he returns from his current journey. Thank you for bringing this matter to my attention. I will send word when I've spoken to my son."

Joab got up, bowed, and left the chamber, leaving Maacah wondering how different her life might have been had it taken another direction.

Hesel did not always accompany Absalom on his travels. As Absalom's campaign began to transition into a recruitment drive, Hesel was able to be with Tamar and Maacah while Eliza, Absalom's wife, was away visiting relatives. As Hesel and Tamar enjoyed the first fruits of the grape arbors in the garden, Hesel said, "Your brother is pushing forward with his campaign. He's asked me to begin recruiting officers for his army.

"No. It seems he expects to become king soon, not years from now. I can't believe it. If my father doesn't do something soon, Absalom will successfully take the throne."

Hesel replied, "I need to see the king while Absalom is out of town. Since you brought word that King David doesn't want to meet with me in his official chambers again, did he have any suggestions for a meeting elsewhere?"

Tamar nodded vigorously after tasting a sweet grape. "Yes, he said you can meet in Nathan's room on the second floor of the palace."

"I know that area well. Did your father set a time?" Hesel took a grape from the basket that Tamar held.

"He said that morning rounds are finished around noon. If you can be there at that time on the second day, he will see you then."

The meeting took place as planned. King David had arranged to have Nathan busy elsewhere, so they had the chamber to themselves. David said, "I don't want to take any more time than necessary. What do you know about my son's progress with his rebellion?"

"Absalom's words to the people have turned strongly critical. His strategy is working. The people are saying he is an angel sent from heaven to lead them; you know how fickle the crowds can be in celebrating their heroes."

"I know very well," the king said, recalling his youthful glory days.

"But now Absalom's ploy has been to describe you as a lost soul. The towns and villages are thronging to see him. I believe he will be able to field a large army before long. He has me recruiting officers now. My lord, you must do something soon to stop him."

The king replied simply, "I will move when God tells me to move."

With a sigh, Hesel replied, "It is time for me to confront Ahithophel. I have been directed to take a message to him tomorrow. I hope he retains his past regard for me. Maybe I can learn when they plan to make their move. Is that acceptable, sire?"

David hesitated. "Very well. But be careful. Leave yourself an escape route in case Ahithophel's feelings have changed." David looked intently at the valiant young man who now stood before him. "You will make a fine son-in-law, Hesel." The king clasped Hesel's shoulders and kissed his left cheek, then his right. "Now, be careful, my son. Go in peace."

When Hesel arrived in Hebron the next evening, Ahithophel was drawing water from the well in his backyard. Hesel walked over to lend a hand, taking the bucket of water and saying to his mentor, "Sir, you are looking well. Can we talk inside?"

The old man said, "It's good to see you again, Hesel. Certainly, my boy. Let's go inside, and I'll prepare a meal."

As the two men sat down to eat, Ahithophel said, "What's on your mind? You seem uneasy."

Hesel swallowed the bite of bread he had just taken and responded, "I have loved you, admired you, served you gladly, and have been thankful for all you've done. You have been like a father to me. So, I hope you can trust me and tell me what you and Absalom are up to."

His mentor looked surprised. "What brings you to ask that question?"

"Absalom has been traveling through the provinces along with meeting and patronizing the people in Jerusalem, and now he is expanding his campaign. I believed him when he said that he was obeying his father's directives. He says that David is preparing to retire and that he wants Absalom to get out to meet the people."

"Yes, so what's wrong with that?" Ahithophel munched on a piece of cheese.

"I thought it seemed fine at first, but now it's absurd. He has me recruiting officers to help develop an army."

Ahithophel's eyes brightened. "How is his campaign working? Are the people in Jerusalem responsive?"

"Yes, they are."

"Well then, what's the problem?"

Hesel sighed. This wasn't going the way he'd hoped. "What he is saying is not true. King David is not encouraging him to do this. The king has no intention of turning his crown over to Absalom. So, I want to know what the two of you are plotting."

Ahithophel sat back in his chair and got quiet. His brow furrowed as his eyes squinted at the young man. "Where did you get such an idea? How would you know what the king's intentions are?"

Hesel got up and stepped back from the table. "Princess Tamar overheard you and her brother talking in the farmhouse in Geshur. She told her father what she heard. Later, the two of us did have an audience with the king, and he revealed that he knew about your plan. But he is not trying to stop Prince Absalom."

"Hmm...the princess has an active imagination. I assume her father feels the same way about her report since he has done nothing to stop his son's activities."

"No! The king knows all about it. He said God knows and will take care of it. He doesn't seem overly concerned."

"Really? That makes no sense. The David I remember was edgy, suspicious, and quick to snap at anyone who offended him. The David you are describing seems passive and meek. Not the same man at all."

Silence swept over the room as both men thought about the words that had been spoken. Breaking the silence, Hesel said, "When you left King David's service, I heard there were harsh words spoken between the two of you. Can you tell me what happened?" Hesel stepped forward and leaned on the back of his chair.

Ahithophel squirmed, unable to find a comfortable position while searching his mind and soul for a way to respond to this young man for whom he cared deeply. He began to speak, slowly at first. "Hesel, you know I have always loved you like a son. I don't want you to get mixed up in this. The truth is that I left David's service because he threatened me with Goliath's sword and told me to get out of Jerusalem if I wanted to keep my head on my shoulders."

"But why? You and the king have been friends for decades. What could make him threaten you?"

"I confronted him with his crimes."

"What crimes?"

"He violated my granddaughter, then murdered her husband so he could cover the resulting pregnancy. He turned Bathsheba and my son against me. David destroyed my life. He betrayed me. He said if he ever saw me again, I would be a dead man. So, I have been exiled from all who were dear to me. Then I had to lose you too. Hesel, I have become a very bitter man. Your King David has taken everything I hold dear."

Hesel's face paled. "Sir, I didn't know you felt this way. But all that happened years ago…and now, how does your relationship with Absalom figure into this?"

"It happens that Absalom is an ambitious man. He burns with the desire to be king. He will do anything to take his father's throne. Anything!"

"Are you saying that you are helping Absalom to steal the king's crown? After all this time?"

"Ah, young man, taking a strong man's kingdom isn't something that can be done overnight. It demands much time and hard work. If anything goes wrong, it would be the end of our lives."

Hesel insisted, "But you're talking about a coup. This could start a civil war! A long and bloody civil war."

"Yes it could, and it probably will. That is why I am cautioning you. Now, keep this to yourself, but take measures to ensure your safety and the protection of those closest to you. We will soon declare Absalom the rightful king of Israel and Judah. The coronation will be held here in Hebron, where we will gather an army from all the people Absalom has won over."

Hesel drew a sharp breath. "Can you raise an army large enough to defeat those loyal to King David?"

"I'm sure we can. We will march from Hebron to take Jerusalem. If what you heard Tamar's father say about non-resistance is true, there will be little violence."

"What will happen to King David?"

"What always happens to leaders who lose. He will be no more. I hope to be his executioner after all the harm he has done to me and my family."

"But he is married to your granddaughter. They have several children who are your descendants. Your son is one of his top officers. How could you do that to your loved ones?"

"I hope to convince them to support me. I don't know if that is possible, but I hope so."

Hesel fidgeted as his mind tried to comprehend what he was being told. He spoke quietly with sorrow in his voice, "Sir, as much as I respect you and as thankful as I am to Absalom for hiring me, I cannot be a part of this revolt. Here you are, a broken man, seeking revenge out of anger, and here is Absalom rebelling against his own father, driven by greed and ambition. On the other hand, David has returned to his former self, a godly man who loves his family and has repented of his sins. He is God's chosen one, a good ruler of his kingdom. As far as I can see, you are on the wrong side of this conflict. I must withdraw further assistance to you and Absalom."

Ahithophel looked at his protégé with sorrowful eyes. "I'm not surprised, Hesel. You are a good man, raised to love and fear God. Here's what you should do. Remove yourself and your loved ones far from what may come. If King David doesn't surrender willingly or if we have miscalculated our strength, there could indeed be a bloody war. The losers will die. Bring your loved ones to Hebron. If it looks like Absalom's side is losing, take your people to Geshur where they will be safe." The old man paused, letting his mind review this advice. Then he added, "I will not tell Absalom about our meeting. I wish you Godspeed and peace."

Hesel bowed to his mentor. "Farewell, sir. I will pray for a way you can resolve this crisis without bloodshed. I wish you shalom." He turned and left the house, never to return.

Chapter 26:

King Absalom

W hen Absalom was ready to launch his revolution, he made one last visit in secret to Hebron to meet with his mentor and advisor. Absalom told his confidant that everything they had planned had been accomplished, and he was ready to launch the overthrow of King David's government.

The old sage asked, "How certain are you that the people outside Jerusalem will answer your call to arms?"

The prince replied, "I am convinced that most will. There are a few old-time warriors who are dubious about my claims. Those men may hold back. But I don't think they will persuade their townspeople to follow them. No, the people are ready to remove the king from his throne and put me on it."

"Excellent. You've done well," Ahithophel said. "I agree with you to the extent that the people I know here in Hebron and in Giloh are behind you. There is a small contingent of older folks who will be faithful to David, I'm sure. They will be the ones to run to David with the news of your coronation. That's all right. It's time for him to know."

"Of course," Absalom agreed.

"Now, here are the main reasons I suggested you launch from Hebron. First, while you may have convinced some people in Jerusalem to follow you, many of King David's faithful warriors are around him in Jerusalem. At the first word that an uprising is beginning, Joab would have a sizable force together immediately. Therefore, if you launch in Jerusalem, King David's people would crush you at once before you could amass enough troops."

"Yes, that makes good sense," Absalom said thoughtfully.

"However, if we launch from Hebron, we will have time to assemble a large enough army to march on Jerusalem with the odds in our favor. We won't move from Hebron until we're sure we have enough troops. When King David gets word of our advance, he would be a fool to stand and fight. In addition to that, we still have the king's word that he would not try to stop you. So, unless I'm wrong, Jerusalem will be ours without a struggle."

Ahithophel paused to be sure that this made sense to Prince Absalom, and then he continued. "The other reason for launching from Hebron is that it is here, in the first capital of King David, that we will crown you king—right here where your father was first crowned. When the trumpets blow throughout the kingdom, and the cry goes out that 'Absalom is king in Hebron,' we will place the crown on your head. We will hold your coronation here on the steps of the original palace of your father. What a glorious day that will be when we bow before King Absalom. Long live the king!"

Absalom's head was spinning as his mentor's words echoed in his mind. *King Absalom. What a beautiful sound. Finally, it is really going to happen. King! King Absalom!* He then said, "It will be you, Ahithophel, my advisor, my mentor, and my guide, who will officiate at the ceremony. We will need a senior priest to be there, and whoever else you decide. Thank you, my friend, for helping this come to pass."

The mentor said, "Wait. There is one more thing I advise you to do. When you are ready to leave Jerusalem for the last time, I'm sure you will want to ask for an audience with your father. You can ask his permission to go to Hebron, the place of your birth, to pay a vow you made to the Lord while you were in Geshur. I think he will give his approval. That will be your farewell to him."

"Yes, that should work," Absalom mused.

"Before you leave, make one last tour around the city, announcing that you are going to make a pilgrimage to Hebron to keep a vow to the Lord. But tell the people that any who want to accompany you are welcome. If I'm not mistaken, there will be many affluent citizens volunteering to make the trip with you, just to be a part of your adventure. However, you must not let them know that the real reason for your trip is to proclaim your ascendance to the throne."

Absalom listened closely to his mentor, but asked, "Why do I want to do that?"

Ahithophel answered, "First, you will remove many important decision makers from your father's influence. That will weaken his position in Jerusalem. Second, if you bring a sizable group, you will impress the people in Hebron with your importance in Jerusalem. That will further strengthen our position here. When you are crowned king, those who came with you will either join in your celebration, or if they make a fuss, they will be held as hostages in case we need them. I'm sure we will need every advantage. There's no telling what may happen when we blow the trumpets and announce that you are taking your father's throne."

Joab arranged one more visit to Maacah while Absalom was away. The queen reported that she had talked to her son about his activities. "I told him that you claimed he was campaigning without his father's approval. But he said, 'That's not true at all. Father told me personally that I could do what I wanted, and he wouldn't stop me.'"

Joab gave her a challenging look, but she continued.

"I asked if his father instructed him to do what he's doing. Absalom said, 'Not in so many words, but that wasn't necessary. We both know what my plans are.'"

Joab held up his hand to stop her and asked, "Did he tell you that he is trying to turn the citizens against his father so he can take the throne?"

Maacah stood up, agitated. "No, of course not. He wouldn't do that."

"That's exactly what he is doing, and somebody has to stop him," Joab said sternly.

"Then why don't you?" she asked in curiosity.

"I told you. Because David won't allow me to touch him." Joab's tone was frustrated, and he ran a hand through his hair.

Maacah, relieved for her son, sat down again. "Then I guess you'd better let him be."

"Are you saying you approve of your son starting a civil war that could leave either him or his father dead? Or all of you and many others?"

Looking around to be sure no servants were listening near the open doorway, Maacah said, "Oh, Joab, don't be ridiculous."

Joab paced back and forth. Then he stopped and stared at the floor. Finally, he said, "This will be my last visit to this home. We may be on opposite sides of what could be a bloody war."

"Oh, Joab, surely it won't come to that. Absalom wouldn't hurt his father or any of us."

Joab frowned at her. "You'd better decide whose side you are on because the one who loses will risk everything, including his or her life. If you want to go back to King David at the palace, I will help you. But if you stay with Absalom, you will share his fate."

With that, Joab wheeled abruptly and walked out the door.

After Absalom and Ahithophel finalized the details of how the coronation and the military launch would be executed, Absalom returned to Jerusalem and visited his father one last time. In the prince's mind, it was a ceremonial farewell wherein he would kneel before his father, the king, for the last time.

When King David received him, Absalom fell to his knees and said, without looking up at his father's face, "Father, please allow me to go and pay a vow in Hebron as I promised the Lord I would do while I was still in Geshur. I told the Lord then that if he would allow me to return to Jerusalem, then I would serve Him in Hebron."

Impressed by his son's newfound piety, King David replied simply, "Go in peace." Absalom wondered, *Does my father know what I intend to do? Perhaps that is why he told me to 'go in peace.'*

After Absalom left the palace, he called his team of leaders together, including Hesel (Ahithophel had kept his promise to Hesel that he would not tell Absalom about their talk). After giving his men an inspirational speech, Absalom instructed them on their sworn duties. Through Hesel's organization, each of them had been assigned villages, towns, and cities where they were to contact the local representatives who had been recruited. "At midday on the first day of the week (the day after the next Sabbath), a trumpet is to be blown and the announcement made that "Absalom is king in Hebron." That will be the signal for each village, town, and city to gather their fighting men and march to Hebron."

Absalom packed up his family, including Tamar. However, Maacah resisted. Joab's words had troubled her. Maacah said to her son, "Maybe I'd better stay here. I could move back into the palace."

Absalom said, "Mother, please come with me. I want you there with me for my coronation. If you stay with my father, I can't be responsible for what might happen. I think you will be safer in Hebron."

Maacah responded, "So it is true. You are planning to take your father's throne. But why? Why do you have to do this?"

Absalom's eyes blazed fiercely. "Because it is my destiny. I know this is God's will for me. Everything has fallen together perfectly. Father is passive about it, and I hope I can get him to see that he will be better off if he surrenders the throne to me without a fight. But I can't guarantee he will. There is risk, so I would rather have you with me. When my army marches on Jerusalem, it could become dangerous. Please, come with me now."

Maacah was full of conflicting emotions. She would be leaving her life in Jerusalem and the king, but she was committed to her son and daughter and also the grandchildren she had come to love dearly. It was finally the grandchildren that convinced her to go with Absalom. She said to him, "I will come with you. I pray there will not be total war. Will you promise me that?"

"No, I can't promise, but I will try to prevent it. You and Tamar will be safe with my wife and children. Come, we need to go now."

Along with his family, Absalom led a procession of over 200 people from Jerusalem to Hebron. Many of those accompanying Absalom did not realize they were participating in a coup. They were simply attaching themselves to Absalom's rising star as a beloved regional leader.

Upon arriving in Hebron, Absalom immediately brought Ahithophel forward to address the large crowd that had been assembled by local conspirators. Ahithophel announced to the crowd that in a few days, there would be a momentous celebration and that they would participate in making history. This was the first time Absalom and Ahithophel appeared together in public.

The next Sabbath was given over to prayers for Prince Absalom. Earlier in the week, orchestras and choirs were assembled and rehearsed in preparation for the coronation. Absalom labored over the coronation message he would deliver to the gathered masses.

Ahithophel was also preparing a speech and pouring into it all the vitriol that had consumed him since he left David's service almost eleven years before. He had attempted at times to rid himself of the bitterness he harbored, but any attempts to seek out David's favor had been soundly rebuffed; that made his hatred even more intense. His former life of honor and respect was destroyed. He had been transformed from a wise, compassionate grandfather to an angry and bitter old man. His effort to displace David and destroy his life consumed the old man day and night. He prayed that his speech on Monday would convince the crowd to show no mercy to the aging king.

The coronation day arrived with a flurry of color and sound as the crowds began arriving at the town center for the celebration. Absalom's elite core of fighting men paraded through the streets of Hebron, then took up their position before the royal palace. Several dignitaries took their places on the front porch as trumpets blew. The crowd began to shout as Absalom appeared, accompanied by David's former advisor, Ahithophel. Most people in the crowd only knew Ahithophel as a respected figure—King David's personal counselor, thus affirming Absalom's credibility.

The old advisor stood before the crowd and delivered a speech that convinced even the most skeptical citizens that it was time for King David to step down. Absalom would lead them to glory that the former ruler could only dream of.

The head priest, assisted by Ahithophel, placed the crown on Absalom's head and voiced a loud prayer, asking the Lord

God's blessing on the new young monarch. The crowd roared approval as Absalom faced the multitude, drinking in the honor he had dreamed of so long.

Finally, he motioned for the crowd to quiet down. When they were settled, he delivered a speech building on his advisor's theme. It was time for change. It was time for their new king to rule as God would. It was time for King Absalom to wear the crown and sit in the seat of David.

The crowd shouted in unison, "Long live the king! Long live King Absalom!"

Over the next two weeks, large contingents of fighting men began to arrive in Hebron. Absalom's senior officers began immediately to organize his army. His officers had been preparing for this time leading up to the launch. As the contingents arrived, they were oriented and placed in the appropriate positions for marching and attacking. The majority had fought with King David and Joab previously and therefore fell into place without much effort. Within two weeks, Absalom's army was ready to march.

As Hesel witnessed the coronation and military buildup in Hebron, he said to Tamar and Maacah, "I don't like this. Now I understand why Absalom sought Ahithophel's advice. Their position looks formidable from a strategic military point of view. Men continue to arrive, and it looks like they are going to have a sizable army. Yet, King David is not building up a counter force to defend Jerusalem. It looks like Absalom and

Ahithophel will be able to defeat the king and take the throne. Absalom has already been crowned king."

Maacah stared out the window and said in agitation, "I cannot understand why the king has allowed this to happen."

Tamar stood by the door and said, "It's not fair for Absalom to deceive the people about our father. Yes, the king made mistakes, but he repented, and from what Nathan told me, God forgave him and restored him years ago. Where is God in this uprising?"

Hesel responded confidently, "I think God is watching, and He may turn the tables on Absalom before it's over. I would be surprised if Absalom is king by this time next year. God will not let evil defeat good. Absalom is motivated by ego and greed. Sadly, Ahithophel is driven by hatred and vengeance. He has allowed a root of bitterness to consume him.

"King David is God's chosen ruler, a man after God's heart. If God turns this around, everyone who has supported Absalom is going to be in trouble. That includes the people here in Hebron. That includes us."

Maacah said, "I don't think King David would allow his daughter and grandchildren to be harmed. I don't think he would allow me, one of his first wives and queens, to be harmed."

"He may not be able to control what happens when Joab's army marches on Hebron. Here's what I think we should do. I will take you two and Absalom's wife and children to Geshur to wait out the war. We can monitor developments from there. When it's over, we can see about coming home if we want to at that point. What do you think?"

Tamar said, "Geshur is safe. Yes, let's seek refuge there."

Maacah nodded. "I would feel protected in Geshur, with my father watching over us."

Hesel glanced at both of them and said, "I'll make arrangements so we can leave right after Absalom's army departs."

The coronation of Absalom and the gathering army in and around Hebron was bound to cause excitement among the local populace. Many had connections in Jerusalem. When word of Absalom being declared king and the army gathering in Hebron reached King David, he called in Joab and Hushai, as well as the elders who were available.

Joab reported, "I cannot count on most of my officers who live in the outlying areas. I've heard reports that Absalom has turned the populace against you, and their fighting men have joined Absalom in Hebron. But I think I can put a sizable force together to defend Jerusalem and the palace."

King David looked sad and tired. Raising his hand, he said, "We are not going to fight. My son Absalom is leading them. This is what God told me would come to pass. We are experiencing the judgment of God due to my failures. I was not surprised when word came that Absalom was to be crowned in Hebron and he was assembling his army."

Joab started to speak but caught himself to let the king finish.

"However, we will not wait to be consumed by Absalom. We will evacuate Jerusalem immediately."

Several people spoke at once, but the question on everyone's lips was, "Go where? Absalom has turned the whole country against you while you've watched and done nothing."

King David spoke quietly, "No, that's not entirely true. We have received no reports that Absalom has ventured across the Jordan. That's where we must go. We will take the Jericho road. Everyone must begin preparing our people and provisions. Joab, what is your best estimate of when Absalom will reach Jerusalem?"

Joab replied thoughtfully, "They will need a week or so to get organized, then a few more days to move a large force here. But we will need several days' head start before they arrive. I would say, to be safe, we should depart within two days. The road down to the Jordan River is narrow and treacherous. The sooner we leave, the better our chances of survival."

As everyone left to get ready, Joab was talking with David when Hushai invited himself into their conversation. Joab paused, and with raised eyebrows, looked at the man, saying, "What is it, Hushai?"

The new advisor responded, "I have something to share with King David, but you may be interested as well, General." Then he said to David, "Your Majesty would want to know what I heard this afternoon."

David looked intently at him and said, "Go on."

Hushai said, "I am sorry to tell you this, but it seems that Ahithophel is with Absalom. Apparently, he has been working with him for some time."

The king replied, "I have known that Ahithophel is helping my son. I could see his thinking in the things my son is doing. Tamar told me she overheard them plotting in Geshur. The man was angry when he left me, with good reason. I told him to get out and stay out of the city. He hates me, and I don't blame him."

Joab's ears perked up at the mention of Ahithophel being with Absalom and helping with the rebellion.

Hushai continued, "But, sire, I fear the advice of Ahithophel. He could lead Absalom to our vulnerabilities. So far, he has been successful. If he has indeed been guiding your son, he has led well; Absalom has put us in a precarious position."

At this point, Joab interjected, "I can speak to Hushai's concern, sire. Ahithophel was with Absalom when I went to Geshur to fetch your son home. I didn't mention it when we returned to Jerusalem because they convinced me that Ahithophel was just helping a friend. They said Ahithophel was advising the prince about how to convince you to let the boy come home. I see now that the two of them tricked me into helping with their plot. Or there may have been three of them."

King David replied, "Who's the third?"

Joab said, "Maacah. I let her deceive me into thinking I was helping you."

"Ah, don't be too hard on yourself, Joab. I understand her wanting to protect her son and his claim as my successor. So that widow from Tekoa was Ahithophel's idea, wasn't it? That explains much."

Joab exclaimed, "But, sire, I blame myself for allowing this rebellion to take root. It's been three or four years since I saw them together in Geshur. I should have dispatched both of them on the spot."

David responded, "No, Joab. I have forbidden you to oppose Absalom because I'm sure the Lord God is bringing this rebellion against me. We will see what God's will is. Don't touch Absalom. That is my command. When we reach Gilead, we should find people there receptive and helpful to their king."

Joab grunted, then turned on his heel and stormed out of the room.

David watched Joab leave, then continued his conversation with Hushai, saying, "Hushai, please pray with me." King David raised his hands to heaven and prayed, "Oh Lord God, we are in a difficult situation. We know that Ahithophel is with Absalom, advising him how to attack and destroy us—not only me but my family and all of these other innocent ones who are faithful to your servant. Lord God, please confuse the advice of Ahithophel. Make his counsel foolishness to Absalom."

David completed his prayer silently while Hushai remained quiet, waiting to resume their conversation. Then David turned to his counselor and said, "Hushai, you may not like what I am about to say, but I think God may have already answered my prayer. You could be the key to defeating the advice of Ahithophel."

The sage advisor looked puzzled but listened carefully.

"I want you to stay behind and offer your support to Absalom. Say this: 'I will be your servant, oh King, as I have been your father's servant in times past.' If he accepts you into his inner council, then you will be in a position to thwart the counsel of Ahithophel."

Hushai responded, "Anything you desire is my command, King David. I was thinking it would be helpful if we could find a way to get word to you of Absalom's plans. Do you know how we could do that?"

Pausing momentarily, David said, "Yes. The priests will stay behind when we leave. They are supposedly beholden only to God, not to any man. However, Zadok and Abiathar have been with me for decades, and I'm sure they will help me if they can. Each of them also has a son who can help: Ahimaaz and Jonathan. Pass any messages to those two priests, and they will tell their sons to bring your words to me. May God be with you, my friend. I know you won't let me down."

A flurry of activity ensued over the next two days to move the king's household and court. Just counting his family and their attendants, they numbered over two hundred people, many of them women and children. Bathsheba alone, with her little ones and their helpers, constituted thirty people. King David was determined to save as many as possible.

The court of King David rendered dozens of souls to the exiled group. Others in Jerusalem who feared for their lives wanted to join them. The records show that all his servants passed by him, all the Cherethites, Pelethites, and Gittites, six hundred men who had come with him from Gath. Many remained loyal to God's anointed ruler.

Over 1,000 people, plus Joab's men, pledged to make the journey with the king. Their escape would be on foot, women and children included. There would be donkeys weighed down with personal effects, plus mule and ox-drawn wagons or carts for supplies and necessities. Anyone too weak to travel would remain behind.

Chapter 27:

David's Flight

Pressing responsibilities weighed heavily on David as he watched the busy activities of his royal court. He summoned the seer Nathan, pacing nervously as he awaited the holy man's arrival. When Nathan was ushered into his reception chamber, the king said, "Nathan, please come with me to seek the Lord's guidance on some pressing issues that are on my heart."

The two men walked out of the palace and across the way to the tabernacle, which housed the ark of the covenant. As they entered the holy place, both men fell to their knees before the Shekinah Glory of the ark, the place where God dwelt on earth.

Nathan prayed first:

> *Oh, Holy Lord God, Creator of the heavens and the earth, hear Your humble servants as we dare to come into Your presence. Please favor us as we seek Thy guidance in these perilous times. Your servant, our king, needs to know Your will concerning the heavy issues that are on his mind. Hear our prayers, oh God.*

David knelt quietly for a few moments as he focused his mind on the Holy Presence. Then he prayed in a humble, hushed voice:

Oh, Holy God, I love You, my Lord, my Savior. How great Thou art. We thank You, Oh God, for Your tender mercies and Your covenant promises that You have spoken to our fathers. Oh Lord, these people You put in my care are following my directions, trusting me to lead them to safety. But Holy God, I am a blind man, trying to find my way in a time of great danger. Oh Lord, I love to come here and feel your closeness in your tabernacle. But now I must take these, your servants, on a flight over treacherous trails to escape the danger caused by my failures and disobedience to You.

Lord, my first supplication is for You to help me know if I should take this ark of the covenant with us, or should we leave your ark here in this tabernacle? We know You are not restricted to any one place, but we feel your presence so much more when we are in your holy house. Should I leave Your ark here or take it with us?"

Silence filled the holy place as the two men waited on their knees.

Then Nathan prayed:

Lord, I feel You are saying that Your ark belongs to the people, not to their king alone. Many of your people will be traveling with us, but the entire nation comes to this holy place to offer sacrifices. So, the ark should remain here, but your presence will be with us, wherever we go. Thank You, Lord, for giving us that assurance.

Then David prayed:

Oh Lord God, I can't forget the third judgment you spoke to me through your servant. You said my wives would be violated in public by someone close to me. I feel I must protect those women who have been part of my rule, my kingdom, and my life for so long. But Lord, I have also had these concubines whom You have convicted me about repeatedly. I realize they are forbidden fruit. They have been a stronghold of the enemy in my soul and spirit. Therefore, I have sworn that I will set them aside. I cannot provide for them in exile, but I trust that if I leave them behind, Your will shall prevail here in Jerusalem and wherever we must flee.

Silence again filled the holy chamber. David began to feel peace settle into his soul and spirit, building in intensity and in such power that he began to weep. He fell on his face before the Lord with a mighty emotional outpouring that drained him of energy and left him prone on the ground. His body was racked with sobs he was powerless to control. As they subsided at last, he felt Nathan's hand on his shoulder and heard him say, "I believe we have our answer."

David choked out a few words. "I didn't expect that."

"Did you feel approval or God's displeasure?" Nathan asked.

"It feels like a blessing of healing. I feel like God's Holy Spirit has filled me to overflowing. I will do all I can to save our people, and God will do the rest."

Later, when the priests sought to bring the ark, David said to them, "Return the ark to the tabernacle. God has spoken." King David then announced to his elders, "I have made the decision that my concubines will remain behind to take care of the palace. Absalom should not have a reason to harm them since they are no threat to his rebellion."

Their escape route would be over the Mount of Olives, then eastward down the steep, rugged trail through the wilderness to the Jordan Valley over 3,000 feet below. David was familiar with the trail from his years of running from King Saul in the wilderness.

He advised his leaders, "The trail is little more than a wide footpath. It skirts the edges of cliffs and ravines that at times are hundreds of feet deep. This is roughly a twenty-mile dangerous journey, especially with women and children. However, armies have used the narrow road for centuries, so it is well enough traveled to ensure a reasonably safe route. When we reach the Jordan River, I will have to make a decision about our ultimate destination. To be sure of survival, we need to cross the Jordan by the time Absalom's army reaches Jerusalem."

Joab told David, "I am dispatching a small group of soldiers in advance to ensure the way is clear and alert the elders of Jericho that a large group of civilians will be arriving soon with the king. We will need all the ferries and river men available to help with the crossing."

Before the caravan left Jerusalem, Joab assembled over two hundred of his loyal men to guard the caravan. He left several trusted men behind to gather intelligence and distract Absalom's army however they could without putting themselves at risk.

Joab called Eliam, the son of Ahithophel, and directed him, saying, "I'm leaving you in charge of the soldiers who remain behind."

Eliam wanted to protest since his daughter and the grandchildren would be with David in the caravan. However, being a loyal soldier, he held his tongue.

Joab instructed the soldiers with Eliam to disguise themselves as villagers and observe Absalom's movements. "Be alert and ready to spread the word for a call to arms as soon as King David's royal party establishes temporary headquarters."

Then Joab looked right at Eliam and said, "And hear this, if any of you happen to have the opportunity to approach either Absalom or Ahithophel, I will give a hundred pieces of silver to anyone who cuts either of them down."

Eliam uttered a startled response. "Why, Ahithophel? What has my father to do with this rebellion?"

Joab replied, "I have just been advised that Ahithophel has been plotting this rebellion with Absalom for years. More than that, they used me deceitfully to convince the king to let his son come home from Geshur. I am telling you now, I will not rest until both of them are in the ground. This uprising will be defeated, and the sooner we cut off its heads, the sooner it will end."

Eliam sat in stunned silence, his head spinning.

Finally, the caravan was ready to leave Jerusalem. It stretched over half a mile as David led them down into the Kidron Valley, then stood by the road to watch them pass up the Mount of Olives. David and Joab could see right away that it was going to be slow going, even while the path was easy. As the caravan turned east and began the descent, it became obvious to David that with the size and makeup of his caravan, they would have to proceed too slowly. When they reached the beginning of the narrow trail down the mountain, there was only room for six or eight people abreast much of the time. It would take much too long to reach the river.

In some places, the steepness of the rough trail required that the wagons and carts be held back with ropes held by several men to prevent the wagons from barreling out of control and over the edge into the yawning canyons. David prayed constantly and encouraged those around him to pray for God's protection. It would take a miracle for them to reach the river alive.

David knew that with Ahithophel's experience and wisdom, he would be advising Absalom to pursue, overtake them, and slaughter the entire party. He wondered if having Ahithophel's granddaughter and her children in the caravan would cause him to hesitate. David couldn't count on that, and he continued pleading with God:

> *"Please, oh God, make the advice of Ahithophel foolishness to my son. Please give Hushai words to confuse Absalom and turn him away from pursuing us. Keep us safe in the shelter of your wings, Oh God."*

David continued in unspoken prayer as the caravan made its laborious way down the treacherous path to the Jordan River.

Ahithophel rode beside his young monarch as they led their army toward Jerusalem. Absalom's army numbered in the thousands, easily large enough to subdue any force that David and Joab could muster. Neither man was certain what kind of resistance they would meet when they arrived in Jerusalem, but they were prepared for whatever, or whoever, came out to meet them.

Ahithophel couldn't help but think about his son and his granddaughter. It was hard enough to face battling his son, Eliam. He wondered if he could strike down King David and make Bathsheba a widow again while she stood by and watched. But he knew he could.

As the advance guard approached Jerusalem, scouts were sent ahead to assess the situation. They reported back to Absalom's general, Amasa, saying, "There is no resistance. Jerusalem is a ghost town. David and his army have fled." Amasa hurried to inform Absalom about the findings of the scouts: "Jerusalem is ours! David has fled."

As Absalom and Ahithophel entered the royal palace, they were accompanied by General Amasa and a group of elders. They found that a few of David's people had stayed behind. Zadok, the head priest, welcomed them graciously. Of course, both men knew the priests well, having lived and worked in the palace for many years. They accepted their welcome gladly.

Absalom slyly asked the priest, "And is my father in his chambers today? Will he welcome his son home?"

Zadok went along with the jest and replied, "I'm so sorry, Your Majesty. The king...I'm sorry, your father is not in his residence today. In fact, I don't know where his residence is at the moment." The hint of a smile indicated he was going along with Absalom's humor.

Ahithophel was not amused. He was no longer the kind grandfather as he asked sternly.

"Who is in residence then? Is his family in the palace?"

Zadok quickly adopted a serious expression and answered, "Only the concubines of his harem. They remained to mind the palace and host any visitors. Everyone else has been evacuated."

Ahithophel pressed the priest further: "When did they leave? How long ago? Which way did they go?"

Zadok said, "A few days ago."

Ahithophel thundered, "I want to know exactly when they left, to the hour."

It had been three days since they left, but Zadok tried to equivocate, giving David's refugees more time to make it to the river. He said, "It must have been five days ago, to this very hour, when the last of them left. I don't know where David was leading them."

Ahithophel was sure it couldn't have been that long ago since they left, considering the number of days since the coronation. It would have taken David a few days to prepare such a large caravan.

General Amasa asked, "How many fighting men did Joab have to protect the caravan?"

Zadok again tried to mislead Absalom and his men, "I'm not sure, my lord. There were too many to count."

Ahithophel raged back at the priest, "Stop trying to confuse us. Answer the question. How many soldiers?"

Zadok, struck by fear, managed to utter, "Maybe a few thousand men. There must have been at least three to five thousand men. But I truly don't know for sure."

Ahithophel spoke to Absalom and Amasa, "I think he's lying. They couldn't have raised that many men on short notice. I don't see how they could have been gone that long. They must have taken the Jericho road to the Jordan. Their progress will be slow with the wives and children. We have an excellent opportunity to overtake them if we leave immediately."

Absalom responded, "Not so fast. We've only just arrived. I want to see who is still here and give the men a rest. Let's see what luxuries my father may have left behind in his hasty departure."

The old sage warned, "The longer we wait, the worse our chances of catching them before they cross the Jordan."

Absalom replied, "All in good time."

While Zadok talked to the two leaders of the occupation, Abiathar, the other priest, and Hushai, David's counselor, walked in and took their place behind Zadok. When Absalom spotted Hushai, he interrupted his discussion with Abiathar and addressed the counselor, "Hushai, why are you here? Aren't you my father's advisor?"

Hushai came forward and bowed before Absalom, saying, "Oh, King, I serve the people of Israel, and now you are the leader of my people. My place is now with you, my lord."

Ahithophel witnessed the exchange with suspicion. He tried to get Absalom's attention, but he was waved aside, rather rudely, he thought.

Absalom said to no one in particular, "Well. This is a good stroke of luck. Let's see if there is anyone who can cook some food. I'm hungry."

Hushai took command of the concubines and set them to work preparing a meal for their new king. Although unused to domestic chores, several had learned food preparation as children or from the servants, and now they had no choice as new duties were demanded of them.

Ahithophel was visibly upset about the delay. He was beginning to resent the devil-may-care attitude of his new king, and he didn't try to hide his feelings. That didn't escape Absalom's notice, but he tried to ignore it.

An hour or so later as the men finished eating, Absalom faced Ahithophel and said,

"What is your problem, my friend? Try to relax."

Ahithophel responded from his seat near the wall, "I'm trying to decide what my role is now that you have attained your father's throne. You have rebuffed my opinions while you seem enamored with this man Hushai, whom I do not trust."

"Oh, nonsense, Ahithophel. You are my counselor and mentor. I count on your advice at every turn."

Ahithophel growled, "You haven't followed my advice about pursuing your father. I consider that our highest priority."

Absalom considered what his old sage had said and thought, *The old man has been a big help, but now that I've come this far, I'm not sure he is important anymore. He's getting too pushy; he thinks he's in charge here. Now I have Hushai, who is also respected as an advisor. My father trusted him. I think I can as well.*

As Absalom continued to consider what his advisor was recommending, he thought, *I'm not sure I want to chase down my father and his followers. If we did, my soldiers would wipe out every man, woman, and child. That would include not only my father but my brothers and sisters, as well as all the friends I've grown up with. Do I want to do that? Would I be able to control the carnage to spare my family members?*

He spoke to Ahithophel and said, "Old friend, you know I depend on you to guide everything I do. I'm not ready to hunt down my father's caravan right now. I need to think about that carefully. But come, here we are in the royal palace in Jerusalem. So, what do we do next? What should I do to establish my control and authority?"

Ahithophel sat up and leaned forward as the shadows cast by the warming fire leapt around him. Becoming quiet, he asked in a husky voice, "Are you serious about severing all ties to your father, with no hope of being reconciled to him?"

Noting the gravity in his advisor's voice, Absalom also became serious. "Yes, Ahithophel, I am prepared to do that." He thought, *Anything would be better than wiping out my entire family.*

Very well then," said the sage. "You must let the people see you claim your father's concubines."

"What?" said Absalom, astonished. "Why?"

"That act will show everyone remaining in Jerusalem and in all the kingdom that you have permanently destroyed the bond between you and your father—between his rule and yours. Violating his concubines is, in effect, violating his family sanctity and wounding David as your father and ruler."

"But concubines don't hold the same position as the official royal wives," Absalom started to argue.

Ahithophel cut him off. "They are legitimate members of his household, and their sons are heirs to the crown. If you violate them, it is as if you violated David himself."

Absalom stared at his mentor.

Ahithophel continued, "I suggest you erect a tent on the roof of the palace. As the crowds assemble to see what is going on, you will go to the concubines in view of the city. I can think of no other way to prove that you have made yourself odious to your father. When you violate David's wives, you violate him personally. Ten times emphasizes the point. Can you do that?"

Absalom liked the idea of flouting his virility, although he thought the public spectacle was a bit extreme. He stated, "Yes, I will do this on the roof of the palace. That is where my father conceived of his sin of adultery with Bathsheba. It is fitting."

"Yes, that is as it should be," Ahithophel agreed.

Absalom explained, "We will do it in the morning. Then we shall sit down with the advisors, the elders, and our military leaders and decide what to do about David."

It did not escape Ahithophel's notice that Absalom lumped him with Hushai as his advisors. Ahithophel's resentment of Absalom was growing. *Where is the man's loyalty to the person who brought him to where he is now? He is a spoiled youth.*

The next morning, several servants began erecting a large tent on the palace roof. The news quickly spread, and the townspeople began to gather at the palace gates to see what was happening. Behind them stood many from Absalom's amassed army, Israelites drawn from every tribe. Ahithophel stood on the steps to watch the crowd's reaction. He didn't recognize his disguised son with his men in the crowd.

"Your former ruler, King David, has fled; long live King Absalom."

Many in the crowd roared, "David is dead; long live King Absalom."

The throngs of warriors shouted as one, "David is dead. Long live King Absalom."

The servants on the rooftop began escorting the concubines into a row across the palace roof. They weren't sure what to expect. Several of the women looked down at the crowd, some drawing back in fear or embarrassment. The women were all beautiful, although they differed in age and nationality.

After a few moments, Absalom appeared on the roof and walked around the parapet as though admiring the views of the city. Finally he moved toward the concubine at the far end of the line, took her hand, and led her into the tent. The other women were mercifully guided into a group behind the tent, obscuring them from the crowd by the servants to await Absalom's visits.

Absalom spent the next few hours with the concubines, bringing them in full view of the crowd, into the tent one at a time. The women remained in the tent after he left them. Most of the citizens in the crowd remained still, unsure of what to think. A few men shouted approval with each glimpse of Absalom.

The people who were secretly faithful to King David were disgusted by the spectacle, as were most women in the crowd. Mothers with children hurried home when they realized what was happening. It was a day that would live in disgrace, a low point in the history of Israel.

Chapter 28:

The Kingdom Restored

After his rooftop performance, later that day, Absalom met with his advisors, elders, and military leaders to discuss their next step. Ahithophel repeated his concern that David's caravan would soon be out of reach if they didn't move immediately. His proposal was met with silence until Absalom spoke up, "All right, Ahithophel, now let's hear what Hushai has to say."

Hushai bowed slightly to Absalom and said, "I'm afraid our esteemed Ahithophel is allowing his personal feelings toward David to cloud his judgment. I don't agree with him. David is well protected with some of the fiercest warriors in Israel. David himself is a mighty warrior and as wise as a serpent. I foresee him setting an ambush on the narrow road and defeating us if we attack him now. Word will spread across the nation that there has been a slaughter among the people who follow Absalom."

Absalom leaned back, listening carefully.

Hushai continued, "I think we should wait and call in more troops, especially from the further reaches of our territory—from Dan to Beersheba, as the sand of the sea is in abundance. Then, Your Majesty, you should lead them into battle. We will find David wherever he goes, and we will fall on him as the dew falls on the ground; of him and all who follow him, not even one will be left."

"No! No!" shouted Ahithophel, standing abruptly. "We must hit him now while he is vulnerable. Please—let me choose a regiment of men, and I will pursue David. We will come upon him while he is weary and exhausted and terrify him so that everyone in that group will flee. Then I will strike down your father with my own hand! Then all of Israel shall be at peace." *And*, Ahithophel thought, *I will finally be at peace.*

As silence filled the room, Absalom leaned forward and scanned the faces around the table. "Does anyone have any thoughts?"

Continued silence.

"No? Then I will speak. I think Husahi's counsel is better than Ahithophel's. Does anyone disagree?"

A few heads nodded agreement.

Absalom stood up. "So it is agreed. The counsel of Hushai the Archite is better than the counsel of Ahithophel."

The Lord saw fit to answer the prayer of David, His anointed ruler of His chosen people.

When Ahithophel saw that his counsel was not followed, he stared at Absalom, who kept his eyes down, refusing to meet the old sage's gaze. By that act, Absalom effectively discharged Ahithophel from his service.

Ahithophel understood; he turned and strode out of the room, head held high. Crossing the threshold with the door closing behind him, his proud, erect stature and his entire posture seemed to melt as his shoulders sagged, and with head down, he headed to his belongings. Gathering his things, he loaded them on a donkey and began trudging the dusty road to his home in Giloh.

As Ahithophel passed through the city gate of Jerusalem, a hooded man stepped out of the shadows and blocked his way. The old sage had his head down and didn't see the man until his donkey stopped. He looked up and studied the man but couldn't make out his features. Then the stranger pulled back his hood and said, "Hello, Father."

Ahithophel gasped. "Eliam! Oh, my son. I never expected to see you again. What are you doing here?"

Eliam said, "Let's go sit under that tree yonder where we can talk."

The two men sat on the ground in the shade of the voluminous branches, and Eliam began to speak. "Father, I know that you have been working with Absalom and advised him in all that he has done. I didn't want to believe that, but then I saw you at the palace helping to orchestrate Absalom's defilement of King David's concubines. Everything began to make sense. I know our last words together years ago were about your accusations against David, but I never would have believed you would go so far as to lead a civil war against him. How could you do that when Betta and I are part of his family?"

Ahithophel spoke slowly, "I am wondering that myself after the events of today."

He paused several seconds and decided not to talk about what had just happened. He went on, "I always worried about the two of you and the children, fearing for your safety. But my anger toward David took control, and all I could think of was getting even with him for destroying my life. When Absalom asked me to help him take the throne, I thought surely God was providing a way for me to punish David for the terrible things he did to our family."

Eliam stared at his father, trying to comprehend the older man's version of events.

The sage went on, "I tried to talk to King David about what he had done before all this business with Absalom began. I told him that I knew exactly what he had done to Betta and Uri, but he ordered me out of his home and threatened to kill me if he ever saw my face again. So, he destroyed my life also. All I had worked for over decades, all my dedication to him—everything was gone. I went into exile a broken man. That was when Absalom came to me in my despair and asked for help. It seemed like God was offering me hope. What else could I do?"

Eliam spoke. "Father, I can see how you came to join Absalom, but at some point, you must have surely understood what was happening. It has been over ten years since you were exiled. How could you hold onto your anger so long? You saw how Betta settled into her new life with the king. Their babies are my grandchildren, and I love them dearly. How could you not see you were arranging our destruction by joining Absalom?"

Ahithophel sat slump-shouldered with his head down, ashamed for the part he had played in Absalom's revolt. Then he looked up and said, "I felt both you and Betta had rejected me in favor of King David. Betta said she didn't want to see me again—ever. Do you know how much that hurt me? Worse than anything David had done. I blamed him, and I still do. Losing the two of you has kept my pain alive all this time, fueling my hatred of that man. I knew in my soul that I should let go of my resentment, but when I got involved with Absalom, I couldn't stop."

Eliam felt sympathy rise up for this father, but he could hardly believe he had helped the prince to rebel against the king.

"My son, I wanted to see you and Betta, but David banned me from Jerusalem under penalty of death. There was no way I could see you while you were living in the palace."

Eliam said, "Father, I'm sure David would have welcomed you back if you had asked."

"No, he wouldn't. He made that clear when he threatened to take off my head if he saw me again."

"But that was before he changed. After Nathan confronted him, the king recognized his wrongdoings. He became compassionate and merciful like he was in the old days. If you had sent word that you wanted to see your family and your great-grandchildren, I believe that King David would have welcomed you back with open arms."

"No. Absalom reported several times that his father wanted my head. He told me again recently that King David would not allow my name to be spoken in his presence. I was surprised his father held onto his hatred of me for so long."

Eliam continued, "But Betta told me that David has spoken of you kindly and even with affection almost since the day you left. He told her he was sorry that he had sent you away. He said you were right to confront him, and he was wrong."

Ahithophel was speechless and stared at Eliam to see if he had exaggerated. Seeing his son's sincere face, the old man sat silent. Then he muttered with contempt in his voice,

"Absalom...Oh, I see it now. Absalom was lying all along. He kept warning me that David still hated me. He wanted to keep David and me apart. If we had reconciled, he wouldn't have been able to keep me in his camp. If I had only known. Do you know if it was true that King David told his people to make sure I couldn't come to their wedding?"

Shaking his head no, Eliam said, "When I was called home for their wedding, David told me he was saddened that you didn't respond to his invitation, and that all was forgiven. He said that you sent a message back that you would never countenance his wedding to Betta. He said that your message indicated you would never forgive him, and if he married Betta, you would kill him outright if the opportunity arose."

The old man's countenance drooped even more. He sighed, "I see it all now. Absalom was playing me the whole time. And I thought I was playing him. Now we are both getting what we deserve. I have nothing to live for, and he will surely be defeated by King David's troops when he follows the advice given by Hushai."

After a moment of reflection, he asked his son, "Do you know what happened when Nathan confronted him?"

Eliam said, "Only what Betta has told me. She said the message from God was that even though God had blessed him so much, time and time again, David despised the Word of the Lord by doing evil in His sight. Then he went through all of David's evil acts and revealed God's judgments against him."

"So, divine justice prevailed," Ahithophel mused.

"David told Betta that God had disciplined him severely, but he deserved it. He was a broken and contrite man. He wrote in a psalm afterward, 'A broken and contrite heart, oh God, you will not despise.' Father, I'm sure that King David will welcome you back. I will escort you to him right now."

Ahithophel shook his head and said softly, "No, my son. I can never return to King David. It's not because I've conspired with Absalom, but because of what I advised Absalom to do with David's concubines. That destroyed any chance of reconciliation. I see now that was a tragic mistake, but it is done."

Reaching over to clasp his father's shoulder, Eliam said, "Joab has put a price on your head. If he finds out that I had a chance to slay you but didn't, he will have my head. You must go on home. If we are able to put down this rebellion, Joab will search for you. Maybe you could go to Geshur, but even there, Joab would look for you. Your options are limited."

Ahithophel said as he looked into Eliam's face, "No, my son. Don't worry about me. I have a plan. I am grateful to see you one last time. I have no doubt King David will survive this war. I see clearly now that God will protect his anointed one. I have been fighting God all this time, but couldn't see it."

"Father..." Eliam started to say, but Ahithophel continued.

"I have been humiliated by the man I supported to carry out my vengeance. I can't go back to Jerusalem. Go in peace, my son. Tell Betta how much I love her and my great-grandchildren. And Eliam—I love you. You have been a good son. I am proud of you. Now we must say goodbye."

With that, the sad elderly man rose from the ground, embraced his son, took his donkey's reins, and resumed his journey. As he trod that lonely road out of Jerusalem, the city he had planned in his mind to control, his thoughts took him back over the eleven years since he first parted company with his old friend, the king. *In our early years together, I watched David as a fugitive on the run from King Saul. I remember when he had the opportunity to slay King Saul but refused to do it, even though Saul tried to kill him before. David respected Saul's position, and more important than the position was that God had put him in that office. David would not attack Saul because he was God's anointed.*

The donkey stumbled over an unseen rock under a weed in the road, and the sage old man helped the donkey regain his footage. Settling into a steady pace, his thoughts resumed. *I wasn't as wise as David. Now, I have nothing to live for. I saw in Absalom the potential to hurt my friend, the true king, and perhaps even to destroy him. I focused on this effort to punish David, and it consumed me day and night. But now my world has crumbled.*

He paused to stare at the afternoon sunshine that lay on the surrounding valleys, but he found no pleasure in the view.

No matter what crimes he committed, David has always prospered. I now know he was under divine protection. The Lord God is on King David's side, no matter how much he transgressed God's laws. Because he repented wholeheartedly and changed his life for good, God forgave him and preserved his life.

As the afternoon waned, Ahithophel looked around and saw no other travelers. He began speaking his thoughts aloud as though to make them more real.

"I have anguished in my soul and blamed God for letting David flout the laws that governed other men. Now I have been dealt the final blow by the man I have fashioned and guided to power. Absalom, egotistical whelp—can you hear me? You rejected my counsel for the flawed advice of a man who had no doubt been planted there by your father, the rightful ruler. You were blinded by ego, Prince Absalom. Your cowardice gave your father the upper hand and will lead to your defeat...possibly your death."

He stopped speaking, watching a flock of geese pass overhead before resuming his monologue. "Yes, I can see now that I have been fighting God all this time. "King David is God's man, and there is no path to reach David, either to destroy him or be reconciled to him. Like your father, young Absalom, you have rejected me—the one who molded and guided you. There is nothing left for me now. Even God is against me for turning against his proclaimed ruler."

Tears trickled down his cheeks as he continued along the dusty road.

Not so far away, David sat at a campfire by the bank of the Jordan, preparing to ford the river in the morning. He was lost in thought as he plucked aimlessly on his harp, wrestling with images of his old friend. Word had been brought by the sons of the priests about Absalom's desecration of King David's concubines. *In my heart, I recognize that Ahithophel was behind that act. He knew that by giving such counsel, he broke forever the chance of reconciliation.*

He paused to look down at the river flowing southward through the wilderness and felt kinship with these natural surroundings. Exiled from Jerusalem, David knew he must wander uncertainly until God made his path clear.

If I could talk to Ahithophel, I would say, 'I know you must detest me and want to kill me, but that is not for you to do. Further, you couldn't do anything that would hurt me more than what God has done. He has judged me well; I deserve everything He put on me. There will be violence and bloodshed in my family forever.

In Jerusalem, Absalom followed the advice of Hushai, fulfilling David's prayer that God would confuse Ahithophel's counsel, that the Lord might bring calamity on Absalom. The counsel of Hushai allowed David and his caravan to cross the Jordan River and find safety in the land of Gilead, in the community of Mahanaim, where they were provided with sustenance by David's subjects living there.

"Do not kill the young man Absalom if you find him," David sternly told the military leaders.

But God's justice will not be denied by human plans. As the armies lined up for battle, Absalom rode his mule under the branches of a mighty oak tree where his famous head of hair got caught firmly in the tangle of branches. His mule spooked and ran away, leaving the traitor hanging by his thick hair, a visible target, suspended between heaven and earth, rejected by both.

One of Joab's men saw Absalom hanging there and ran to tell the general.

"Why did you not kill him and make me pay you the reward?" Joab scolded the man.

"No, not for a thousand pieces of silver would I do such a thing because I heard our king instruct us to not harm his son."

Joab said, "Take me to him."

When Joab saw Absalom hanging from the tree, he took a bow and three arrows from the soldier. He drew the first arrow and let it fly, piercing the helpless body of the prince dangling in the air. He followed that with the two remaining arrows. Then ten of his armor bearers lurched forward and hurled javelins at the youthful prince. "Bury him under a pile of rocks and cover the place with leaves so no one will find his body. He erected a monument to himself in the King's Valley; he needs no further recognition here."

With Absalom and Ahithophel's absence, the war quicky ended. The men loyal to David came to his defense. The battle took place in the forest of Ephraim. David's fighters prevailed against the Israelite troops, and altogether 20,000 of Absalom's men died. But the return of the victors to Jerusalem was solemn, marked now and then by high-spirited laughter or raucous yelling. Anyone who heard or saw the troops would not be sure whether they had been victorious or defeated.

Ahimaaz, the son of Zadok, said, "Let me run in advance of the military and inform the king of the good news that the Lord has saved him from his enemies."

Joab said, "This will not be welcome news to King David that his son has died. Another time, you can be my messenger. You!" he called a paid soldier from Ethiopia. "Run and tell the king this news."

The Ethiopian bowed and took off at a run.

Ahimaaz begged to carry the news as well.

"It will not be good for you to tell the king his son is dead," Joab said.

"Come what may," Ahimaaz replied, "let me tell him."

"Go," Joab said. Ahimaaz took the smoother route and got ahead of the Ethiopian.

As David waited between the town's inner and outer gates, the watchman announced two runners approaching Jerusalem. Ahimaaz arrived first, breathless, and then bowed to the king with his face to the ground. "Praise to the Lord your God, who has handed over the rebels who dared to stand against my lord, the king."

"And Absalom, my son, is he also well?" the king demanded.

Ahimaaz faltered and said, "There was a lot of noise. I'm not sure."

"Wait here," David said, and the young man stepped to the side of the road.

"The Ethiopian arrived and knelt before King David: "I have good news for my lord, the king. Today, the Lord has rescued you from all those who rebelled against you."

"What about young Absalom? Is he all right?"

The Ethiopian permitted himself a small smile of triumph. "May all of your enemies, my lord, the king, both now and in the future, share the fate of that young man!"

The king was overcome and left the group to go up to the room over the gateway and burst into tears. As he went, he cried, "Oh, my son, Absalom! My son, my son, Absalom! If only I had died instead of you! Oh, Absalom, my son, my son."

When Joab arrived, he bitterly chided the king about mourning the man who sought to murder him and usurp his kingdom. He warned David to pull himself together in a show of unity with the kingdom. So the king arose and sat in the gate, and the people came to him as their true king.

King David didn't confront Joab about his defiant disobedience, but he held resentment in his heart. Years later, Joab gave up his life to David's son, Solomon, in recompense for his rebellious acts.

It was only because Ahithophel nurtured a root of bitterness within his spirit that he was unable to release his hatred of David. Ahithophel's bitterness also fed Absalom's ambition so that he was able to raise an army and mount an offensive that produced widespread death.

Ahithophel returned to his ancestral home of Giloh. He took some time to put his affairs in order and perhaps to wait for hope to return. But he found none. According to local legend, he built a gallows and hanged himself. His once-prosperous life deteriorated into rage and disgrace, and eventually led to his self-destruction.

The concubines who had been left to tend the palace were allowed to remain when David returned to Jerusalem, but they were kept separate in their own area of the great structure. David did not have relations with them again.

Queen Maacah, having surrendered her role as lead wife in the harem to Bathsheba years before, went into discreet mourning with Tamar for their son and brother Absalom. But the pair did not remain secluded for longer than necessary.

Maacah and Tamar happily planned for the young woman's long-awaited wedding to her beloved. Hesel was rewarded by David, who appointed him to a position of honor and prestige in the royal court.

King David and Bathsheba devoted themselves to raising their sons. Keeping the promise he made to Bathsheba after the death of their first son, David's last official act was to ensure that their son Solomon would be his successor on the throne. Bathsheba became the mother of the king of Judah and Israel.

Her name was forever enshrined in the Scriptures in the bloodline of the Messiah.

David paid a steep price for his sins, but he reaped earthly and heavenly rewards for being a man after God's own heart. That he was God's chosen one is clearly seen in the many psalms he penned to honor God, both before and after his fall from grace and restoration to God's favor.

Chapter 29:

David's Last Words

These are the last words of David (2 Sam. 23:1–5)

The oracle of David son of Jesse,
the oracle of the man exalted by the Most High,
The man anointed by the God of Jacob,
Israel's beloved singer of songs,
the psalmist of Israel.
The Spirit of the Lord spoke through me;
His word was on my tongue.
The Rock of Israel said to me:
When one rules over men righteously,
when he rules in the fear of God,
he is like the light of morning at sunrise.
Is not my house right with God?
Has He not made with me an everlasting covenant,
arranged and secured in every part?
For all my salvation and all I desire, will He not make it
endure and grow?

THE END

Author's Notes

This book includes two unusual, if not supernatural events which were experienced by the author and his wife personally. The first was the beautiful ice display seen by Maacah and Tamar in Geshur. My wife and I witnessed the same sort of display in the Bavarian Alps near Neuschwanstein Castle. On our second anniversary, my wife and I had the same unique spiritual experience described by Hesel and Tamar during the sunset at the scenic lookout in Geshur. We interpreted our experience as the Holy Spirit consummating our union spiritually to prepare us for ordeals we were to face later in our marriage.

There are some points and questions that I know will be raised by readers. Here, I address a few of them.

Question: Why are you so hard on David? Most Christians and others hold David in very high regard, and why shouldn't we?

His psalms play an important role in our theology, worship, and devotions; they help us express our love to God. We have admired his strength and valor since we were in preschool. David slew Goliath. He was a man after God's own heart. He was God's anointed one. The episode with Bathsheba is hard for us to accept. But we recognize that he was only human, so we can relate to him when he makes a rare mistake. He is our hero, and we are relieved when he repents and confesses his sin.

Answer: One of the purposes of this book is to show that David's sin was probably not a momentary lapse in judgment. It may have been premeditated over months or even years. We don't know. It was an intentional act of adultery, or possibly rape, which he did not anticipate leading to murder.

The way the Scripture writer presents the story leaves out much detail that further incriminates David. However, Nathan specifies that David "despised" God, and he had "contempt" for God's Word. He despised God's Word. Think about that. Nobody develops contempt for someone in an instant. This damning verdict indicates clearly that David's actions were not a momentary lapse but more likely spread over a prolonged length of time.

As I mentioned in the preface, several authors have written of the changes in the life of the aging David, none of them for the better. The text of 2nd Samuel after Chapter 7, leading up to Chapter 11, hints at what is to come. It's clear that David's religious life had suffered, probably without him noticing. So, even though I picture his moral life in disarray leading up to his affair with Bathsheba, I think the damning language used by Nathan in his confrontation with David is accurate. However, I tried to be generous with him in the years following his repentance.

I believe the first sentence in 2 Samuel 11 is key to interpreting the story. "In the spring, at the time when kings go out to battle, David sent Joab and his servants, and all Israel .. but David stayed at Jerusalem." We are not told why he stayed home, but failure to meet his responsibilities is implied. Immediately, in the next sentence, the writer launches the sordid story of David seeing and summoning Bathsheba to his bed. One must assume the two sentences are closely related. What is the writer implying? Did David remaining behind have something to do with his summons to Bathsheba?

Once we see that Bathsheba's grandfather is David's personal advisor and counselor and that her father and husband are members of David's bodyguard, the inescapable conclusion is that David had known Bathsheba, possibly since the day she was born.

But why does the writer omit that information and allow the reader to think David didn't know her? Was it to minimize David's guilt? No, but he reveals enough information to establish that the affair is sordid and more than a momentary failure. In fact, it is much more egregious, but it is better to let the reader find the depths of David's fall for themselves. The clues are all there and easy to find.

Question: The Bible says that Bathsheba was very beautiful. Why was she bathing where the king could see her?

I think most men believe she may be the one who instigated the whole affair. Let's cut David some slack, they say. She probably seduced David. We prefer to think David just let his hormones get the best of him because of her immodest exposure. It was an impulsive, momentary mistake.

Answer: In this book, I have portrayed Bathsheba as a young newlywed in love with her husband. She was an innocent victim. Why have I pictured her thus? To remove the temptation to lessen David's sin and blame some or all of it on her. I believe David's sin was far from being a brief stumble. David's lust consumed him, causing him to turn from God to indulge his basest desires, which had already led to collecting several concubines, in addition to fifteen to twenty trophy wives who bore him many children. His lust took over his life so completely that he even abandoned his responsibility to lead his nation in time of war. And yet, when God confronted him in the person of Nathan, David's repentance was profound. David owned up to his mistakes, confessing his vile sins and recommitting himself to the Lord. His life from that point on was diametrically opposed to his previous period.

You may have noticed in this novel that the roles of protagonist and antagonist reverse after David repents. At the beginning of the book, Ahithophel was the sympathetic grandfather and wise counselor, while David was the antagonist, aloof and sinful. After David's repentance, he becomes the sympathetic hero, and Ahithophel becomes the antagonist, full of hatred and malice. The change in Ahithophel illustrates the wisdom of Hebrews 12:15. In this role reversal, the story is somewhat like a Shakespearian tragedy.

Question: Why would God punish His anointed one so grievously?

After pronouncing the first three judgments, the text clearly states, "Because you have given the enemies of God a reason to blaspheme Him, the baby will die." *That* certainly sounds like severe punishment for a specific sin.

Answer: We know that on this side of the cross, God does not punish us for our sins. Jesus took all of our punishment on Himself. We also know that God chastises or disciplines us as a loving father would. As John MacArthur says in his sermon on 2 Samuel 11 and 12,[9] "We may not be able to tell the difference (between punishment and chastisement) because it feels the same. *But the purpose is different.* We know that judges mete out punishment, but a loving father disciplines his son to teach him." In this case, God chastised David for his actions, and His chastisement was effective. David changed his behavior and blessed God for his discipline.

Question: How do you come up with the number of fifteen or so wives? Only eight are listed by name in Scripture (including Michal).

Answer: That is true. We cannot state with certainty how many wives David accumulated. However, since the writer of 2 Samuel documents that the six wives in Hebron all had only one son each, that seems to establish a pattern. Some commentaries think the treaty wives who he collected through international agreements were expected to bear one or more male heirs for their king-husband. Possibly, David only slept with each wife until they had a son. However, the following verses specify that Bathsheba had five sons in Jerusalem, including the one who died. But then, nine additional sons born in Jerusalem are listed without naming their mothers (the writer of 1 Chronicles names eleven sons besides Bathsheba's five who were born in Jerusalem, again, without naming their mothers). Bathsheba is obviously an exception to David's policy. That implies, again, one son per wife for the others. It's true that all nine (or eleven) of the sons born in Jerusalem could have been born to the previously named wives in Hebron. However, in 2 Samuel 5:7, the author states specifically that David took more wives and concubines in Jerusalem. Seeing how this writer thinks, it seems more likely that he is saying Bathsheba is special, but the other wives were limited to one son each. So, it seems safe to assume that several additional wives were taken in Jerusalem. The total number of wives was probably at least fifteen, and possibly as many as nineteen.

This analysis ignores the concubines, but the writer again implies in 2 Samuel 5:13, and another writer states specifically in 1 Chronicles 3:9, after naming fifteen sons born in Jerusalem, that "All these were the sons of David, besides the sons of the concubines." If David was only fulfilling his duty with his treaty wives, perhaps he used the concubines for his abnormally strong sexual drive. In Psalms 38:7, David writes, "For my loins are filled with burning; and there is no soundness in my flesh." Men with strong passions and drives usually experience a high level of virility as well.

Question: How do you justify David becoming monogamous after he repented?

Answer: There is not a lot of evidence in the biblical text, but since the writers and chroniclers specify David's other wives had only one son each, only Bathsheba is shown to have multiple (five) sons by David. Also, it was Bathsheba who was with him when he died in 1 Kings 1 and 2, and David selected Bathsheba's son to follow him as king, despite the fact that there were many other sons, all of them older than Solomon.

Regarding the concubines, my thinking is that when David brought Bathsheba into his harem, it was his intention to stop consorting with the concubines. However, the temptation may have been too much for him. When David left the concubines behind as he fled Jerusalem, it was not just to have someone there to take care of the palace. He was offering them up to God as a sacrifice of righteousness, as he wrote in Psalm 4:5, "Offer the sacrifices of righteousness, and trust in the Lord" (NASV). By leaving them behind in a vulnerable position, he was both offering his "sinful playthings" to God as a sacrifice, but was also giving God an opportunity to fulfill his third judgment through them. It is notable that in 2 Samuel 20:3, we learn that when David returned to Jerusalem, he locked away the concubines and provided for them, but "did not lie with them."[11]

Why do you say that David changed after the affair with Bathsheba?

Answer: David does nothing noteworthy in the remainder of 2 Samuel. The only initiative noted was a negative one when he ordered a census of the people. God ended that action by slaying 70,000 of his citizens.

Following are some points made by other authors in the referenced works:

The only published book I could find on Ahithophel available in print was written by an African-English pastor and author named Oghenebrorhie.[10] He feels that Eliam's first allegiance was to his commander-in-chief, David, and not to his son-in-law, Uriah. In the author's dispassionate view, Eliam was pleased that his daughter, Bathsheba, ended up with David, where she became the new First Lady of Israel, and eventually, Queen Mother of Solomon, the successor to David's throne. This author faults Ahithophel for deserting David because of a "minor sin" that ended up as a blessing for his family.

Bill Purvis[11] states in his Leadership CD on Ahithophel that he was a great, godly man, but he let anger and bitterness destroy his life and his witness. There was nothing wrong in feeling those emotions when David betrayed him and his family, but he should have surrendered them to God (which isn't a trivial task) and trusted that God would take care of David because he was God's anointed one.

From our vantage point on this side of the Cross:

We see that Bathsheba was in the direct line of Jesus himself, not just once, but twice. In Matthew's genealogical line, Solomon is listed as the son of the woman who was Uriah's wife (Matt. 1:6). In Luke's genealogical line in 3:31, he traces Jesus's line through David and Bathsheba's third son, Nathan, who

David must have named after the prophet who confronted him with his sin. I will let someone else explain why the two genealogies are different. Either way, Bathsheba and Ahithophel were in the lineage of Jesus.

Despite his hateful actions, it is ironic that Ahithophel himself is in the bloodline of Christ. But Ahithophel didn't have the benefit of knowing how everything would eventually work out for this "man after God's own heart." He only knew that David had committed horrible travesties of justice and decency to his family. However, he let that anger smolder and allowed that root of bitterness to eat at his soul for over ten years, and that eventually led to a civil war and his own death.

David's Sin Changed History

After the prophet Nathan helped David realize that he was the man who had sinned so grievously, Nathan pronounced what amounted to an everlasting curse from God on David's progeny. Even though David repented and he wrote more glorious psalms, he was never quite the same. Even though he truly and completely repented, the consequences of his sin continued in accordance with the prophecies of Nathan. God restores us to full fellowship with Himself, but the consequences of our sin continue to run their course. As Alexander MacLaren says, "Pardon is not impunity."[12] For example, the consequences of Nathan's prophecy continued to be fulfilled after David's son Solomon died. The nation split into the Northern and Southern kingdoms with wars and conflicts between the two kingdoms and other surrounding nations. I suppose we can still see the conflicts today, 3000 years later, as modern Israel, all descendants of Judah, is continually beset by enemies on every side. God said forever.

But on the other hand, we can also see, even today, the blessings of God's earlier covenant with David in 2 Samuel 7, that his descendant would always sit on the throne. In verses 12-13, God promises, "I will raise up your descendant after you, who will come forth from you, and I will establish His kingdom... and I will establish the throne of His kingdom forever." That descendant is, of course, our Lord Jesus Christ, who eventually came from the union of David and Bathsheba. Yes, God redeems, and He redeems completely. His true Anointed One has come to deliver each one of us from sin and death. We don't have to fear everlasting punishment because Jesus took the punishment for our sins upon Himself, setting us free from fear of death and death itself. So, we can praise God for His lovingkindness and mercies forever. Praise be to His name.

Appendix

The following Scripture passages are incorporated in the text of this novel. Some are quoted verbatim but many are paraphrased to fit into the flow of the text. Unless noted otherwise, the quotes are taken from the New American Standard Bible. The Scripture verses are listed below by the chapter of the novel in which they are used.

Chapter 1. Deuteronomy 2:4–5

Chapter 2. Samuel 7:18–29; Deuteronomy 17:17

Chapter 4. 2 Samuel 11:2–25; Deuteronomy 22:24–27

Chapter 7. 2 Samuel 17:26

Chapter 11. 2 Samuel 12:1–15; Psalms 51:1–7. Romans 7:18–24; Psalms 32:3–5; Psalms 139:23–24; 2 Samuel 12:18–24

Chapter 13. 2 Samuel 13:1–22, 23–29, 30–33, 34–39

Chapter 19. 2 Samuel 14:1–24

Chapter 23. 2 Samuel 14:26–33

Chapter 25. 2 Samuel 15:1–12, 18, 25

Chapter 26. 2 Samuel 16:20–23

Chapter 27. 2 Samuel 18:5–7, 9–14, 33; 2 Samuel 19:5

Bibliography

Books on Ahithophel:

Cohn, Ronald and Jesse Russell. *Ahithophel.* Bookvika, 2012. (https://smile.amazon.co.uk/Ahithophel-Ronald-Cohn-Jesse-Russell/dp/B007KLNASQ/ref=sr_1_1.?ie=UTF8&qid=15506 0102&SR=8-1&keywords=Ahithophel)

Oghenebrorhie, Emmanuel. *AHITHOPHEL: Humbly Mind Your Business.* Xlibris Corp, 2010.

DVDs:

Purvis, Bill. *Leadership Series: Lessons from Ahithophel: Facing Betrayal and Bitterness.* Bill Purvis Ministries. GA: Columbus.

Old Sermons:

Baker, Aaron. *Achitophel Befool'd: A Sermon Preached November V. 1678 at St. Sepulchres* (Classic Reprint). Forgotten Books, 2018.

Carpenter, Nathanael. *Achitophel: Or, the True Picture of a Wicked Politician.* Gale Ecco, 2018.

Long, Thomas. *King David's danger and deliverance, or, The conspiracy of Absolon and Achitophel defeated in a sermon preached in the Cathedral Church of Exon, ... discovery of the late fanatical plot (1683).* EEBO Editions / Proquest, 2011.

About the Author

Author Don Clifford has led adult Bible Studies for over 50 years, many of them team teaching with his wife, Karen. The couple also teamed up in writing about their experience as life-long Christians whose marriage and faith survived the loss of three of their living children. Don authored *Grace Enough for Three, Losing Three Children*  but Finding God's All-Sufficient Grace.* The couple co-authored *Heavenly Grief, a Guide to Spiritual and Emotional Healing.* Their two living daughters have blessed them with six grandchildren and nine great grandchildren. Karen died of Parkinson's Disease in 2020.

Don had a rewarding career as a physicist and aerospace engineer. He specialized in studies of atmospheric electricity and its effects on aircraft. He worked with NASA and the Defense Department, leading groups who designed lightning protective measures for the Space Shuttle and several military aircraft.

After his retirement, Don and Karen traveled extensively, leading mission tours in Europe and South America. Don is president of Agape Communications, owners and operators of Christian radio station KSGL in Wichita, Kansas. Don served on the Executive Board of the Missouri Baptist Convention. He now lives in Missoui and leads Bible studies at the First Baptist Church in St. Charles. He would be happy to hear from readers of *Widom Betrayed*.

Acknowledgements

I owe so much of this novel to several people who guided me in the art of writing fiction, and others who corrected and suggested much of the material in the book. First, my wife Karen, who reviewed, encouraged and motivated me to never give up. My greatest regret is that she was not able to see the finished work. She passed away in April, 2020, a victim of Parkinson's Disease. Some of her last words when I promised her that I would see her soon were, "Not until you finish your book."

My daughter, Becky, the wife of Paul Harcourt, an Anglican vicar in England, helped fashion my initial brain dump into the beginning of a fictional novel. Paul helped research the centuries of archives for previous writings on Ahithophel. My pastor and close friend, Buddy Perstrope, reviewed several early versions and added significant insights into the characters in the book. Rob Phillips, Apologetics leader of the Missouri Baptist Convention, encouraged me and edited much of the material for the book. Author/editor Brianna Boes mentored me early in the basics of writing fiction. Dr. Bill Victor, Resident Scholar for the Convention added corrections and suggestions based on his expertise on the life and times of David and of the Old Testament in general.

As the novel began to look like a credible commentary on the 2 Samuel text, Debra Johanyak of THGM Writers assisted in refining the text and adding insight from her years of living in the Middle East. I also want to acknowledge the coaching of the Uberwriters team, especially in the technical area of character development.

Don Clifford

Endnotes

1 John Dryden's Classic Poem "Absalom and Achitophel", published 1651. Available at Poetry Foundation.org/poems/44172/Absalom-and-Achitophel

2 *The Aggada*, (Legends of the Jews) http://www.book-lover.com/legendsofthejews/4/4lotj10_ahithophel.html

3 Steve Maltz, *Shalom: God's Masterplan (2019) Saffron Planet*, Ilford IG1 9TR, UK

4 Alexander Whyte : Vol. 3 of 6, *Bible Characters: Ahithophel to Nehemiah*; Publication date 1836-1921 : Publisher Edinburgh : Oliphant, Anderson & USA 1983-1999.

5 Alexander MacLaren, *The Life of David: As Reflected in His Psalms*. A digital copy is available at WordSearchBible.com/MasterWork

6 Jonathan Kirsh, *King David: The real life of the man who ruled Israel*; A Ballantine Book published by the Random House Group (2000)

7   Coffman's Commentary on the Bible. Re: 2 Samuel 15:7 – The KJV and other ancient versions have "forty years" here instead of four; but the RSV's four years is doubtless correct here in following the Syriac and certain texts of the LXX. Coffman Commentaries on the Old and New Testament. Abilene Christian University Press, Abilene, Texas, USA 1983-1999.

8   David Wolpe, *The Divided Heart*; Yale University Press, (2014)

9   John MacArthur, *Sermon on 2 Samuel 11-12*. Gracetoyou.com

10 Oghenebrorhie, Emmanuel. *AHITHOPHEL: Humbly Mind Your Business*. Xlibris Corp, 2010

11 Purvis, Bill. *Leadership Series: Lessons from Ahithophel: Facing Betrayal and Bitterness*. Bill Purvis Ministries. GA: Columbus.

9 781662 826771